The Stone Boy
and other stories

OTHER BOOKS BY THICH NHAT HANH

The Stone Boy
and other stories

THICH NHAT HANH

Parallax Press
Berkeley, California

Parallax Press
P.O. Box 7355
Berkeley, California 94707

Cover drawing by Vo-Dinh Mai
Drawings by Vo-Dinh Mai and Nguyen Thi Hop
Cover and text design by Legacy Media, Inc.
A list of translators from the Vietnamese appears at the end of the book.

The first three stories appeared previously in *The Pine Gate* (White Pine Press), and the final four stories appeared previously in *The Moon Bamboo* (Parallax Press). Both books are now out of print.

LIBRARY OF CONGRESS CATALOGING-IN PUBLICATION DATA
Nhât Hanh, Thích.
    The stone boy and other stories / Thich Nhat Hanh.
        p. cm.
    ISBN 0-938077-86-4 (pbk.)
    I. Title.
    PR9560.N47 1995
    823—dc20   95-36105
                                                    CIP

Contents

The Stone Boy

and other stories

∞

The Ancient Tree

Dᴇᴇᴘ ɪɴ ᴛʜᴇ ꜰᴏʀᴇsᴛ highlands stood a great, ancient tree. No one knew how many thousands of years it had lived. Its trunk was as large as the armspans of eighteen people. Its great roots pushed up through the ground and spread to a radius of fifty meters. Its bark was as hard as rock; if you pressed a fingernail against it, it would hurt your finger. Its branches held tens of thousands of birds' nests, sheltering hundreds of thousands of birds, large and small. The earth beneath the shadow of the tree was unusually cool.

In the morning when the sun rose, the first rays of light were like a conductor's baton, beginning a grand symphony, the voices of the birds as majestic as any great philharmonic orchestra. All the creatures of the forest arose, on two feet or four, slowly and in awe.

In the great tree there was an opening as large as a grapefruit from Bien Hoa. It was twelve meters up from the ground. In that opening lay a small brown egg. No one could say if a bird had brought that egg there or if it had been formed by the sacred air of the forest and the life energy of the great tree.

Thirty years passed and the egg remained intact. During some nights, birds would be startled from their sleep by a brilliant light shining from the opening in the tree, illuminating an entire corner of the forest. Finally one night, under a very bright full moon and a brilliantly starlit sky, the egg cracked open and a tiny strange bird was born.

The little bird gave a small chirp in the cold night, and it continued to cry throughout the night until the sun appeared— a cry neither tragic nor bold, a cry of strangeness and surprise. It cried until the first rays of light opened the morning symphony and thousands of birds' voices broke forth. From that moment on, the little bird cried no more.

The bird grew quickly. The nuts and grains that mother birds brought to the opening in the tree were always plenty. Soon the opening became too small, and the bird had to find another home, much larger. It had taught itself to fly, and it gathered sticks and straw to build a new nest. Although the egg had been brown, the bird was as white as snow. Its wingspan was vast, and it always flew slowly and very quietly, often to faraway places where white waterfalls tumbled day and night like the majestic breath of earth and sky. Sometimes it did not return for several days. When it returned, it lay in its nest all day and night, thoughtfully and quietly. Its two bright eyes never lost their look of surprise.

In the ancient Dai Lao Forest, a hermit's hut stood on the slope of a hill. There, a monk had lived for almost fifty years. The bird often flew across Dai Lao Forest, and from time to time it saw the monk walking slowly down the path to the spring, holding a water jug in his hand. One day, the bird saw two monks walking together on the path leading from the spring to the hut, and that night, concealed in the branches of a tree, it watched as the light of the fire flickered inside the hut and the two monks conversed the whole night long.

The bird flew high over the ancient forest, sometimes for days without landing. Below stood the great tree, and the creatures of mountain and forest concealed by grass, bushes, and trees. Since the day the bird overheard the exchange between the two monks, its bewilderment grew. Where have I come from and where will I go? How many thousands of years will the great tree stand?

The bird had heard the two monks speak about time. What is time? Why has time brought us here, and why will it take us away? The nut that a bird eats has its own delicious nature. How can I find out the nature of time? The bird wanted to pick up a small piece of time and lie quietly with it in its nest for several days to examine its nature. Even if it took months or years to examine, the bird was willing.

High over the ancient forest, the bird felt like a round balloon drifting in nothingness. It felt its nature was as empty as a balloon's, and that emptiness was the ground of its existence and the cause of its suffering as well. If I could find time, thought the bird, I could certainly find myself.

After many days and nights of flying and contemplating, the bird came quietly to rest in its nest. It had brought with it a tiny piece of earth from the Dai Lao Forest. Deep in thought, it picked up the piece of earth to examine it. The monk from the Dai Lao Forest had said to his friend, "Time is stilled in eternity, where love and your beloved are one. Each blade of grass, each piece of earth, each leaf, is one with that love."

But the bird was unable to find time. The clod of earth from Dai Lao Forest revealed nothing. Perhaps the monk had lied. Time lies in love, but where is love? The bird remembered the waterfalls endlessly tumbling in the Northwest Forest. It remembered the days it listened to the sounds of waterfalls from morn to eve. It even imagined itself tumbling like a waterfall, while it played with the light sparkling on the water and caressed the pebbles and rocks down below. The bird felt that it was a waterfall itself, with endless water falling from it.

One noon, while flying across the Dai Lao Forest, the bird saw that the hut was no longer there. The whole forest had burned, and only a pile of ashes remained where the hut had been. In a panic, the bird flew around searching. The monk was no longer in the forest. Where had he gone? Corpses of animals. Corpses of birds. Had the fire consumed the monk? The bird was bewildered. Time, what are you? Why do you bring us here, and why will you take us away? The monk had said, "Time is stilled in eternity." If that is so, perhaps love has returned the monk to itself.

The bird flew swiftly back to the ancient forest, where anguished cries of many birds and explosions of bark revealed that the ancient forest was burning. Faster, faster still, the bird flew. The fire spread throughout the sky, and it spread near the great tree. Hundreds of thousands of birds shrieked in fright. As the fire approached the great tree, the bird flapped its wings feverishly, hoping to put it out, but the fire burned even more fiercely. The bird sped to the spring, dipped its wings in the water, and rushed back to shake the water over the forest. The drops just turned to steam. It was not enough, not enough. The bird's whole body soaked in water was not enough to extinguish the fire.

Hundreds of thousands of birds cried. Young birds without feathers to fly screamed. Then the fire began to burn the great tree. Why was there no rain? Why didn't the downpour that fell endlessly in the Northwest Forest flow like a waterfall here? The bird let forth a piercing cry, a cry both tragic and passionate, and suddenly the cry was transformed into the sound of a rushing waterfall. In that moment, the bird felt the fullness of its existence. Loneliness and emptiness vanished, and the image of the monk, the image of the sun behind the mountain peak, and the image of the rushing water falling endlessly through a thousand lifetimes took their place. The cry of the bird had become the rush of the waterfall, and without fear, the bird plunged into the forest fire like a majestic waterfall.

The next morning was calm. The rays of the sun shone, but there was no symphony, no sounds of thousands of birds. Parts of the forest had burned completely. The great tree stood, but more than half its branches were charred. Corpses of large and small birds were everywhere. The forest was silent.

The birds who were still alive called one another, their voices betraying their bewilderment. By what grace had the clear sky suddenly poured forth rain, extinguishing the fire? They remembered seeing the great white bird shaking water from its two wings. They looked everywhere throughout the forest, but they could not find the white bird. Perhaps it had flown away to live in a different forest. Perhaps it had been killed by the fire. The great tree, its body charred and scarred with wounds, did not say a word. The birds turned their heads to the sky, and then began to build new nests in the remaining branches of the great tree. Did the ancient tree miss the child, the child of sacred mountain air and the life energy of its own four thousand years? Dear bird, where have you gone? Listen to the monk: time has returned the bird to the love that is the source of all things.

∞

The Giant Pines

AFTER INVITING THE LARGE bronze temple bell to sound one hundred seven times, Novice Tam The of Phap Van Temple turned the big wooden mallet upside down and tapped the bell twice to alert novice Tam Hien that it was nearly time to begin the dawn ceremony. Tam The waited patiently for the last reverberations of the one-hundred-seventh sound to disappear, so he could invite the bell for the final time.

From another corner of the temple, Tam The heard Tam Hien's gong ring three times, and he responded with three more sounds of the large bell before he laid the mallet down and listened to the beautiful sound of Tam Hien's gong. The monks were all assembled at the main hall for the morning chanting.

Tam The lifted his palm-leafed raincoat over his shoulders—the air was quite chilly—descended from the bell tower, and swiftly made his way in the thick morning mist toward the main gate, where the wandering monk was sitting in deep meditation. His guest had arrived the afternoon of the day before, but had declined the offer of bed and board in the temple, asking only to be permitted to rest on a straw mat under the roof of the temple gate. He insisted that was all he needed. His brown monk's robe, already worn and faded, was thick with dust from the journey. Instead of being clean-shaven as a monk should be, his hair and beard were long and unkempt. His face, hands, and feet were filthy, and a sour, awful stench arose from his body.

Tam The had offered the traveller a basin of fresh water, a hand towel, and a straw mat. When the traveller had finished washing, Tam The took the basin of dirty water away and then returned with a small wooden tray of rice gruel, pickled mustard greens, and soy sauce. The traveller thanked him and began to eat in a most leisurely way. Tam The formed a lotus with his palms, bowed to the old monk, and went back to the temple. An hour later, he returned to pick up the tray, and he saw that the traveller had already wrapped himself in the straw mat and fallen fast asleep.

That morning, Tam The found the monk sitting in deep meditation, although not in the lotus posture. His right knee was up to his chest and his right foot flat on the ground. Tam The was struck by the monk's noble bearing, even though the horrible stench was still there. The monk looked about fifty. His hair and beard were overgrown, but his face had a clarity and distinction that was awe-inspiring. He must be one of those mysterious monks I've read about, Tam The thought. He didn't want to impose his terrible appearance on us. Perhaps I can learn something about him. Tam The was about to go back for a basin of warm water when his guest opened his eyes. Tam The bowed, and the old monk, clearing his throat, said gently, "Dear Novice, how far is it to Cuu Lung Mountain?"

Tam The replied, humbly, "Most Venerable, it isn't far. At most, half a day's walk. I will bring you a basin of warm water for your morning wash."

The traveller raised a hand to indicate that it wasn't necessary. He leaned against the wall and, pushing against it, raised himself with difficulty. Then he reached for his bamboo walking stick.

"Thank you, young monk, but I must go now if I am to arrive before dark. I walk quite slowly."

No sooner had he said that than the monk started limping away, leaning on his stick. Tam The began to walk alongside him, to help him on his way, but the stranger again raised his hand to tell him not to bother. Then he just hobbled off by himself.

He'll never make it to Cuu Lung Mountain before dark walking like that, Tam The shrugged in sympathy. Going all that way and without even a small bag! And he's so skinny. I wonder why he wants to go to Cuu Lung Mountain? Tam The had never heard of any temple or pagoda on Cuu Lung Mountain. He had never seen the mountain itself, but he had heard that Cuu Lung was high and wild, its summit always shrouded in mist and clouds.

Tam The had come to like the old stranger very much. There was something about him that made Tam The wish he could know him better, even be near him. But now there was nothing he could do but go back and help the other novices prepare the monks' breakfast. Morning chanting was nearly over.

The old monk made his way slowly, with much pain. On his left thigh was a boil the size of a grapefruit. But he never complained except while he slept, when he allowed himself to moan softly. He had hoped to reach Cuu Lung Mountain by nightfall, but the boil hurt so much he was not able to walk all the way there in one day, and he had to spend the night under a tree. He was without food, but that was no great problem. For the six months he had been travelling, countless times he had slept under trees without even a grain of rice in his stomach. When there was a pagoda nearby, he would ask permission to sleep under its gate, and a young novice, like Tam The, would invariably bring him a bowl of gruel or rice. The novice he had met the night before was especially thoughtful and kind. He had even brought a basin of warm water and a straw mat that was so clean it still smelled of the sun. But tonight, there was only a big root to lay his head upon. He wanted to sleep, but the mountain air was too cold, and he could only curl up to keep warm, not to sleep at all.

It was not yet daylight when the old monk rose slowly to his feet to continue his journey. He was so weak he fell down several times. One time he thought he would not be able to get up again—but he did, and he went on. After a few hundred steps, he stopped and sat down on a rock, and as soon as his breathing returned to normal, he took his bamboo stick and started off again. He continued this way until the hour of the monkey, when he finally reached Cuu Lung Mountain.

Standing at the foot of the mountain, he looked around. There were no signs of human presence, not even a pale gray strand of smoke in the distance to indicate that someone, perhaps a woodcutter, was boiling some rice. He couldn't even see the summit, for it was covered in mist. How would he be able to find the grass hut of the one he wanted to see? The old monk sat down on a large stone. After six months of walking, he had finally arrived. Suddenly he remembered two lines by the Chinese poet Gia Dao:

> My friend has lived for years on this mountain,
> but in this thick mist, how can I find him?

Sixteen years earlier, the old traveller, then named Tri Huyen, was a young man studying to be a monk. He had met an Indian monk named Kanishka at an old temple in the capital city. Kanishka, covered with foul-smelling sores, stopped at the young man's temple to ask for temporary shelter, and everyone was overwhelmed by disgust. Only Tri Huyen was willing to take care of the stranger. Every morning, he brought the Indian monk a basin of hot salt water and helped him bathe himself. Afterwards, he would bring a freshly laundered monk's robe and take away the one soaked with pus and blood to wash it and hang it in the sun. At noon, Tri Huyen brought him rice, and in the evening, he served him hot tea and took away his dirty dishes. Though Kanishka's illness did not seem to abate, the care

Tri Huyen gave him brought much comfort. Tri Huyen cared for Kanishka this way for two years. His patience was steady and his thoughtfulness constant. Tri Huyen's superiors never said a word of disapproval, because, at the same time, Tri Huyen was diligent in his monastic studies and temple responsibilities.

One morning, the Indian monk said to Tri Huyen, "You have cared for me for a long time. I am very much indebted to you. Now I will be leaving."

Tri Huyen was surprised. "Most Venerable, where will you go? You are still quite ill. Who will care for you?"

Kanishka looked at him gently. "I have unfinished business, and it is time for me to attend to it. Please, do not worry. There are many temples along the way. Surely someone will be kind enough to help an old monk."

The Indian monk could see that the student's face was sad. "Please, don't think this is the end of our friendship. Our paths will cross again. You have a brilliant mind and your studies will bear fruit. One day, you will be a great monk and teacher. Your fame will spread far and wide. Let me say only this: Study the Way to become free, and not for any other reason. Our friendship is deep and true. Please remember what I have told you."

Tri Huyen bowed deeply in gratitude. Then, he asked, "You say we will meet again. When? Where? I'm afraid that on your journey you will not leave behind even a footprint."

"If it is our destiny to meet, even if we try to run away from each other, we will meet! Don't worry! In this lifetime, you will attain all of your goals. But fourteen or fifteen years from now, you will meet a terrible ordeal. Remember me then, and come to me. I will be able to help you."

"But how will I know where to find you?" Tri Huyen asked.

The Indian monk put his hand on Tri Huyen's shoulder, led him out of his monk's cell, and said, "Come to Cuu Lung Mountain, stand at its base, and look up. When you see two giant pine trees standing together, that is where you will find me. Please remember, Cuu Lung Mountain."

After the Indian monk left, Tri Huyen never heard his name mentioned again. Time passed, and the young student became a full-fledged monk whose erudition, wisdom, and eloquence were widely recognized. Every time he preached, thousands of people came to hear him. The capital city was hardly short of great monks and teachers, but Tri Huyen's reputation was so great that even King Y Tong knew of his presence. That year, during the Buddha's Birthday celebration, the king sent for him to come to the palace to preach to the royal family and the entire court. Sitting on an elevated dais above all present, he was the picture of a living Buddha—his appearance handsome, his bearing noble, his voice ringing clear and true. His words swept everyone off into the marvelous world of the Dharma. The king was very pleased and ordered that a purple monk's robe be offered to Tri Huyen. From then on, his fame spread far and wide. He was still only forty-three.

After Tri Huyen had given several such Dharma talks, the king prostrated himself before him and proclaimed him to be the Teacher of the Nation. By royal decree, the king gave him the glorious name Ngo Dat, "The One Who Has Attained Full Enlightenment." An Quoc Temple, next door to the royal palace, was prepared to become the Master's own residence. The king wanted him nearby so he could see him often and benefit from his teachings.

But all these honors paled in comparison with what happened when the Great Teacher reached his forty-fifth birthday. On that occasion, by royal proclamation, the entire population of the country sent representatives to the capital to attend a special month-long retreat to hear the Great Teacher expound on the *Lotus of the Wonderful Dharma Sutra*. Five thousand seats were set aside for the royal family, the court, and the best minds of the nation. The people arrived in the capital city like an avalanche. Standing in row after row, filling every available space in the temple courtyard, they listened as the Great Teacher's voice rose and reverberated over them like the wind. For a month the sermons continued, and the king himself never missed even one.

For the final session of the retreat, the king had a special platform built from fragrant cedarwood by the most skilled craftsmen of the kingdom. It was placed very high so that thousands of the faithful would be able to see him. The installation ceremony was conducted in utmost solemnity. The king stood majestically, walked slowly to the Great Teacher, bowed to him, and invited him to step onto the magnificent platform. As the Most Venerable Ngo Dat did so, the entire audience fell to their knees. Many were so moved they wept uncontrollably. And so the final session began. It was to be one that Great Master and National Teacher Ngo Dat would never forget.

Now, sitting on a rock at the foot of Cuu Lung Mountain, the emaciated wanderer recalled vividly the moment he sat down, with crossed legs, on the cedar platform. Below and all around him, many thousands of people were bowing low, in awe—the king among them. Ngo Dat looked down, and even he was amazed. It was indeed extraordinary for a monk, one who had forsaken everything for the Way, to have reached such a lofty place among mortals. And so, for a moment, for the batting of an eye, he felt pride in himself. Immediately, a strange fire surged to his face, and he knew that evil had penetrated him. He shook himself lightly and tried to regain control, but it was too late. From the distant sky, a minute and luminous object, like a brilliant grain of sand, hurled down and struck his left thigh, sending an excruciating pain through his flesh, deep into his bones and marrow. The pain was so terrible that Ngo Dat let out a cry and clasped his thigh in his hands. The king rose abruptly from his throne and shouted for attendants to help the Great Teacher down from his platform. Thus, what was to have been the last, glorious session of Ngo Dat's preaching on the *Lotus of the Wonderful Dharma Sutra* never took place. Everyone thought the Great Teacher must have been bitten by some small poisonous creature, perhaps a centipede, for immediately afterwards, he began to run a high fever.

Ngo Dat knew that no centipede had bitten him. He had seen that luminous particle from space flying straight down at him like lightning and penetrating his flesh without damaging the purple monk's robe that covered it. He knew, but he said nothing. He let the royal physicians go on with their theories and treatments. The small wound began to fester, and quickly it became a swollen purple mass, as large as a grapefruit and dreadfully painful. After ten days the swelling burst, and the swollen mass became an enormous infection oozing blood and pus, enough each day to fill a large bowl. The royal physicians prescribed all manner of medication, some internal, some external, but none were of any help. King Y Tong came several times each day to pay his respects and to order that no effort be spared to cure him. Yet a year passed, and the Great Teacher's condition only worsened. He lost weight, and his strength just ebbed away. During one visit, the king believed he saw a tear trembling in the eye of the holy man.

During one painful, sleepless night, Ngo Dat decided to leave the great temple, the king, and the people he had made his own. For a year he had lain on his back, waited on by an army of physicians and attendants, without being of any use to the nation. He had reached the pinnacle of honor, and now he was at the nadir of shame and torment. That night, he stole away wearing only a brown monk's robe and holding a staff that was a gift from the king. The sore was excruciating, but by tremendous effort he made his way through the night out of the capital. When he saw a bamboo stick lying alongside the road, he picked it up and threw the royal staff into a swift river. The precious artifact floated back toward the capital while the former

Teacher of the Nation, now a sick, desperate man, limped away toward the mountains.

The first day, at noon, the traveller passed a rural market-place. Seeing a monk in such pitiful condition, a peasant woman offered him two bananas and a handful of sweet rice. He feared that the rice would make his sore worse, and he accepted only the bananas. As he sat down on a mound of earth to eat, he realized that someone might recognize him, so he rubbed his face with mud and dirt. Suddenly, while he was doing that, the image of the old Indian monk came to him like a flash of lightning. He remembered what the holy Kanishka had told him years before, "In fourteen or fifteen years, you will meet a terrible ordeal. Remember me then, and come to me. I will be able to help you. Come to Cuu Lung Mountain."

So, walking by day and resting by night, the monk Ngo Dat set out for Cuu Lung Mountain, despite the dreadful pain. Blood and pus continually soaked through his trousers, but because he had no change of clothes, the foul-smelling secretions poured out and dried up again and again, until his trousers became stiff like old corn stalks, filled with an overpowering stench. His monk's robe had become badly stained, and even where there were no stains, the original brown was so faded it had become the color of dust. Every evening, he stopped at the root of a tree, pulled up his trousers, and looked at the sore. It was still big as a grapefruit, and its festering surface had four small crimson openings. The two low ones, nearest his knee, looked like eyes; the middle one looked like a nose; and the one on top flared out like an angry, bloody mouth. The sore seemed to be rolling its eyes and clenching its teeth in utter fury, and the monk could only stare at it in mute silence, filled with sorrow and desolation.

During his long journey to Cuu Lung Mountain, the former National Teacher slept under many temple gates, and no one ever recognized him. Everyone had been hospitable, but no one was as kind as the young novice at Phap Van Temple, who had brought him warm water and rice gruel. He remembered him with delight. And now, he had finally reached the foot of Cuu Lung Mountain.

The wandering monk, the former Great Teacher of the Nation, flinched. In a murmuring brook, he thought he heard the words of the Indian monk Kanishka, "Stand at the base of Cuu Lung Mountain and look up. When you see two giant pine trees standing together, that is where you will find me."

Ngo Dat looked up, and there were, indeed, two giant pines. On the left side of the mountain, very high up, the mist had cleared, and the two great trees stood together in extraordinary grandeur, their tops still covered by clouds. Ngo Dat reached for his bamboo stick, and step by painful step, made his way up the left face of the mountain.

At the end of his strength, Ngo Dat had to crawl on his belly. But finally, he looked up and could hardly believe what he saw. In the distance, half-hidden by the lush vegetation, were many brilliant, multicolored roofs and gates of an extraordinarily beautiful temple. From afar, the delicate sounds of a windbell reached him, and he thought he was hearing the wind in the leaves of the Tree of Seven Jewels described in the *Amitabha Sutra*. A bird melodiously sang nearby, and he thought it was the sweet voice of the karavinda bird. As he reached the main gate of the temple, he met a novice, who told him that this was indeed the temple of the Most Venerable Kanishka. The novice went back inside to announce the visitor, and a moment later, Kanishka walked out. His old friend, resplendent like a bodhisattva, was such a vision that Ngo Dat fell to his knees and prostrated before him. Kanishka bent down, helped the former Teacher of the Nation to his feet, and, with a gentle hand, led him into the reception hall.

Together, they drank cup after cup of a tea so fragrant that it awakened Ngo Dat from the deep slumber of the past fifteen years. Kanishka asked his friend about his recent life and work, and though he was a man of forty-six who had been the most exalted Great Teacher of the Nation, Ngo Dat could not help feeling as small as a helpless child. He told his host every detail, and Kanishka listened intently, now and then sighing in sorrowful compassion for his friend's travails. Then he asked to see the sore. Ngo Dat pulled up his trouser leg and showed it to his friend. The sore was a terrible sight: it glared at the two men. Kanishka told Ngo Dat, "My friend, at the base of this mountain is a stream called the Brook that Unties All that Binds. Its water can help rid you of this monstrous sore. Stay here tonight, and then first thing tomorrow we will go down together. I will help you wash it. I assure you the sore will go away. Two washings will suffice."

Then the Most Venerable Kanishka left and returned with a basin of warm water and a bowl of salt. Smiling, he said, "Honored Friend, long ago you washed my pitiful body for two years. Do you remember? Now, before the water of the miraculous brook does its healing work, please allow me to clean your sore one time for you."

Ngo Dat was about to decline, but seeing Kanishka's sincere eyes, he knew it would be of no use. Kneeling solemnly, Kanishka poured water on Ngo Dat's festering, foul-smelling sore, and washed it using only salted warm water and a washcloth. Kanishka soothed away the loneliness and pain that six months' wandering had inflicted upon his friend. Ngo Dat was so moved, his eyes filled up with tears. When Kanishka finished, he took the dirty basin away and then returned with clean water and another towel. He took off Ngo Dat's robe and began to bathe him, washing his entire body from head to toe, as if the former National Teacher were a small child. Then he went away and came back with a clean monk's robe and helped his friend dress. Ngo Dat could only let himself be cared for. The clean robe, still smelling of the sun, was light and soothing, and from it the fragrance of cedarwood arose and filled his nostrils. That evening, Ngo Dat ate rice gruel cooked and served by the Venerable himself. Then he was taken to a small room with a clean-smelling cot. Kanishka bade him goodnight, and they agreed that, after early-morning tea, they would go down to the brook together.

But some time past midnight, Ngo Dat could wait no longer. All night long, the sore had been causing him more pain than ever. It would be too long until morning. He remembered that he had heard the murmurings of a brook as he arrived at the base of the mountain, so he rose from his cot, put on his robe, and limped out of his small room. The mist was thick, and Ngo Dat could hardly see his way, but he managed to find the path down the mountain. After limping for awhile, he heard the brook again, and finally, he found it.

He knelt down on a rock and pulled the left leg of his trousers up, exposing the sore. Breathing slowly and deeply, he brought himself to a state of deep concentration. Reciting the name of Lord Buddha several times, he bent down and scooped up some brook water with both hands. The water was icy cold and it stung his hands, causing him to spill at least half of it. But the half that remained in the palms of his hands was enough. When it came into contact with the open sore, he felt a stabbing pain that went straight to his marrow, and he collapsed right on the bank of the brook. Half-conscious, he saw an angry red face, its hair and beard upright, glaring at him and speaking, "Ah! You who are reputed to be so wise and well-read, tell me, have you ever read the *Book of the Western Han?*"

Ngo Dat was taken by complete surprise, but he maintained his composure and replied, "Yes, I have."

"Then you must recall the affair of Vien An and Trieu Pho? Because of Vien An's slanderous statements, Trieu Pho had to die by back-chopping in the middle of the Eastern Market. What a horror! What an injustice!

"Look at me: I am Trieu Pho. And you are no one but Vien An, the slanderer, the murderer! You did me a terrible wrong, and for many lives I have chased after you to make you pay for your crime. For ten lifetimes, I have pursued you, but I have not been able to take revenge because in each existence you have been a great monk, even a saint, and your ways and conduct have been so blameless I could find no opening for an attack. But Vien An, I finally caught up with you! The king's devotion and the people's worship brought you down. You exposed yourself to pride and egotism, and I found a way in. I am the sore you have been carrying on your body!"

The former Teacher of the Nation looked straight at the angry red face and broke into a cold sweat. He wanted to say something, but he knew there was nothing to say. The red face spoke to him again, this time in a less wrathful tone of voice.

"No, of course, you don't have to say anything. In so many existences, I have myself suffered because of this desire for revenge. I have sunk into darkness because of my hatred for you. But the Most Venerable Kanishka proposed using this miraculous water to wash your sore, and doing so has washed away my hatred. I will no longer chase after you. It is your great blessing to have met the holy Kanishka and to be saved by him. Our karmic debt to one another is released! Please, get some water and wash yourself once more! Hurry!"

Ngo Dat woke suddenly and sat bolt upright. He knelt down on a large rock, bent over the brook, and splashed two more handfuls of water onto the big sore. The pain was even more terrible than before, and again he lost consciousness. But this time, he no longer saw the angry red face. He felt only a great peace descend on his body and soul. He saw himself in a forest, running and jumping over rocks and bushes with the ease of a butterfly fluttering along the grass. He was a child running in a spring field of wildflowers. Then he was floating on his back on a cool river looking up at the immense blue sky. Then he was a child again, this time dressed for New Year's, frolicking on a snow-covered hillside. Feeling cold, he ran inside to warm his hands over a fire, and he saw his grandmother sitting with her sewing basket, and his mother, her eyes flowing with tenderness. The hearth was so comforting he did not want to go out into the cold again. Then, suddenly, he heard the howlings of the monkeys nearby.

Ngo Dat woke up and found himself lying on the bank of the brook. All around him the forest was filled with choruses of birds singing. The sun had risen, and Ngo Dat felt warm and contented. He rose swiftly and pulled up the left leg of his trousers. The sore was no longer red. The face on it had begun to dry up, and it was becoming smaller. The boil was beginning to heal.

Filled with energy, Ngo Dat looked for the path leading up the mountain, but there was no path in sight, only stones and bushes. He spotted the large rock where he had rested yesterday upon arriving at the base of the mountain, and he looked up. The sun had cleared the mist, but he saw no temple roofs, no gate, and no giant pines! All that happened seemed like a dream. He sat down and thought about what had occurred: seeing the giant pines, discovering the magnificent temples, meeting the young novice, drinking tea with his friend Kanishka— fragrant cups of tea that rid him of so much weariness, being washed by Kanishka and given a new cedar-scented monk's robe. Then he looked down and he saw that he was still wearing the torn, foul-smelling robes he had been wearing for six months!

Ngo Dat sighed deeply. He understood. The course of destiny had come full circle. He turned toward the mountain and bowed deeply three times, his heart overflowing with gratitude. But his gratitude had a tinge of regret, for he knew he would never see his friend Kanishka again.

∞

Tam The, the Venerable Patriarch of Phap Van Temple, along with two disciples, arrived at Chi Duc, a small thatched meditation hut at the foot of Cuu Lung Mountain. It was a sunny afternoon. As they approached the hut, Tin Co, a gentle monk of forty years, was already on the bridge to greet them. The tall, straight pine trees in the area were not thick in foliage, but they seemed to reach up to heaven in their uprightness. For many years, the Patriarch of Phap Van Temple had heard about this small retreat at the foot of Cuu Lung Mountain, but this was the first time he had actually visited it. He was indeed pleased to have made the journey. Every tree, every rock, and every leaf here were very beautiful. And the brook beneath the bridge was especially clear. The Patriarch lifted his eyes toward the summit of the mountain, which was still covered in mist, and saw many tall pines rising to the sky. He nodded silently, in approval and admiration.

His host ushered him into the delightful small temple-retreat, half-hidden by greenery, and a novice served them tea. Venerable Tam The noticed, lying on a small desk nearby, a bound volume that was obviously being filled in. The calligraphy was excellent, he thought to himself. He asked to see it, and he read on the cover, *The Water of Compassion That Washes Away All Wrongdoing*. Venerable Tam The put the book back down on the desk and was about to inquire about it, when Tin Co, the Abbot of Chi Duc, said to him, "This, Most Venerable, is the text of a repentance ceremony that my master himself prepared. This is the first copy."

Still looking intently at the small volume, Tam The said, "May I assume that your Honored Master is the one who founded this temple? What was his august name, pray tell me."

"You are correct, Most Venerable. My master built this humble abode forty years ago. As long as he was alive, the place had no name. Only after he passed away did I name it. Mindful of my great debt toward my master, I chose the name Chi Duc Zen Retreat. When he came here, there were no settlements for miles around. Only after he built this meditation hut did a handful of peasants and woodcutters start to arrive and build their own places."

Venerable Tam The asked, "I suppose when the Most Honored Master came here, you were with him, as a small child of course?"

Tin Co shook his head, "No, Most Venerable, my master came to Cuu Lung Mountain by himself. I was a child of seven then, and my father was one of the woodcutters I just mentioned who moved here afterwards. When my eyes fell upon him, I became his disciple. All my education, literary and religious, I received from my master. My master used to compliment me on my calligraphy, but to this day, I believe that his brushwork was the work of the gods."

Abbot Tin Co reached for another bound volume and gave it to Venerable Tam The. Tam The recognized right away that it was the original of *The Water of Compassion That Washes Away All Wrongdoing*, in Tin Co's master's own calligraphy. The script was firm yet graceful, bold yet delicate, like a dance of phoenixes. His head shook in delight. "How beautiful! How marvelous!"

Then he looked up and said, "This is a most precious work. Why have you not inscribed the name of your Honored Master on the first page, so that posterity will know about him and pay him homage?"

Tin Co replied, "My master did not want his name on it. He came here and lived the life of a hermit, nameless and unknown. What would be the point of leaving his name on a page?"

Then, after a moment of silence, he continued, "The day my master came here, there was only wilderness. With his own hands, he built the retreat, cleared the bushes, planted beans, and grew rice. He had never done such work before. When he arrived, he sat on a rock on the bank of the brook. He was in great pain, and there was no strength left in him." As Tin Co spoke, the image of the wandering monk who had stayed one night under the gate of Phap Van Temple forty years earlier came swiftly into the mind of Venerable Tam The. He was only the Novice Tam The then, but in his mind's eye, he could still see clearly the old monk's solemn expression and majestic bearing, his robe covered with dust and dirt, and he could still smell that awful stench. Tin Co's master must have been the stranger who had asked for permission to sleep under his temple gate. It must have been he who founded Chi Duc Temple. The Venerable Tam The stood up and clasped his hands in front of his chest. "Most Honored Host, your master once stopped by our humble temple and stayed overnight. It was forty years ago. I myself had the honor of bringing him water to wash and rice gruel for his supper. I dare say that our two temples, Chi Duc and Phap Van, are neighbors, for only a half-day's walk separates us. Won't you, for the sake of that, allow me to know the noble name of your master, for whom, even after such a brief encounter, I have felt until this day a most profound veneration?"

Faced with such genuine respect, Tin Co was moved to stand up, too, and it was his turn to bow deeply to his visitor. "Most Venerable, I will not keep the secret from you. But it is getting late in the day, and if I tell you my master's story, we will speak late into the night. Please accept my invitation for you and your attendants to spend the night here." Tam The accepted, and Tin Co lit two white candles and told the Patriarch of Phap Van Temple all about his master. He began with his master's encounter, while still a student-monk, with the Indian monk Kanishka; told him about when his master had been the Great Teacher of the Nation; about the boil; and about when he scooped water from the brook and splashed it on his sore. The night advanced, and though their disciples had all retired, the Abbots of Chi Duc and Phap Van Temples continued to sit facing one another. The candles burned in silence, and the mountain outside was perfectly still.

Tin Co cleared his throat, and went on, "My master was so grateful to the holy Kanishka for having delivered him from such mortal hatred, he made a vow to remain on this mountain the rest of his life. He broke branches with his bare hands and built a small hut. He ate fruits and wild greens, drank water from the brook, and spent all his remaining time in meditation. From the few woodcutters he encountered, he obtained seeds for beans and vegetables, a hoe and even a machete. I was told later that my master was infinitely more at peace here at the foot of Cuu Lung Mountain than he had been as the Great Teacher of the Nation in the capital.

"After I became his disciple, I enlarged the garden, and from then on we always had enough to eat. Whenever I had extra time, I cut firewood, which, through my brother, was sold at the marketplace. The proceeds were enough to buy ink, brushes, and paper for my own studies. When he saw these implements, my master couldn't resist! He started to write again, and he wrote prolifically. *The Water of Compassion That Washes Away All Wrongdoing* was the first work that came from his brush in this mountain. He called it *The Water of Compassion* to honor the holy Kanishka, who had used the water from the brook to wash away the curse that had hounded my master for ten lifetimes. My master often admonished me, "To follow the Way is to seek liberation, not fame or gain." I understand this well, knowing as I do of my master's vicissitudes! He often told me to keep whatever I knew about him to myself, and, in truth, I should have obeyed him.

"But tonight, I cannot do this. Because you have met my master, you are a friend. Pardon my forwardness, but I can see my master in your presence. Now that I have told you this story, I will never tell anyone else again. Speaking to you about my master's life has lifted a great weight from my shoulders. Please accept my gratitude. It is quite late now. Let me show you your room and wish you a very peaceful sleep. Tomorrow, I will show you my master's tomb."

Lying on his small cot, the Patriarch of Phap Van Temple remained wide awake. Forty years, he thought. What have I done these past forty years? I studied, worked with my hands, sat in meditation, and expounded the Dharma. I was a novice of sixteen, and now I am head of a large temple. For forty years, I have been tied down at Phap Van Temple while so much water has flowed down this brook at the foot of Cuu Lung Mountain.

Suddenly, the young novice that Tam The had been forty years earlier came alive in him, and tears welled up in his eyes. He realized that he no longer wanted to be the Patriarch of a great temple. As Patriarch, he had no opportunity to grow vegetables, plant corn, or cut firewood, and no chance to come to Cuu Lung Mountain in time to see the founder of the Chi Duc Zen Retreat. This mountain is only half a day's walk from my temple, he thought, yet I never came. Tam The cocked his ear and listened. He could hear the murmurings of the brook, becoming fainter and fainter. As he dozed off, Novice Tam The saw two tall pine trees atop Cuu Lung Mountain, their tops shrouded in thick mist. Two giant pines, as tall as the sky.

⚭

The Pine Gate

IT WAS A CHILLY autumn evening, and the full moon had just risen, when the young swordsman arrived at the foot of the mountain. The wilderness was bathed in the light of the moon glimmering playfully on branches and leaves. It seemed that nothing had changed during the seven years he was away, and yet it was surprising that no one was there to greet him. The swordsman paused at the foot of the mountain and looked up. He saw that the narrow path up the mountain was barred by a tightly shut pine gate. He walked forward slowly and pushed at the gate, but it was immovable, even under his powerful hands.

Never, in as long as he could remember, had his master locked that gate. This narrow path was the only way up the mountain. So, holding onto the handle of his sword, he jumped as high as he could, but he was unable to jump over the low gate. A strange force had gripped his whole body and pushed it back down. Next he unsheathed his long sword to cut the gate's bar open, but the sword's sharp blade bounced back from the soft pinewood with so powerful an impact that it sent a shock through his hand and wrist. He raised his sword toward the sky and examined its edge under the moonlight. Somehow, the gate was too hard for his sword. It seemed that his master had endowed it with the strength of his own spirit. It was impassable. The swordsman sighed deeply, returned his sword to its sheath, and sat down on a rock outside the gate.

Seven years earlier, on the day he was to leave the mountain, his master looked into his eyes for a long moment without saying anything. There was a kind expression on his master's face, and yet there was something else, too—a kind of pity. The young swordsman could only bow his head in reverence. After a while, the old man said to him, "I cannot keep you here forever. I know you have to go down the mountain and into the world to carry out the Way and help people. I thought I could keep you here with me a little longer, but if it is your will to leave now, you have all my blessings. Remember what I have taught you. In the world below, you will need it."

Then his master told him what to seek, what to avoid, and what to change. Finally, he put his gentle hand on his disciple's shoulder. "These are the main guidelines for your actions: Never do anything that might cause suffering to yourself or others, in the present or in the future. Go without fear in the direction that will lead yourself and others to complete awakening. And remember the standards by which happiness and suffering, liberation and illusion are measured. Without them, you betray the Way, and will not help anyone.

"Here is my most precious sword. It is a sharp blade that comes from your own heart. Use it to subdue all evil and also to conquer all ambition and desire.

"Here is the *me ngo* glass," he said, handing his disciple a small viewing glass. "It will help you distinguish the wholesome from the unwholesome, the virtuous from the immoral. Sometimes it is called the 'Demon Viewer,' for looking through it, you will be able to see the true forms of demons and evil spirits."

The following day, at the break of dawn, the young swordsman went up to the central hall to take leave of his master. The old man walked with him down the mountain, all the way to Tiger Brook, and there, amidst the murmuring of the mountain stream, master and disciple bade one another farewell. The master put his hand on the young man's shoulder, looked into his eyes, and said, "Remember, my child, poverty cannot weaken you, wealth cannot seduce you, power cannot vanquish you. I will be here the day you come back, your vows fulfilled!" Then he watched his disciple's every step very carefully, as the young man walked away to begin his journey.

The swordsman recalled the first days of the journey vividly. Then, months and years swirled through his mind. Humanity had revealed itself under so many different guises! How helpful the sword and the *me ngo* glass had been! Once, he met a monk, an old sage, whose appearance instantly inspired reverence. The old man invited him back to his hermitage to discuss how they might "join their efforts to help humankind." The young man listened with rapture, but then something struck him as odd about the old monk. He took out the *me ngo* glass and when he looked through it, he saw in front of him a giant demon with eyes sending forth crackling sparks, a horn on its forehead, and fangs as long as his own arms! The young man jumped back, drew his sword, and furiously attacked it. The demon fought back but, of course, it had no chance. It prostrated itself at the young man's feet, begging for mercy. The swordsman then demanded that it swear, under oath, to return to the place it had come from, study the Way, pray to be reborn as a human being, and refrain from ever disguising itself again as a monk to bewitch and devour the innocent.

Another time, he met a mandarin, an old man with a long white beard. It was a happy encounter between a young hero out to save the world and a high official, a "father and mother to the people" bent on finding better ways to govern and benefit the masses. Again, the young man's instinct was aroused, and under the glass, the handsome, awe-inspiring official turned out to be an enormous hog whose eyes literally dripped with greed. In an instant, the sword flew out of its sheath. The hog tried to flee, but the swordsman overtook it in one leap. Standing in front of the gate to the mandarin's mansion, he barred the only escape route. The beast took on its true form and cried out loudly for mercy. Again, the young man did not leave without extracting from the monster the solemn oath that it would follow the Way and that it would never again take the form of a mandarin to gnaw the flesh and suck the blood of the people.

Another time, walking by a marketplace, the young man saw a crowd surrounding a picture and book stall. The vendor was a beautiful young lady with a smile as radiant as a lotus opening to the sun. Seated nearby was another beautiful young lady singing softly while plucking the strings of a lute. The young ladies' beauty and the grace of the songs so captivated everyone present that no one left the stall once they had stopped. They could only stand and listen, enraptured, and buy pictures and books. Also drawn to the scene, the young man managed to make his way to the front and he held up one of the pictures. The elegance of the design and strength of the colors overwhelmed him. Yet an uneasiness arose within him, and when he reached for his *me ngo* glass, he saw that the two beautiful girls were actually enormous snakes whose tongues darted back and forth like knife blades. The swordsman swept everyone aside in one movement of his arms, and with his sword pointing at the monsters, he shouted thunderously, "Demons! Back to your evil nature!"

The crowd scattered in fright as the big snakes lashed at the young man. But as soon as his fabulous sword drew a few flashing circles around their bodies, the reptiles coiled at his feet in submission. He forced their jaws open, carved out their venomous fangs, and extracted the solemn promise that they would never come back to bewitch the village people. Then he burned down the bookstall and sent the monsters back to their lairs.

The young swordsman went from village to village and from town to town on his mission, using his sword and his viewing glass to vanquish demons and offer them priceless counsel. He began to see himself as the "Indispensable Swordsman." He had come down from the mountain into a world where treachery and cunning reigned, and the world was surely better for his presence. He experienced great exhilaration in his actions for the good. At times, he even forgot to eat and sleep, the joy and satisfaction from helping people was so great.

Years passed quickly. One day, as he was resting alongside a river watching the water flow quietly by, he realized that he had not used the *me ngo* glass for some time. It was not that he had forgotten it. He just had not felt like using it. He remembered that at first he had used the glass reluctantly, and then had fought to the death every time he saw, through the *me ngo*, the true natures of the many evils that faced him. He recalled the great happiness he felt each time he saw, through the glass, the image of a virtuous man or a true sage. But, obviously, something had happened to him, and he didn't know what it was. He no longer felt much joy or fury whether he saw a sage or a monster. In fact, the monsters began to have a certain familiarity to him, even their horrifying features. The *me ngo* glass just remained safely in his pocket. The young swordsman thought about returning to the mountain some day to ask his master's advice. Why was he reluctant to use the *me ngo* glass, that had obviously been of great help to him in the past?

On the twelfth day of the eighth month, seven years after he had left the mountain, he was walking through a forest of white plum trees, when suddenly, he yearned for the days when he studied under his old master, whose cottage also stood in an old plum forest. Covered with snow-white plum blossoms under the autumn moon, he decided to return to the mountain.

He climbed many hills and crossed dozens of streams and, after seven days and seven nights, he reached the foot of the mountain. As he arrived, darkness was descending, and the rising moon revealed that the pine gate to the path up the mountain to his Master's abode was tightly shut. There was nothing he could do but wait. He could not go any further until one of his brothers came down to open the gate. At dawn, he thought, one of them will surely come down to fetch water from the stream, and they will open the gate for me. Now, the moon had risen and the entire mountain and forest were bathed in its cool light.

As the night wore on, the air became chillier. He pulled his sword out of the sheath and watched the moon's reflection on the sword's cold, sharp edge. Then he sheathed it again and stood up. The moon was extraordinarily bright. Mountain and forest were still, as if unaware of the swordsman's presence. He dropped onto another rock, dejected, and the past seven years passed before him again. Slowly, the moon edged toward the summit of a distant mountain, and the stars shone brightly. Then they, too, began to recede, and there was a hint of glow in the east, as dawn was about to break.

The swordsman heard the rustling of dry leaves. He looked up and saw the vague form of someone walking down the mountains. It must be one of his younger brothers, he thought, though it was not light enough to be sure. The person was carrying something like a large water jug. As the figure came closer and closer, the swordsman heard it exclaim, happily, "Elder Brother!"

"Younger Brother!"

"When did you arrive?"

"As the moon was just rising! I've been here all night. Why is the gate locked like this? Was it the master's order?"

The younger disciple raised his hand and pulled, ever so lightly, at the heavy gate. It swung open with ease. He stepped through it, and, grasping the swordsman's hands, looked at him and said, "You must be chilled to the bone. Look, you're covered with dew!

"My job used to be to come down here all day to pick herbs and watch the gate. If someone came who deserved an audience with the master, I'd bring him up. If I thought someone was not ready to see him, I'd just stay behind the bushes, and eventually they'd just give up! As you know, our master doesn't want to see anyone who does not have a true determination to learn.

"Lately, the master has allowed me to move on to more advanced studies, and as I stay up at the retreat most of the time, he told me to close the gate. He said it would open itself for anyone who is virtuous, but that it would bar the way for those too heavy with the dust of the world!"

The swordsman asked, "Would you say I am such a person? Why did the gate stay shut for me?"

The younger man laughed heartily, "Of course not! Anyway, we can go up now. But wait a moment, Elder Brother! I must first fetch some water. Will you come with me? Smile, Brother! Why are you so angry?"

Both men laughed. They made their way down to the stream. The sun was not yet up, but the east was already glowing brightly. The two disciples could now see each other's faces clearly. In the water, which was tinted a pale rose by the dawn, they could see their reflections next to one another. The swordsman was bold and strong in his knight's suit, the long sword slung diagonally over his back. The younger disciple's figure was gentler in his flowing monk's robe, a jug in his hands. Without speaking, they looked at both reflections, and smiled to one another. A water spider sprung up suddenly and caused the rose-tinted surface to ripple, sending their images into thousands of undulating patterns.

"How beautiful! I would certainly destroy our reflections for good if I dipped the jug in now. By the way, do you still have the *me ngo* viewing glass with you? I remember that our master gave it to you when you came down the mountain years ago!"

The swordsman reached in his pocket to get it, and he realized that for all the years he was away, he had used the glass to look at others, but never once had he looked at himself through it. He took the glass out, wiped it on his sleeve, and aimed it at the water's surface. The two men's heads came close to look through the small glass together.

A loud scream escaped from the throats of both of them. It reverberated through the forest. The swordsman fell forward and collapsed. A deer, drinking water farther upstream, looked up in fright. The younger disciple could not believe what he had seen. There he was in his flowing robe, jug in hand, standing next to a towering demon whose eyes were deep and dark like waterwells and whose long fangs curved down around its square jaw. The demon's face was bluish gray, the shade of ashes and death. The young man shuddered, and, rubbing his eyes, looked again at his senior, who was now lying unconscious on the blue stones of the riverbank, the older man's face still expressing shock and horror. Suffering had been etched upon his brother, who, for seven years, had ceaselessly braved the rough and cruel world down below their mountain retreat.

The young disciple reached down to the stream to fetch water to douse his elder's face, and a moment later, the swordsman came to, his face ravaged with despair. His true image had appeared in the *me ngo* glass so unexpectedly, bringing him self-knowledge in such a swift, brutal fashion that he could do nothing but collapse under the blow. His energy had vanished. He tried to stand up, but he had no strength in his legs or arms.

"It's all right. It's all right, my elder brother! We'll go up now."

To the swordsman's ears, his brother's voice was like a faint breeze murmuring from afar. He shook his head. His world had collapsed, and he wanted to live no longer. He felt as if he had just stood in the path of a hurricane. How could he bring himself into his beloved master's presence?

The younger man brushed the dirt off his brother's shoulder. "You need not worry about it. Our master has nothing but compassion for you. Let's go up now. We'll live and work and study together again."

The two figures made their way slowly up the steep, rock-strewn path that wound its way up the mountain. It was not yet day, and the silhouettes imprinted themselves on the thin veil of dew stretching over trees and rocks. The first rays of sun finally reached the two men and heightened the contrast—the swordsman seemed only more broken in body and spirit walking next to the younger disciple whose steps were firm and whose mien was gentle.

Over the mountaintop, far away, the sun rose.

∞
A Bouquet of Wildflowers

Many years ago, the wife of a good-natured farmer passed away after giving birth to their second child. The farmer raised the children alone, until, when his son was sixteen and his daughter eleven, he too fell ill and died. Following his last request, the children buried him in one of their rice paddies, surrounded by *o-moi* and *so-dua* trees.

The children knew that six generations ago, one of their ancestors—a scholar who wanted to flee his difficult career—had moved south from central Vietnam, cleared a forested area, and established four fertile rice fields. For six generations, his children and their children worked hard and became real farmers.

Before his death, the farmer called his two children to his deathbed and made this last request: "After I die, do not sell any of our rice fields. Take care of them and continue to plant and to harvest. You know that for five generations, our ancestors have believed that a treasure of gold and jewels was buried by the founder of this land somewhere in our fields, but so far, no one has found it. Our ancestors left a poem, and my father was told this poem would help us find the buried treasure. But for several generations, no one has understood the meaning of the poem. Your grandfather told me that to uncover the meaning of the poem, one must contemplate it for a long time. During your grandfather's lifetime, our country went through many adversities, and he had to move often as a refugee, although he always returned to the land. Other houses fell in ruins, but your grandfather had worked hard to rebuild and maintain our house. Grandfather never had time to reflect upon the poem and he asked me to find the time to meditate on it. But I have not had the time to do it. I have only been able to work in the fields.

"So I pass the treasure and these instructions on to you. Don't be as busy as I have been. Work just enough to live, and take the time to find the deep meaning of the poem and uncover the treasure. That will be the best way for you to show your gratitude to our ancestors. The poem is on page forty-four of the family register, which is in the wooden case on the ancestors' altar."

The day after their father's funeral, the brother and sister prostrated before the altar and took down the family register. Ceremoniously, with great respect, they opened the register to page forty-four and read the poem:

> No tile roof above
> no land to settle below.
> Don a new robe
> and tread forward with your staff.
> With just one step, the world will tremble
> like a dragon leaping on its prey.

Brother and sister sat still for a long time. Their incense stick had almost burned to the end before the young lady's voice broke the silence, "Brother, do you understand? The poem sounds wonderful, but I don't understand a word."

The brother did not reply. He just closed the family register and put it back in the wooden case on the altar, respectfully. Then the two of them prostrated before the ancestors again. After several minutes more, the brother said, "Grandfather was right. We will need a lot of time to understand. Let us do as we were told. After we settle down, we must carve out time to meditate on that poem."

∽

Time went by quickly. For six years, brother and sister had excellent crops, and they were able to rebuild their ancestors' house. The tile roof was shiny-red. In the yard, the jackfruit trees grew green and dense, laden with fruit. The rice granary was always full. Two strong water buffaloes shared the plowing to break up the ebony soil of the rice fields and allow the young green rice plants to grow. Brother and sister were very success-ful and very generous, and the people of the village loved and respected them both. When someone needed to borrow rice, they always received more than they asked for. Everyone who worked for them was honest, treating their masters' property as their own.

The young ladies of the village all had eyes for the young man, but the thought of marrying never occurred to him. In fact, he was determined not to get married so he would have time to look deeply into the poem. When his sister came to mar-riage age, the young men in the village all courted her. She was beautiful and compassionate, and many intermediaries came to propose marriage. But she always refused. She too wanted to have time to penetrate the meaning of the poem.

But the two of them were too busy in their daily work to have enough time to contemplate anything. Not that they had any debts, or major repairs, or farm problems. Their many work-ers helped with the house and the fields, and their crops flour-ished. It was just that the time went by so fast.

Finally, the brother began to have sleepless nights worrying about all of this. He was taking good care of the rice fields and the house inherited from his ancestors, but he did not feel hap-py. He could not feel peaceful until he had found the deep meaning of the poem. Why? Did he really need his ancestors' treasure? He already had success and riches, yet the very source of that success—the house, the garden, the rice fields—were obstacles to his search. There were only twenty-four hours in a day, and those hours were completely filled. At dawn, he ate breakfast and went to work in the fields. At noon, he had a light lunch and a nap. In the afternoon he continued working in the fields with the buffaloes. And in the evening, there was only time for washing, eating, and sleeping. When would he ever have time to contemplate?

If he were without his house and rice fields, he would be just a homeless wanderer. But with a house and rice fields, he had time only for them. He tossed and turned all night, thinking of the hermits of old who had left their homes and gone into the remote jungle to seek the Way. Yes, to have time, he thought, I may have to leave everything behind. But how can I leave the fortune inherited from our ancestors? The treasure is in the rice fields. To leave would be to lose everything.

Time continued. When he was thirty years old, the brother's aspiration to understand the poem had only grown deeper. His fields were thick with golden rice and the harvesters talked, laughed, and sang joyfully as they worked. During moonlit evenings at threshing time, young men and women gathered and sang together. But none of these things made him happy. His sister noticed this and offered to take complete charge of the house and all the field chores, so he could devote himself to studying the poem.

Her idea seemed wise, but to put it into practice was not easy. Even after his sister had begun to take care of everything inside and outside, he still could not stay idle. He was too accustomed to working, and he felt unhappy when his hands were free from chores. He realized that he would need to leave home and find a remote temple if he really wanted to contemplate the poem.

So he did. He left home and went to a remote region of central Vietnam, where he was accepted at a temple. During his retreat there, his sister sent five hundred pounds of rice every month to the temple as a donation. Undistracted by chores, the brother was finally free to meditate on the poem.

∞

Three years passed. Now the young man walked slowly on the sunny, deserted village road back to his farm. He had not seen anyone yet. When he got to the crossroads, he put down his bag and sat in the shade of an old banyan tree. Everything was completely still.

For three years, he had worked in the monastic community—planting potatoes, cleaning vegetables, chopping wood, and carrying water. At the temple, hard work was very much a part of the practice. In fact, he now worked harder than he had at home, but somehow he also had time to memorize each line of the poem. He recited it silently countless times during sitting meditation, walking meditation, and work. But even after three years, nothing had been revealed. The first two sentences seemed to be the most mysterious:

> No tile roof above
> no land to settle below.

Where was this place? Could it be a pond? No, a pond still had "land to settle below." And how could there be a pond in the rice fields? There was only the duckweed pond, and that was in the backyard. Besides, how could a treasure be buried in a pond? Perhaps the treasure was under a large stone? But there were no large stones in the fields either. The place where there is no tile roof must be the open air, he thought. He felt he finally understood the first line. However, he was not at all sure about about the second line and even more unclear about the next two:

> Don a new robe
> and tread forward with your staff.

This must refer to his ancestors' burial site, he thought. These lines suggested a funeral: people putting on mourning robes, a monk holding a staff. But his ancestors' tombs were in the village cemetery, not in the rice fields. In the field surrounded by o-moi and so-dua trees, there were only his parents' tombs. The final two lines confused him the most:

> With just one step, the world will tremble
> like a dragon leaping on its prey.

He thought of geomancy. Perhaps a good geomancer would be able to locate the "dragon's mouth" in the four rice fields. But how could there be a blue dragon or a white tiger in such a vast, flat area?

At the temple, he had once given the poem to a venerable monk and asked him to explain it, but the old monk could not help at all. After three years at the temple, the young man felt he did not have much better an understanding of the poem than when he had arrived there. But his mind and spirit had changed. He looked at things more attentively and somehow began to feel a connection between his daily life—eating, sleeping, and working—and his ancestors' poem. His life and the poem felt as close as the blood circulating in his body.

The rays of the sun lengthened, and the afternoon air became cooler. The young man stood up, put his bag back on his shoulder, and continued walking. The rice plants surrounding him were tender and green, and they waved to him in the afternoon breeze. A light happiness permeated his whole being. Suddenly, the sound of singing caught his attention. He stopped to listen, and he heard a voice as joyful as the young rice plants swaying in the breeze. The voice grew clearer and clearer, and the man recognized it as his sister's. Feeling as excited as the New Year, he ran ahead, looking for his sister, and he saw her walking up from the mulberry field, singing to the water buffaloes, a bouquet of wildflowers in her hand. When she caught sight of her brother, she ran toward him and spontaneously handed him the wildflowers she had picked in the field. Smiling widely, she looked him over from head to toe, at his brown clothes and the gray bag on his shoulder. Then she looked directly into his eyes. Her gaze was as clear as a fresh stream, bringing comfort and peace to his whole body and mind. His sorrows suddenly vanished, and he felt as light as a floating cloud. She was his sister, but the look in her eyes was as generous and protective as a mother's.

∞

Brother and Sister drove the herd down to the meadow and sat on a mound of earth beneath a cool shade tree. Then he began to tell her about his three years of temple life and his insights about the poem, and she listened attentively, without interrupting him or missing a single detail. When he finished, he looked deeply at his sister. Her skin was tanned, her body healthy, her eyes bright, and her smile fresh and compassionate. She used to be somewhat quiet. Now she was completely silent. When he saw her manner and the look in her eyes, he knew she had found peace, joy, and happiness.

She understood his mind, and she said, "After you left, I took care of the house and the fields alone, but I didn't consider it a burden. I felt completely at ease doing all the chores. I did them slowly, and I enjoyed it. You were always able to plow the fields in seven days; it took me twelve. I realized that whether I finished quickly or slowly, it would come to the same end. Whenever I held the plow and pushed the buffalo forward, I thought, "This might be where the treasure is buried." Realizing that any spot in the field might be the place where the treasure was buried, I plowed even more slowly, giving my full care and attention to each inch of soil.

"On the afternoon of the eighth day, while plowing the last furrow in the field close to the pagoda, I realized that in all four fields, every spot is a treasure! The treasure is not hidden in the soil. It is each inch of the land itself. I saw that the land is precious not just because it produces rice, but because it is the land. I looked at the plow, the buffalo, the white clouds, the sky, and the plumeria trees behind the pagoda and I saw that the plow is precious because it's a plow, and the buffalo is precious because it's a buffalo, and the clouds are precious because they are clouds, and the plumeria trees are precious because they are plumeria trees. I realized that what we have been looking for is not one particular treasure, but the unique presence of all beings in the universe, including ourselves.

"I felt happier than if I had discovered a treasure chest. I walked home after a day's work in the fields. I felt an enormous love for all life and all beings. The next day and the three days that followed, as I plowed, my mind was very clear. I could see that each drop of my sweat was nothing less than my entire soul watering the soil. I realized that I am not any more important than the buffalo or anything else.

"If I had been able to write, I would have written to you to let you know that whether or not you found the meaning of the poem or discovered the treasure, our lives would be filled with happiness. I continued to send rice to your temple each month, hoping that you would be inspired to find the meaning of the poem *for its own sake* and not just for finding our ancestors' treasure.

"What would we do with the treasure anyway if we found it? Would we buy more land? Build more houses? Aren't our four fields enough for us to plow? And who would take care of the houses? This house and fields were already enough to make you take refuge in the temple.

"I have no wish for the treasure. But I know that there is something in the poem of our ancestors that is deeply connected to our lives. Since the first time you read it to me, I've repeated the words many times, without comprehending the meaning at all. Still, each time I read it, my heart pounds, as when I hear the wind blowing between the so-dua leaves. I don't know what the wind is trying to say. I only know that I enjoy its sound and feel very close to the wind and the trees.

"Thanks to eight days of plowing on the treasure itself, I discovered myself, the plow, the buffalo, the white clouds, and the plumeria trees behind the pagoda. Then one night in a dream, I saw father smiling at me. His face was radiant. 'It was Brother, not I, who discovered the treasure,' I told him.

"Since that day, I've lived freely, singing with the buffaloes, the cows, the fields and the rice plants, awaiting your return. Now you are back, and I am very happy!"

∞

The brother listened carefully to his sister's words, which came deeply from her heart. He understood that his sister had truly discovered the treasure. He had gotten close to the treasure once, but he had not reached it. Sometimes, he, too, felt that he did not long for the treasure anymore. He felt a close connection between the poem and himself, as close as his ancestors' blood circulating in his veins. He realized that he had not found the treasure *because* he was looking for it. His sister had found it because she had not intended to look for it. "Tomorrow morning," he thought, "I will walk down to the fields, see the old plow, the buffalo, and all of the treasures there, and I will find myself again."

Then he stood up and looked at his sister, filled with love and gratitude, and walked with her up the hill. Together, they drove the herd ahead of them. As they walked back to the farm, the brother felt the earth, the sky, and the wind as kind, loving arms embracing his whole being.

∞

There Are Beautiful Eyes

SHE LIVED WITH her mother, in a small house made of mud and straw that was built high up on the hill. In front of their house grew one sturdy cypress tree that stayed green throughout the year. Every afternoon, her mother, although old and weak, would set out to collect firewood and also wild vegetables for soup. That was all her mother could do. The young woman had to work from before sunrise till sunset to eke out a living for them both. She would plant, tend, and harvest all the vegetables and fruits in the garden, and every third day, she had to bring whatever was ripe down to the marketplace to sell in exchange for rice and other necessities.

Everyone in the village knew she was pious, hard-working, gentle, and good, a woman of perfect virtue. Her smooth, black hair flowed over her slender shoulders, her face was the color of persimmons in summer, and her mouth blossomed every time she spoke. If her eyes had been clear, she would have been the most beautiful young woman in the village. But her eyes, those horrible eyes! Every time she looked in the mirror, she cried her eyes out! The young men in the village paid no attention to her at all. They cared only about the young women with bright, clear eyes. How she envied those with beautiful eyes. They are the ones who are happy, she thought. Looking in the mirror, she knew she had no future.

Then one autumn morning, a handsome young man paid her a visit. He stepped down from his horse, tied the reins to the cypress, and walked slowly yet confidently toward her house. He looked like a scholar—a high forehead, two clear eyes, and a square, determined chin—and he had a bright smile on his lips. She put down her basket and looked up at him, and she was suddenly overcome with shyness. Calmly offering her greetings with kindness, respect, and familiarity, the young man put her at ease. She went to the kitchen to prepare him some tea, and she brought it out to serve him.

The young man said he had come from far away because he had heard about her. His voice was very warm. She listened joyfully, as obedient as a small child listening to her older brother telling a story. She felt so much affection toward him she thought they must have had some connection in a previous life.

The young man opened a package wrapped in a cloth and revealed to her a collection of ancient texts. From the pile, he picked out one thin volume and handed it to her. "This is my most treasured book. It is for you. You are the only person with this miraculous book.

"Tonight before you go to sleep, light one candle. Then, every time you turn a page, think of me. If anything appears on the page, place it under your pillow and go right to sleep." After he said this, he left as suddenly as he had appeared. Their meeting had been short, but she knew that the stream of love that had opened in her heart was pure. It was not the kind of love in which a girl becomes shy when standing in front of the man of her dreams, but a more natural love—straightforward, gentle, and sweet.

That night she lit her candle, and, with a peaceful mind, she opened the beautiful old book. As she looked at the first page, she began to think of the young man. She saw that the book contained matters of the heart that were simple but extremely deep. In fact, the words seemed to speak only to her, and each time she turned a page, she thought of him. She felt touched to the core of her being, and she began to cry.

When she got halfway through the book, the page began to move. Then the last two words radiated a brilliant light and transformed themselves into two shining pearls, as bright as the early morning dew reflecting the rising sun. She picked up the pearls and, closing the book as the young man had instructed, placed them under her pillow and drifted to sleep.

The story continued in her dream, and she slept peacefully until the birds began to sing as the sun rose. When she reached under her pillow, nothing was there. Had it been a dream? No, the old book was still there beside her bed. She gazed at it for a long time until her mother called, reminding her to go out and crop some fresh vegetables for the marketplace.

The young woman put on her usual blouse, arranged all the flowers and vegetables into one basket, and said goodbye to her mother. That day her vegetables sold quickly, and she noticed that as people were buying her vegetables, they were staring at her. Perhaps there was some soot on her face, she thought, and she rubbed her cheek with her sleeve, but nothing came off.

When she returned home, she hurried to look in the mirror to wipe off the soot, and she was astonished! She had two very clear eyes! Her face was totally changed! Sparkling dark pupils shone forth as, for the first time, her eyes truly reflected her radiant being. Her eyes had become windows for the world to see her virtuous, compassionate soul. Suddenly she remembered the young man, and she fell to her knees in gratitude, sobbing with joy. Her tears only made her eyes deeper and more radiant.

From that day on, her life changed. The villagers all praised her, and all her vegetables and flowers sold out in a matter of minutes. The young men in the village all took notice of her, carrying wood or water for her whenever they could. At night, when the moon was bright, she sang to the many young men who gathered outside her small house. In the past, when her eyes were displeasing, no one had listened to her, but now they were pleased to listen to her sing for hours on end. In just a few weeks, her beauty had become known in every village in the province, and horses and carriages lined up at her door. Sons of wealthy families came and offered her gifts of diamonds and ivory. Sons of noble families built her a castle on that very plot of land. Princes built a gold and silver wall around the castle, and young kings planted trees with branches of gold and leaves of diamond. Quickly, she became wealthy and famous.

It was not long before things changed. She became cool and aloof, ignoring the gentle and simple young men from the village. Pride began to grow in her eyes and in her heart.

One day, the young man returned. He tied the reins of his horse to the cypress, and raised his head at the sight of the charming castle surrounded by a wall of gold and silver. The young man smiled as he entered. She was sitting inside listening to two noble gentlemen praise her beauty and talent. She began to sing for them, but when she saw the young man, she suddenly stopped. Facing his calm demeanor and radiant smile, she felt embarrassed and began to cry. Immediately, the two shining pearls fell from her eyes, rolled across the floor, and vanished into the earth! The two gentlemen, seeing her lusterless eyes, became frightened and, thinking she must be a sorceress, left in a hurry.

The young man looked at her, his eyes filled with deep compassion. He spoke to her in a comforting voice, saying that she might be able to retrieve her clear eyes. But she realized that it was he who had caused the problem. His calm presence had made her feel awkward and somehow lose the beautiful pearls. Standing before the one who had given her beauty, she was unable to sustain her pride, just as when the full moon rises, the nearby stars no longer seem bright. The young man advised her to read the book again, and when the two shining pearls appeared, to pick them up once again and place them under her pillow. Then he asked her if she would show him around the garden, and she did. Seeing that her life was of such great ease, he appeared happy. He looked at her for a long time, and then, understanding that it was in fact his presence that had caused the pearls to fall, he vowed to her never to return again. It was late afternoon when he mounted his horse and departed. She closed the door tightly behind him so no one would see her, and she waited impatiently for night to descend. Once again, she read the ancient text, and the miracle did indeed take place a second time. Her eyes became as clear as the water in an autumn lake, capable of drowning countless young men.

Several months later, about noon, while she was hosting a banquet for seventeen noble gentlemen, the two shining pearls fell to the ground once again and vanished into the earth. Her eyes again lost their luster and became ugly, and her guests fled, convinced that she was certainly a sorceress. Overcome with grief, she staggered out of her castle and down the mountain, wandering the streets of village after village until nightfall, finally losing herself in a small village in a remote region. She knocked on the door of a simple old house and was surprised to see the lovely young man answer. She burst into tears and told him what had happened. Immediately he understood. Because she had become so admired and famous, her pictures were everywhere. At noon that day, he had happened to see one of these pictures pinned to a tree, and that must have caused the pearls to fall from her eyes. The young man promised to go far, far away, to a place where he would never see her picture again. He would do anything to ensure her happiness. Then he escorted her home, suggesting that she try the old miracle again.

That night, she felt anxious and agitated. Would he keep his promise? What if he did see her picture one more time? Her suitors would abandon her forever. Seeing how sad she had become, her maid asked what was the matter. In deep distress, she revealed everything in her heart.

The maid said that there was only one thing to do. She had to murder the young man to prevent him from ever seeing her or her picture again. The idea frightened the young woman, but the more she thought about it, she realized there was really no other recourse. As long as the young man lived, her happiness was in jeopardy. So the two of them devised a plan. The maid would go to the house of the young man and offer him some poisoned food.

It worked. The young man died immediately, and peace came to the young woman and her charming castle. But it was not long-lasting. In less than a month, even though her eyes were beautiful and young men came from everywhere to lavish praise upon her, something heavy was pressing on her heart. She felt no peace at all. In fact, she was becoming more and more agitated. Unable to stand it any longer, she left her castle and went to the house of the young man. The simple house was still there, and the man's elderly servant came out to greet her. The servant knew everything that had happened, and he took her to the young man's grave by the stream and then back to the house, and he cooked her a warm meal. She asked him many questions about the young man, and the old servant explained quite frankly that the two pearls had been the result of many years of practice and purification, the crystallization of the young man's mental and physical essence. The young man had told his servant many times that as long as she was happy, he would not regret anything. Even as the young man was being poisoned, he understood what was happening, and he told his servant that if he had any more precious pearls, he would offer them to her. The young woman cried and cried, realizing how evil and destructive she had become. To comfort her, the servant showed her a picture of the young man. The moment she set eyes on the picture, the two pearls fell to the ground and returned to the earth.

She ran out of the house. She ran and ran until she reached her castle, cursing everything she saw along the way. When she saw her maid, she cried even louder. She was crying for the young man, but mostly she was crying because the miracle had ceased once again. The maid told her that there was no use in trying to bring about the miracle again, because those shining pearls, his essence, had now returned to him in the earth. "Surely he is filled with hatred for you. I am sure that this time the miracle will never return." She wailed and wailed, and cursed her fate.

But before going to sleep, she decided to try one more time. She took the young man's book down from the shelf and read it almost to the end, but still there were no pearls. She remembered the words of the maid, and tears flowed from her eyes, although this time in silence. Then, as she read the last two words of the book, two shining pearls appeared, sparkling on the page. She picked them up, overcome with pain and joy, and she cried, "Oh, my dear one! My heart is loathesome and ungrateful, but your love is boundless." And the young man, lying quietly in the earth, smiled, once again offering the two shining pearls.

∞

The Bodhisattva on the
Fragrant Mountain

MANY CENTURIES AGO, Bodhisattva Kwan Yin lived along the Nam Hai Sea on the coast of Vietnam. She had begun her life in the land of Hung Lam, which is to the east of India, as a princess named Wondrous Goodness. She and her two elder sisters were all intelligent, kind, and loyal to their parents, King and Queen Dieu Trang.

Because the king and queen had no sons, they focused all their attention on finding suitable husbands for their daughters, so one of these young sons-in-law could be the next king. The royal parents adored their three daughters and pampered them, hoping always to find excellent young men as husbands.

Princess Wondrous Goodness was the most beautiful. Her hair resembled the clouds, her skin the snow, and her mouth a lotus flower. Because she was the youngest, people sometimes called her *Chua Ba*, "Third Princess."

Princess Wondrous Goodness often asked permission to go outside of the palace to be with the people—to see how they lived and to learn more about their happiness and their difficulties. The king and queen always assented, and Wondrous Goodness learned much about the people's real lives. She saw poverty, illness, and injustice throughout the kingdom. Like Siddhartha when he was young, Wondrous Goodness had a strong desire to ease the suffering in the world, to help people.

One day when she was seven, while venturing outside the palace with her two elder sisters, Princess Wondrous Goodness asked her attendants to give all of her snacks and sweets to the children along the roadside. Then she ran toward one little girl her own age and hugged her. The little girl's clothes were ragged, her arms and legs as skinny as rails. Another time Princess Wondrous Goodness saw a woman wandering aimlessly through the streets and wailing, holding in her arms a newborn who had just died of starvation. She stared at the woman, and her eyes filled with compassion. Every time the princess went out of the palace, she brought with her some food and clothing to share. Her elder sisters never told the king and queen about this, nor did the attendant who drove their chariot.

Wondrous Goodness's elder sisters were married first and moved to beautiful homes not far from the palace. They visited their parents and younger sister often. After her sisters were married, Princess Wondrous Goodness was no longer permitted to leave the palace. Still, the scenes of poverty and illness she had seen remained in her mind, and she resolved to help. Every day, after finishing her lessons in sewing and embroidery, the princess walked alone in the palace garden, contemplating how she might help people.

When Princess Wondrous Goodness turned nineteen, the king and queen felt it was time for her to marry. The king called her to him and said, "You have arrived at marriage age. There are many fine young scholars and officials here in the court. Please tell me which one you would like to marry, and I will choose him for you."

Because he had been immersed in his duties as king and had spent little time with any of his daughters, the king was shocked when she said, "Father, I do not wish to marry. I ask your permission to become a nun."

Wondrous Goodness had thought about this for a long time. Several years earlier she had seen a nun taking care of children, washing their sores, and she was determined to become a nun like that and to help poor people. She had observed that her two elder sisters, since marrying, never had time to enjoy the palace garden *or* to be with the people of the kingdom. They spent all their time entertaining royal guests and buying beautiful clothes. Wondrous Goodness did not want to live that way. She only wanted to be with the people of the kingdom and to serve them however she could. She thought that for her, getting married would be a kind of imprisonment.

When he heard this sign of disobedience, the king broke into a rage and threatened to behead her! The queen overheard his shouting and came forward to plead on her daughter's behalf. She succeeded in tempering the king's rage enough so that he only confined the princess to the royal garden, prohibiting her from entering the palace. He thought that after a few days of living on the bare earth under the open sky, she would give up the idea of becoming a nun. What could be more lowly and difficult, he thought, than the life of a nun? He was determined to give her a taste of the nun's regimen to help her come to her senses.

The king did not understand his daughter. Once a day, an attendant brought the princess a bowl of rice and a plateful of salted sesame, which was the basic food of the country's temples. But the rice and salted sesame tasted delicious to her. After a month of living in the royal garden, Wondrous Goodness felt happier than ever. She spent her time practicing sitting and walking meditation, and she learned to take care of the flower beds and the bamboo groves using only a hoe, a shovel, and a rake. The queen and her two elder sisters visited often, encouraging her to give up the idea of becoming a nun, but Princess Wondrous Goodness' aspiration was never shaken.

The king could see that exiling his daughter to the royal park was not bringing about the desired result, so he began to look for another way. He decided that if he allowed the princess to become a novice nun—while secretly ordering the abbess of the temple to assign her only the most arduous work—she would change her mind. The abbess agreed, and Princess Wondrous Goodness was very happy when she heard the news. She was ordained a novice nun at Vu Doai Temple in the Imperial City, one of three hundred nuns. She stayed at the temple, and had to work arduously from three in the morning until eleven o'clock every night, husking rice, carrying water, planting sweet potatoes, cooking, washing dishes—doing the tasks of three or four people. The other nuns were instructed not to help her. Besides all of her manual work, Wondrous Goodness also had to study Buddhist scriptures and perform many chanting ceremonies.

The princess found ways to study while cutting vegetables and to recite the sutras while plowing the earth. Some young nuns, feeling sorry for Sister Wondrous Goodness having to do so much heavy work, secretly helped her. When Wondrous Goodness went to the well to fetch water, they went to the kitchen and washed the rice and vegetables for her. When she arrived at the well again, Wondrous Goodness noticed that two barrels of water were already filled. She only needed to carry them back. Rumors spread that dragons were helping the princess fetch water and birds were cutting the vegetables for her. She managed to work hard the whole day and study and memorize the sutras as well. Sometimes, she even understood the Buddha's teachings better than the other sisters. Six months passed, and the princess did not feel discouraged or exhausted.

The king was losing his patience. The nuns have not been able to make his daughter's life unbearable, he thought, and he ordered the temple burned to the ground while the nuns, including his daughter, were in it.

One dark night, when there was no moon, the king's soldiers surrounded Vu Doai Temple and shot burning arrows into the nuns' sleeping quarters. Awakened by the fiercely burning fire, they began to scream and tried to run outside. Wondrous Goodness was able to run outside right away, and she saw the whole temple enveloped in flames. Then soldiers came forward and blocked the exits to keep the nuns from escaping, and Wondrous Goodness was informed by a Dharma sister who had also made it out that it was the king himself who had ordered the temple burned down.

Sister Wondrous Goodness cried and cried, aware that nuns would die because of her. She placed her palms together to form a lotus flower, and wholeheartedly she invoked the names of the Buddhas and bodhisattvas in the ten directions. She bit her little finger and sprinkled her own blood upon the fire. In an instant, the skies opened, thunder roared, and a torrential rain began to fall. In less than a minute, the fire was extinguished, and the soldiers, thoroughly drenched, left the temple and returned to the palace, where they reported to the king what had happened.

The king was furious and ordered that his daughter, Sister Wondrous Goodness, be killed that night. The queen begged him for forgiveness, but the king's temper could not be contained. Wondrous Goodness' elder sisters kneeled before their father, crying and asking for a pardon, but the king would not grant one. Throughout the kingdom people were shocked, and thousands of subjects gathered at the execution ground to pray for Sister Wondrous Goodness.

That night, King Dieu Trang himself came to witness the death of his daughter. The torches burned brightly, and the people encircled the grounds, wailing loudly. Sister Wondrous Goodness, hands tied behind her back, was led to the center of the execution ground by a guard. She prayed calmly to the Buddha that her father would not receive bad karmic retribution. When the time for execution arrived, the general gave the command to proceed, and the drums began to roll, imperceptibly at first, but soon at a full crescendo. Sister Wondrous Goodness kneeled in the middle of the execution ground, her head down and her neck stretching forward in anticipation of the headsman's blade. As the third round of drumming ended and the headsman lifted his shining sword to the sky, a great gust of wind suddenly blew out all the torches and lamps, and people thought they saw a white tiger leap forward, as if from nowhere. Everyone backed away in terror, and the headsman's shiny sword fell to the ground. When the torches were relit, Sister Wondrous Goodness was nowhere to be seen. People reported that a great white tiger had leaped forward and carried her away.

The tiger carried Sister Wondrous Goodness into the jungle and up the mountain, across the border of Hung Lam to the high plateaus of an unfamiliar country. When they reached another mountain range, the tiger laid her down alongside a tree and disappeared. Sister Wondrous Goodness fell deeply asleep and dreamed that she was being led by two demons with buffalo heads and horse faces into the gates of Hell. As she entered, she saw those who lied having their tongues pulled out, those who had killed others being tossed onto a forest of swords and knives, those who had been disrespectful to their parents wearing rings of fire around their heads, those who had been selfish being locked in a pitch-dark room, those who had traded in weapons having to embrace substances that exploded and tore their bodies into pieces, those who had been greedy being forced to eat molten liquids, and those who had acted cruelly having to embrace a hot metal pillar until their flesh turned to charcoal, emitting a most rancid stench.

Wondrous Goodness thought she was dead and was about to receive some retribution herself. Still, she felt no fear, only compassion. Everyone in Hell seemed very mean, except the demons who were escorting her. They were kind and polite, so Wondrous Goodness asked where they were taking her. One of the demons replied, "Dear Sister, you are not dead. You are here because the King of Hell wanted to see you." A moment later, Sister Wondrous Goodness found herself in front of the vast palace of the King of Hell and the king himself waited at the palace gate to welcome her. He joined his palms to form a lotus to greet her, and he escorted her in. Then he offered Sister Wondrous Goodness a cup of tea and a peach that his attendants placed on a jade table. The king invited her to eat it, saying that it was magical and could revitalize her health.

Then he asked Sister Wondrous Goodness whether she had seen the sights in Hell. Recalling the terrifying and painful scenes she had just witnessed, Sister Wondrous Goodness joined her palms. In a voice was so strong that it shook the whole Kingdom of Hell, she vowed to save all beings. The painful mournings of those in Hell suddenly stopped. The king joined his palms and praised, "Your compassion is immense and miraculous. The pain in Hell has greatly diminished because of your strong vows. I will not keep you here long. I will ask the guards to take you back to the human world. I know you will practice the Buddha's teachings diligently and will attain enlightenment in this very life."

The king then asked the two demons to take Sister Wondrous Goodness back to the human realm. Wondrous Goodness noticed that the two demons no longer had buffalo heads and horse faces; they had transformed themselves into normal humans and looked very kind. As they led her out, through the ten gates of Hell, the scenes she had seen before had disappeared and the realms of Hell were now tranquil. As they approached a bridge, hero escorts joined their palms and informed Sister Wondrous Goodness that the human world was just on the other side of the bridge. They, of course, could not cross with her. Thanking the guards, she gently stepped onto the bridge. Halfway across, looking down and seeing the fierce current, she fainted and fell into the river. At that instant, she awoke from her dream.

When Sister Wondrous Goodness woke up, she found herself lying on a mountainside, under the shade of a tree, with her two hands still tied behind her back, and she recalled everything that had happened. Her father had sent soldiers to burn down the temple. She was ordered to be beheaded by her father. Then a white tiger leaped into the execution ground and carried her away. Unconscious on the back of the white tiger, she had dreamed of visiting Hell. "Where am I?" she asked herself. "Perhaps the white tiger has taken me here."

The princess realized that the rope around her hands was loose. The soldier had not had the heart to hurt the princess and had only tied the rope loosely around her wrists. Easily unraveling it, she freed her hands. At that moment, she heard the sound of a horse, and as soon as she stood up, a handsome young man appeared. The young man stepped off his horse and bowed his head to greet Sister Wondrous Goodness, and she joined her palms in reply. The young man asked her who she was and why she was alone on the mountain. Wondrous Goodness told him the story of her life, and the young man informed her that she was in the territory of Dai Viet, in Son La Province on Tam Dao Mountain.

The young man was Prince Ly Phat Ma of Dai Viet. He had been out touring the beautiful landscape of his country. Hearing Sister Wondrous Goodness' story, the prince was deeply moved. Although a nun in brown robes, she looked as beautiful as a lotus pond in early morning. The prince proposed to marry her, saying that if she agreed, he would take her to the Imperial City of Thang Long to meet his father, King Ly Thai To. Sister Wondrous Goodness politely replied that she was determined to live her life as a nun. Prince Phat Ma, also a Buddhist, understood and respected her aspiration. He said, "Then I beg you to stay here in Dai Viet to practice the Buddha's teachings until you reach enlightenment. If you return to your own country, you may be in danger.

"There is a beautiful cave a few days' walk from here on Fragrant Mountain near Duc Khe Hamlet in Ha Dong Province.

If you agree, I'll take you there. It is an excellent place to practice the Buddha's Way."

Prince Phat Ma then invited the princess to ride his horse. He held the bridle and led the horse, and they walked for three days until they reached a river at the foot of a mountainous area of Duc Khe Hamlet. There, the prince tied his horse, purchased a boat, and rowed the boat himself along the beautiful, still river to take the princess to her destination. The river wound quietly between two mountains and the view was spectacular. The prince pointed out to Sister Wondrous Goodness the elephant shape of one of the mountains. Wondrous Goodness thought the elephant was putting its trunk in the rice fields. There was clearly an ear at the side of the elephant's head. On reaching the shore, the prince escorted Wondrous Goodness up Fragrant Mountain. They climbed and climbed, and they reached the mouth of the cave just as the sun was setting. Then the prince bade Sister Wondrous Goodness farewell, as he had to return to Duc Khe Hamlet before dark, and to return to the Imperial City the next morning to meet his father.

Wondrous Goodness was ecstatic. The cave of Fragrant Mountain was a perfect place to practice sitting meditation, chant sutras, wash her clothes, plant vegetables, and sleep. During her training at Vu Doai Temple, she had learned many things she could now put into practice. She ate root vegetables that she dug from the earth, and fruit from many trees and bushes. For months she did not eat any grains. Then one day, a woodcutter discovered her and offered some rice she could cook for herself. Sister Wondrous Goodness practiced diligently. When even she did sitting meditation, birds and monkeys came close to her and remained silent. Sometimes they even picked fruits or fragrant herbs and placed them in front of her. After four or five years of practicing the Buddha's Way, her understanding deepened and Wondrous Goodness attained enlightenment.

Sitting in the cave, she could see the suffering and hear the mournful cries of all the world's beings. So she descended the mountain to the nearby village to teach the Way, and to help the poor and cure the villagers' illnesses. Many children came to her, and she taught them about love and kindness. One boy and one girl asked if they could follow Sister Wondrous Goodness back up the mountain to study the Buddha's teachings. The boy was an orphan, and Wondrous Goodness named him Thien Tai (Sudhana). The girl was the daughter of a fisherman. Wondrous Goodness had rescued her from drowning at Port Duc. She named the girl Long Nu (Nagadhita).

Thien Tai, Long Nu, and Sister Wondrous Goodness lived in harmony together in the cave on Fragrant Mountain. The children were both intelligent, and they understood all that she taught them. Besides studying language and scriptures and practicing sitting and walking meditation, the children learned to plant vegetables and prepare sweet rice. They also accompanied Sister Wondrous Goodness when she went into the forest to gather medicinal herbs to make medicine for the townspeople. News spread from the Duc Khe and Yen Vi Hamlets all the way to My Duc Town that a bodhisattva who could cure illnesses lived in the cave on Fragrant Mountain. Sister Wondrous Goodness always taught that understanding and love are the best medicine of all. The two children did not know that Wondrous Goodness had been a princess in a foreign country. They only knew she was a person with deep insights and immense compassion.

Thien Tai and Long Nu were hard-working students. They practiced well and became capable assistants, loving and revering their teacher. They did not know that their teacher was already a Buddha, but some nights they saw a bright light radiate from the inner cave. Their teacher sat very still, and light emanated from her forehead and from everywhere in her body. Some mornings, when sitting next to a spring listening to Sister Wondrous Goodness explain the scriptures, they noticed birds perching on nearby branches and fish swimming close to shore in order to listen to her. The two young students vowed to practice diligently and reach their teacher's level of attainment.

One morning when she was bringing plum tea to her teacher, Long Nu noticed that Sister Wondrous Goodness' eyes were sad. Long Nu asked what was wrong, but Sister Wondrous Goodness said only that she had to meditate that morning.

During her meditation, Sister Wondrous Goodness saw her father, King Dieu Trang, lying in bed in his palace in Hung Lam with both his legs and arms paralyzed. She realized it was retribution for the wicked actions of his past. The king had initiated many wars, and thousands of people had lost their lives because of him. He was proud and hot-tempered, and because of that he had made many wrong decisions. Now in bed and in excruciating pain, the king announced that if anyone could cure his illness, he would reward that person by yielding his throne to him or her. Without leaving her cave, Sister Wondrous Goodness used her meditative powers to transform herself into an old medicine man, and she entered the palace gate. She took the announcement of the king's illness off the walls of the palace wall and told the guards that she had come to cure the king's illness. The guards took the old medicine man into the palace.

The medicine man told the king, "This illness is very difficult to cure. But there is one way, and that is to ask an enlightened person for an arm and an eye to use as medicine."

The king was shocked, "Has anyone ever given an arm or an eye like that?"

The medicine man knelt down to reply, "I know of one enlightened goddess on Fragrant Mountain in Dai Viet. She is a bodhisattva with great compassion. If you send delegates to ask her, I think she will give them to you." Then the medicine man drew a map showing the way to the boshisattva's cave.

The king commanded a delegation to leave immediately for Dai Viet, and he had the medicine man locked up in his palace, threatening that if the delegates were unable to obtain the arm and eye of the goddess, the medicine man would be executed.

The delegates from Hung Lam arrived at Duc Khe Hamlet after thirty days of climbing mountains and crossing rivers. Sister Wondrous Goodness instructed Thien Tai and Long Nu to welcome them at Port Duc. Then she poked out her left eye and cut off her left arm and when the delegates arrived, she presented these to them.

The delegates carried these treasures home, and with the goddess' arm and eye, the medicine man prepared a solution and was able to cure half the king's body. The king could now move his left arm and leg, but his right arm and leg remained paralyzed. The medicine man suggested that they ask the goddess for her other arm and eye.

Even the king thought that request would be too much. But the medicine man insisted, "A Buddhist practitioner has a generous heart. I believe that if you send someone to ask, the bodhisattva will offer them."

The delegates set out again. When they arrived at the bodhisattva's cave a second time, she gave them her right eye and arm. When the medicine from these was made and taken by the king, he recovered completely. The king and queen's hearts were filled with deep gratitude and admiration. Faithful to his promise, the king ordered the transmission of his throne to the old medicine man. But the man declined, saying that his job was to heal people, not to be involved in politics. The medicine man departed without saying even a word.

During his illness, the king had contemplated his past and recognized his many wrongdoings. He repented and vowed to be worthy of the generous heart of the bodhisattva of Fragrant Mountain. So he ordered a chariot for himself and the queen to go to Fragrant Mountain to pay their respects to the bodhisattva in person.

The king, queen, and escorts had just crossed the border when a scheme to usurp the throne arose in Hung Lam. The two sons-in-law of King Dieu Trang headed the conspiracy, using their regiments to overthrow the government and seize the throne. The first son-in-law became the king, and the second son-in-law became the prime minister. They imprisoned those who were against them, including the two princesses, the regent officials, and the mandarins. At her cave on Fragrant Mountain, Sister Wondrous Goodness witnessed these events in Hung Lam. She saw her two elder sisters become awakened while in prison. They began to practice sitting meditation, recite the Buddha's names, and observe a vegetarian diet.

Wondrous Goodness and her two disciples sat in meditation, entered into deep concentration, and transported themselves to Hung Lam to rescue the country. The three of them, disguised as students, managed to get the people and the regiments to take back the throne, free the prisoners, and return power to the regent officials, all within five days. When matters were settled, the three students escorted the two princesses to pursue the pilgrimage of the king and queen to Dai Viet. Ten days later, the princesses caught up with the pilgrims and reported every detail of the *coup d'etat*. The king and queen discussed the matter and decided to continue on their pilgrimage to see the bodhisattva of Fragrant Mountain. The two princesses joined them.

On Fragrant Mountain, Thien Tai and Long Nu prepared to welcome the royal pilgrims. The two disciples of Sister Wondrous Goodness knew that their teacher had been a princess once and was now a Buddha whose insights and actions were generous and immeasurable. Although she had sacrificed two arms and two eyes, her Dharma body of one thousand eyes and hands had not diminished one iota. Her embodiment was lim-itless.

Thien Tai and Long Nu waited at Port Duc to greet the royal pilgrims from Hung Lam. When the king, queen, and two prin-cesses arrived, they invited them into a large rowboat, and rowed them gently on the still river. Everyone was silent, just observ-ing the sky, the clouds, the mountains, the water. The moun-tains alongside the river were truly beautiful. An hour later, when they arrived at the other shore, they all began to climb slowly up Fragrant Mountain. When they arrived at the cave, Thien Tai invited the king, the queen, and the two princesses to rest on the stone platforms, while Long Nu prepared plum tea. After they had rested and enjoyed some tea, Long Nu rose from her seat to show the king, the queen, and the two prin-cesses to the inner cave.

As they advanced slowly toward the inner cave, the atmo-sphere was so still that even their soft footsteps resonated deeply. Thousands of stalactites drooped from the ceiling like a curtain, reflecting a thousand colors. As they walked further into the cave, the sunlight diminished, until it had become completely dark as they stood in front of the stalactite curtain that sepa-rated the outer cave from the inner. Standing just outside the inner cave, King Dieu Trang respectfully greeted the goddess who had saved his life, "We, the royal delegates from Hung Lam, respectfully appear before you, O Goddess." His voice echoed in the cave, then became silent. There was no reply. The king looked at the queen and said softly, "Since I am a man, it would be impolite for me to go behind the curtain. Please go and see if the goddess is there."

The queen heeded his request and, holding a candle, stepped to the other side of the stalactite curtain. The inner cave was cooler and even darker than the outer cave. Looking about, the queen suddenly saw a young woman standing on a stone plat-form with long hair flowing behind her back, her eyes broached, her arms dismembered, and blood dripping from the sockets where her eyes and her arms had been. The bodhisattva had transformed herself into Princess Wondrous Goodness at age nineteen so the queen would be able to recognize that she was her own youngest daughter. The queen screamed and fainted immediately.

Hearing their mother scream, the princesses rushed in to help and King Dieu Trang followed closely behind. They all saw the princess without eyes and arms, and all of them began to sob uncontrollably. The king had never imagined that his youngest daughter might still be alive, and that it was she who had sacrificed her eyes and arms for him.

Wondrous Goodness descended her stone platform and invited everyone to sit on the platforms nearby. Then she told her father, mother, and sisters about her wonderful life in the cave. The king expressed remorse for all of his misdeeds and declared, "I have lived miserably while you attained enlightenment and were able to save not only my life but also our country's. Because of me, you are without eyes and arms. What can I do? How can I help you, my dear daughter?" He held his face in his hands, sobbing uncontrollably. Sister Wondrous Goodness consoled him. "If you and mother vow to practice the Buddha's teachings wholeheartedly, you will end your own afflictions and begin the task of saving all living beings. If you do that, my body will be restored as before." The king and queen both knelt down, joined their palms, and declared, "Homage to all Buddhas in the ten directions. We vow to practice the Five Wonderful Precepts to work to end our greed, hatred, and delusion, and to work to protect the lives of people, animals, plants, and minerals with all our energy."

When the king and queen looked up, Sister Wondrous Goodness had regained both her eyes and both her arms. The king, queen, and two princesses embraced Wondrous Goodness and cried, vowing to stay on Fragrant Mountain and study with her for one year before returning to their homeland.

News about the enlightened bodhisattva who saved countless beings spread from Ha Dong Province to nearby provinces and all the way to the Imperial City. King Ly Thai Tong heard the news and immediately organized a pilgrimage to visit the bodhisattva on Fragrant Mountain. The king was the same as Prince Ly Phat Ma who had led Sister Wondrous Goodness to the cave on Fragrant Mountain ten years earlier. The king brought many white lotuses to offer Wondrous Goodness. It was in the summer of the year Dinh Ty.

It is rumored that after meeting Wondrous Goodness and receiving teachings from her, the king announced that the princess who had attained enlightenment on Fragrant Mountain was none other than Kwan Yin, the Bodhisattva of Great Compassion.

∞

The Stone Boy

Tô STOPPED PLAYING her bamboo flute. She could taste the bittersweet saltiness of the tears streaming down her cheeks. Resting the flute on her thigh, she lifted a corner of her peasant blouse and wiped her tears. The forest was crisp and cool that April morning. Listening to the rustle of young, spring leaves, Tô remembered how irresistibly tender and green they had once appeared to her. But her memory of colors was already beginning to dim, just six months after she had lost her sight.

The night before, like every night for weeks, Tô had carefully, even desperately, touched her mother's face, hoping never to forget a single line. When she tried to picture her father, who had died two years before, no image came to her. Touching her flute, Tô remembered how her father, a woodcutter, had brought her this piece of bamboo and helped her to make it into a musical instrument. He taught her how to rub the flute with a dry banana leaf to give it a rich color, and he taught her how to play.

Father would always walk with Tô partway to school, to the place where the road forked at the foot of Fragrant Hill. With his machete on his shoulder, he would go into the deep forest, and little Tô would walk up and down two more hills to the Upper Village Road, carrying a wooden box filled with school supplies and her flute, and swinging an ink bottle tied to her finger. Father had made her school box from the thinnest wood available, and it was very light to carry. After just a few months, the wood became dark and shiny like the flute.

Each day Tô would return from school to have lunch with her mother. In the afternoon, her father would come home with a heavy load of wood on his back, and after supper, she and Father would take a leisurely walk alongside the stream or in the forest.

On Wednesdays, the family would rise at dawn and go to the Lower Village market, hauling the big cart filled with firewood. By the time they reached the Upper Village, Tô's legs were already tired, and Father would stop the cart and let her sit on top of the woodpile. When all the wood was sold, Mother would buy rice and other essentials, and one special treat for Tô. By noon they would be back home, and Mother would cook a pot of rice. But Tô was never hungry on Wednesdays. Satiated by her special treat, she asked permission to go outside and play, and usually she walked to the edge of the forest. Tô loved playing the flute along the bank of the gentle stream that ran near their house, and she loved gathering beautiful wildflowers whose names she did not know.

∞

Then Father died. Less than one year after joining the army, he was killed in combat. When the news reached home, Mother screamed uncontrollably. Tô, only seven at the time, did not understand what death meant. She saw her mother rolling in the dirt, crying, and she felt torn apart inside. Holding Mother in her arms, she understood that she would never see Father again. He was dead, just like the bird she had seen on the bank of a stream, decomposing to become soil. Sadness entered Tô's spirit. He would not be back to play or talk with her. He would not lift her in his arms or look deeply into her eyes again. As the days passed, Tô became sadder and sadder.

After Father's death, Tô stayed home and helped take care of the house—cooking rice, cropping and sorting vegetables and herbs—while Mother went to the forest to gather firewood.

Mother's loads were smaller than Father's had been, so the family could not afford as much rice. Tô continued to take walks after supper, and she always brought her flute with her. She would go to the place where she and Father used to sit, and she played the short melodies he had taught her.

Sometimes while playing, Tô's sadness became so intense that she could hardly breathe. She felt as if she were in the grip of a strong vise. Breathing deeply a few times, she would refresh herself, pick up the flute again, and create songs which expressed her grief as well as her joy. As the days went by, she composed more and more tunes, and playing these made her feel better. Crying also brought a kind of relief. Tears poured from her heart, and the more she cried, the lighter her heart became.

One day while Tô was sitting in the woods, deeply absorbed in playing her flute, a number of airplanes passed overhead so low that they barely missed the treetops. The forest shook. Tô looked up and saw a thick, white cloud. Within seconds she felt her eyes burning and her lungs gasping for air. Choking and crying, she fell unconscious to the ground. She had no idea that the planes had spread clouds of chemical defoliants.

Tô's mother was horrified by the roar of the planes and the sight of the cloud above the forest. She ran out to find Tô, but it was more than an hour before she came upon the unconscious body of her daughter. Unable to revive her, she ran to the Upper Village to get a nurse. When they returned, Tô was sitting, screaming that her eyes were on fire. Both eyes were badly swollen, and she could hardly see. The nurse washed them with cotton dipped in medicine, and gave her an injection. She told Tô's mother to bring her to the district hospital, a day's travel away. But at the hospital, the doctors were not able to do anything.

When Tô visited the forest for the first time after losing her sight, it was a dark, silent dungeon. Gradually, though, she began to notice things that she had not been aware of when she could see. In the sound of the stream, she heard an old man talking and singing. She felt the branches and leaves of the trees standing up to dance. In the sound of the wind rustling in the leaves, Tô saw thousands of hands rising into the air to wave at her. The light itself had become brighter and begun to dance. Tô came to know the sounds of thousands of friends dwelling harmoniously in the forest. From the blankets of moss, the bark of trees, and even the soil itself, creatures talked to her, telling her about their lives. Hundreds of bird songs each brought a different message. Tô responded to each one by raising her flute and playing a new and utterly beautiful melody.

Tô came to feel that heaven had created her so that she could play the flute and communicate with the creatures of the forest. Once, a strange bird called to her and she responded with a song. Tô could see the bird clearly in her mind: it had a long tail, golden feathers, and a white patch like a crown on its head. Its bright, quick eyes darted left and right. The bird sang for a while and stopped. Tô raised her flute and played in response. The bird replied with a song which communicated surprise that Tô could speak the bird's language, and pleasure to be able to sing with her. Tô played again, telling the golden bird about herself and imitating the bird's song. Delighted, Tô began to laugh, and her laughter carried through the forest like a flurry of young finches at dawn.

For nine days in a row, the golden bird came to converse with Tô's flute. Then it flew away and did not return. Tô went on playing the flute, but her heart was heavy. She would begin with soft, distant notes, as if to share her sadness with the small creatures beneath the ground. Then the sounds of her flute rose and blended with the multitude of sounds coming from the leaves and branches above. Little by little, Tô forgot that she was a young girl playing an instrument, and she became a tiny creature living in the forest with thousands of friends. The sounds of the flute resonated with the cries of the other creatures. She was at one with the forest—trees, moss, grass, and roots began to dance, and her pain dissolved. Tô was no longer only Tô. Tears streamed from her sightless eyes—warm tears like the spring sunshine, and sweet, cool tears like the pure water from the stream— and she felt a great relief.

Tô was enjoying the same warmth and lightness that she imagined the young buds felt after the cleansing rains of winter. She remembered how the defoliant chemicals had stripped the trees of their leaves. But during that winter, unusually heavy rains had washed away the spray, and healthy young trees grew back. Insects and worms were again crawling, flying, and buzzing everywhere. Just as the forest had regained its will to live, Tô had recovered her spirit.

Tô realized that someone was standing in front of her. Completely absorbed in the life of the forest, she had not heard the approaching footsteps. Someone with sweet breath and a light, gentle presence was definitely there. Tô had never before known someone with breathing so fine and pure.

"Who are you?" she asked in a shy, small voice.

There was no answer.

"Who's there? What is your name? Where are you from?" she asked again.

"Stone Boy," came the hesitant reply. "My name is Stone Boy, and I come from up the mountain."

His voice was fleeting, like a wisp of a cloud, as light as the singing of the golden bird who had visited Tô for nine straight days. Stone Boy spoke only a few words, but these words were enough for Tô to envision him. He was about eleven or twelve, with delicate features in a full, oval face, like a mango. His eyes were bright and clear. Tô liked her new friend. She pointed to the foot of the tree next to her and invited him to sit down. "Please tell me, Stone Boy, where is your home on the mountain?"

The boy remained silent. A moment passed, and Tô spoke again, "How old are you, brother—eleven?"

"I don't know how old I am. I may be very, very old...."

Tô burst out laughing and motioned him to come closer. She raised her hands and touched his face, while Stone Boy sat perfectly still and allowed Tô to explore. Yes, his face was shaped like a mango, and his skin was cool like the water of a mountain stream in summer. His hair was long, covering most of his forehead and hanging down over his neck. When she finished, Tô laughed, "Just as I thought. You must be about eleven. Twelve, at the most. Tell me where your home is and what your parents do. My name is Tô. I live with my mother nearby. My father is dead."

But Stone Boy remained silent. He certainly is quiet, Tô thought. His being seemed to be made of innocence and wonder. He had said his home was up the mountain, and he obviously did not want to say any more. I shouldn't bother him, she said to herself, and she sat down quietly next to her new friend.

Finally, Stone Boy spoke up, "Elder sister, please play your flute."

Tô laughed again. "Please don't call me elder sister. I am only nine. Please say, 'Younger sister, play your flute for me, your elder brother Stone Boy,' and I will gladly play for you." Stone Boy repeated her words exactly, and Tô raised her flute and began to play.

Never before had Tô's flute sounded so joyous. She felt as though she were floating on a cloud amidst the sunshine and spring breezes. The entire forest floated up with her and formed an enormous cloud. Tô's flute became a large vessel carrying all of springtime. She forgot that she was blind and that her father was dead. She had returned to her source. She was running along the hillside, her hand in Father's, and they were laughing happily. Tô heard the birds' songs falling like pearls from heaven. She heard the loving calls of the forest, hills, and gardens—calls as familiar as Mother calling her home to wash her feet before coming in to light the lamp and sit down for supper.

Stone Boy sat still and listened. Tô knew that he must have seen the tears welling up in her eyes, and she said, "I'm crying, Stone Boy, but I am not sad. I am very, very happy."

Stone Boy asked her, "Why haven't you played such joyful tunes before? I've listened to you, and the music you play is usually so mournful."

Instead of answering his question, Tô asked, "Where were you when you heard me playing?"

"I was high up on the mountain. Every day your music reaches the top of the mountain."

"How can the sound of my flute reach the top of the mountain?"

"Oh, it can reach the clouds. I hear you every day. I heard your flute, so I came to see you. It took me two days to walk down," Stone Boy said.

Two days? His home must be far up the mountain, Tô thought. She never imagined that her music could travel that far. Her flute had actually found her a new friend. Sitting next to Stone Boy, Tô did not want to move even a hair, as she was afraid to disrupt their fragile world. She did not dare talk and laugh as she would have done with her classmates at Upper Village School. She was not afraid of Stone Boy, but she felt a great respect for this quiet, but not shy boy. He was like a clean sheet of rice paper, open and ready, and she did not want to write or draw on him without the utmost care. So they sat quietly. Then Stone Boy said, "Please tell me, younger sister, what it is like down there."

Tô told him about her parents and her life in the little house on the hill. She told him about school, her teacher, the marketplace, and the people of the Lower Village. She spoke slowly, stopping to explain words she thought he might not understand.

He seemed to know very little about her life, or even her language. She explained that a marketplace was a large area where people gathered to buy and sell vegetables, rice, fish, and firewood. From time to time, Stone Boy asked her to stop and tell him more details. This made Tô feel like a teacher, carefully sharing her knowledge of many things.

The sun was already at noon, and Tô had to return home to prepare lunch for Mother. She invited Stone Boy to join her. Reaching out, she took his hand, and the two new friends walked out of the forest together. Even though she could not see, Tô showed Stone Boy the trees and bushes in her yard, the tools, the garden, and their small wooden house. She had only to tell him the names of things once, and he remembered.

Tô asked Stone Boy if he was hungry, but he did not seem to understand what "hungry" or "eating" meant. This amused Tô, and she laughed as she brought Stone Boy into the alcove that she used as a kitchen. Tô took out a pot, rinsed some rice, and put it on the fire. Then she went out—somewhat self-consciously, as she could feel Stone Boy watching—to pick some garden vegetables. He helped her prepare the vegetables, and soon the meal was ready.

Stone Boy and Tô sat on the front doorstep, waiting for Mother. Stone Boy asked her how her father had been drafted into the army, and how she had been blinded by the cloud of chemicals, but their conversation stopped abruptly when Mother arrived. Tô introduced her friend from the mountain with such thoroughness that there was nothing for him to add. Mother asked him about his home and parents, but his replies were so hesitant that she concluded that Stone Boy, like thousands of other children during the murderous war, must be an orphan. So, breathing quietly to calm herself, she went to the yard and washed her hands. When she returned, she invited the children to sit down to lunch.

During the meal, Tô could tell that Stone Boy was eating very little, and that, in fact, he was watching her to learn how to eat. When they finished, Tô asked Mother if Stone Boy could stay. Delighted to meet such a loving, gentle boy, she agreed, and suggested that the two of them take a walk along the stream to enjoy the afternoon breeze.

As they sat on the stony bank of the stream, Tô asked Stone Boy to describe everything he saw. Hesitant at first, he soon was telling her of the blue sky, the white clouds, and the dark green forest. Tô's face shone with delight. She felt as if she could see everything through his eyes. She heard in his voice the earth itself, deep and resonant. When dusk fell, Stone Boy became silent. Tô lifted her flute and began to play. She felt herself on a rocky peak, lost in the mist, and she saw the birds, the earth, and the wind.

Mother called Tô and Stone Boy home. She lit an oil lamp and served a delicious supper of rice, lemongrass, carrots, and greens. Stone Boy was already more comfortable using his chopsticks, and chewing and swallowing. After dinner, Mother found a mat and invited Stone Boy to stay overnight. Tô was delighted. This was the first time in her life she would have a friend stay in her house.

The next morning the children woke up like two young birds. Tô brought her friend into the garden and taught him hide-and-seek. They played on the grassy hillside, which was dotted with thousands of yellow and purple wildflowers. Stone Boy invited Tô to sit with him again by the brook, and he looked at the sky and earth and told her everything he saw. Tô was happy just to sit and listen to Stone Boy—she loved his voice so—and he no longer had difficulty speaking. Tô had the impression that, not only was this a boy speaking to her, but the earth and sky were speaking to her as well. Even after Stone Boy stopped talking, Tô continued to hear the voices of Heaven and Earth. With Stone Boy by her side, Tô was not blind.

After lunch, Mother made a brown cotton peasant shirt for Stone Boy. Imitating Tô, the boy said, "Thank you, Ma." Tô was sure that this expression pleased Mother because she invited him to come along for their weekly market trip the next day. Tô was overjoyed, for she could explain many more new things to Stone Boy, and he could see for both of them.

In the morning, they loaded the cart with firewood. Mother stood in front with the harness over both shoulders and her hands gripping the handles. She leaned forward to pull the cart to market, and noticed how much easier it was to pull than usual, as Stone Boy and Tô helped push from behind.

Tô talked all the way from the Upper Village to the Lower Village. She told Stone Boy to look at everything en route and asked him whether he was seeing this or that house, tree, or garden, for she knew where they were every inch of the way.

The market at the Lower Village was only a small "pocket market," yet there were more than one hundred people there that day. After selling all the firewood, Mother bought rice, salt, fish sauce, and a handful of tiny live fish wrapped in a banana leaf. She also bought one orange cookie and one sweet rice cake for the two children. Then she asked them to load the cart and wait while she went to a nearby shop to buy lamp oil.

The children sat on the roots of a shady flame tree and slowly ate their sweets. Tô had barely finished hers when the sounds of shots and screams filled the air. In an instant, the market became frantic, like a beehive burst open. Bullets whistled overhead and people threw down their belongings and ran wildly in every direction, fleeing for cover. Tô pulled Stone Boy to the ground and held her hand on the back of his head to keep him from looking up. Then the ground trembled from a huge explosion, and debris fell everywhere. Tô and Stone Boy were covered with dirt. They heard tragic, painful screams, and Tô realized that a bomb had landed in the marketplace, wounding and killing many, many people. From beyond the market, gunfire blazed. Realizing that Mother might be wounded or even killed, Tô cried out, "Oh, Ma, Ma, where are you?" Trembling, she held Stone Boy tightly to her, but Stone Boy sat up calmly and told her, "Don't worry, Ma is all right. Sit here and I will find her."

As Stone Boy stood up, bullets whizzed over his head and another terrifying explosion shook the market. Tô quickly pulled him back down, and they both lay flat in the dirt again. The second explosion was even more powerful. Blasts of hot air scorched them, and they heard buildings collapsing dirt and debris raining down everywhere. There was a moment of stillness before the heartwrenching screams began again, but the guns were now silent.

Tô and Stone Boy lay perfectly still and listened to the crackling sounds of bamboo houses going up in flames. Stone Boy described men with guns tying the wrists of people who had no guns and herding them off in small groups.

"A lot of people are hurt," he said. "We must try to help them." Tô grasped his arm tightly. "No, not yet. We must wait until the men with guns are gone."

After a while, Stone Boy told her, "There are only wounded people in the market now," and the children made their way to a group of victims lying on the ground, moaning and crying. Villagers were trying to help with improvised bamboo stretchers. Stone Boy told Tô that many people had lost arms or hands—some had their feet crushed, while others' faces were torn apart and the small children lay in puddles of blood.

More and more people were coming out of their houses. While the villagers carried the dead and the wounded away, Tô and Stone Boy began searching for their mother. Stone Boy led Tô down to the heap of smoldering ash where the oil shop had been.

"Oh Ma, Ma, where are you, Ma?" Tô burst out crying. "Has anybody seen my mother? Please tell me if you've seen her." Several women standing nearby heard her and shook their heads.

"They haven't seen Mother, I can tell," Stone Boy said. "They're looking for their own families. Let's go."

They walked around the market into the village. Though Tô could not see, she could feel and hear the desolation and sorrow around her. It was spring, but all was agony and despair. Each time Tô heard footsteps approach, she would ask, "Oh Uncle," or "Oh Aunt, have you seen my ma?" Every time the reply was no. No one had seen Mother. Mother was not among the dead or the wounded in the marketplace. Where could she be? They returned to the spot where the market had been, and an old lady said she had seen her.

"Yes, I saw your mother with a bottle in her hand," she told them. "She was leaving the oil shop, walking toward the market, when the bomb exploded."

It was the first piece of helpful information. Tô tugged on Stone Boy's sleeve, and they continued to search the neighborhood, knocking on every door and asking, "Have you seen my mother? She was carrying a bottle of oil." They left no corner or shelter untouched, but they could not find Mother.

Dusk fell, and it quickly became dark. The children were ravenous by now, so they returned to the big flame tree to find their sweet rice cake. After they had eaten, they climbed up onto the cart, which was still parked where Mother had left it. The night was chilly. Though the leaves of the flame tree protected them from the heavy dew, they were cold all night. They huddled up against each other and slept on and off until morning.

As soon as Tô woke up, she knew there was a large crowd at the marketplace. Stone Boy was already awake and sitting quietly, watching her. He told her that a group of men with guns were standing around talking to the villagers. Tô surmised that government people had come from the district headquarters. She climbed down from the cart.

"Let's go, Brother Stone Boy. Let's ask them to help find Mother."

Stone Boy and Tô approached a soldier, and Tô asked him, "Sir, can you please help us find our mother?"

Stone Boy spoke up, "Sir, my little sister is blind. We came from the Upper Village yesterday with our mother. She was at the market when the fighting started, and we don't know where she is now."

Stone Boy's fluency and politeness surprised Tô. The soldier did not reply. Instead, he walked over to another man and spoke with him in a low voice. The second man, in a very authoritative voice, asked them their mother's name.

"Ba Ty," Tô said. "She is a woodcutter, and our home is near Dai-Lao Forest, near the Upper Village."

Tô gathered that this man was the group's commander. He turned to the villagers and asked if anyone knew anything about Mrs. Ba Ty. Someone reported that she was neither among the dead nor the wounded. Another speculated that she must have been taken away by the attackers. The commander told the children to go home and wait.

"Don't worry. If we get any news of her, we will let you know right away."

Tô and Stone Boy returned to the big flame tree to get their cart. Pushing and pulling, they managed to make their way back to the Upper Village by early afternoon. Stone Boy brought Mother's purchases into the house, and Tô followed him. The little house seemed cold and empty without Mother. Tô asked Stone Boy if he was hungry, but neither of them felt like eating, so they just sat on the doorstep and stared blankly ahead of them. Neither spoke for a long time.

Then Stone Boy remembered the little fish that Mother had bought at the market, and he said, "The little fish must all be dead by now." Stone Boy filled a bucket with water and placed all the fish in it. After a moment he spoke. "They're dead except for two survivors. One is orange, the other silver. Let's release them in the stream, Tô."

Stone Boy knelt, scooped the two little fish out of the bucket, and let them go. Tô could imagine two tiny fish happily swimming away, and her lips relaxed slightly into a half-smile. In this moment of calmness, she recalled the desperate cries of villagers in the marketplace. Tô became agitated and overwhelmed by the images of children her own age with crushed skulls and torn limbs. She saw the huge flames from the burning houses, and adults lying in the dirt with their bloody insides exposed. She thought of her own mother being led away with her wrists bound together. She knew that Stone Boy must be thinking about the same things, and she asked him if he thought they would ever see Mother again. Had Mother also died like a bird lying in the forest, with its head crumpled onto its chest, its feet folded under?

Tô felt enormous pressure on her lungs, and it was difficult for her to breathe. She wanted to cry but instead she gasped for air like someone who has been underwater too long. The stone on which she sat was burning.

At that moment Stone Boy began to sing a strange, miraculous song. Tô had never heard anything so solemn or beautiful. It began like a thin strand of smoke rising from the thatched roof of their house as Mother cooked the evening rice. The strand of delicate sound spread out horizontally and hung suspended in the air, motionless; then it opened up like the wings of a huge, beautiful bird flying in endless, open space. The giant bird beat its wings and, high up in the sky, the wind was born and beckoned to the clouds from the four corners of the heavens to gather around. Fire-colored, luminous clouds joined in rhythmic formations. Tô heard the whistling of pine trees swaying in the wind and the distant murmur of a fine spring drizzle descending upon the willows along the stream. She heard tiny footsteps of small children dressed in colorful clothes, holding hands, playing and singing on the grassy hillside.

The pain in Tô's chest released, and she breathed easily. The stone under her felt like a cloud. She heard the thunderous patter of wings beating in the sky, then tens of thousands of birds crying together. Suddenly, one bird flew very low, just above their heads, and delivered its song like a string of pearls stretched across the sky. Tô recognized the song as that of the golden bird who had replied to her flute music for nine days. She put her flute to her lips and played a very sad song, as sad as the purple sky at dusk, while the birds circling above listened attentively. Tô asked the birds to fly everywhere and look for her mother. The simple music cried, prayed, and begged. It flew skyward, then plummeted beseechingly to the ground. The birds scattered in every direction, and only one golden bird with a very long tail and a few small white feathers on its head remained. It sang one more short song, flitted about briefly, and then flew off toward the forest with the others.

Tô and Stone Boy sat silently for a moment. Then, Tô asked him, "Please tell me, who taught you how to sing like that?"

"No one. I lived for a long, long time at the top of the mountain, listening to the clouds, the wind, the rain, the mist, and many other sounds. One day I discovered that I knew how to sing. But I only sing when the sky and the earth are ill at ease, sad, and angry, when the black clouds come down toward earth and the sky is about to explode."

"And who taught you how to play your flute so beautifully? Did your mother teach you?"

"No, when Father was still alive, he taught me a few folk songs, peasant music. Like you, I listened to the voices of the trees, the wind, the stream, and the birds. But your singing is so much better! It makes me feel wonderful. It revives me. Even the birds in the forest fly down to listen to you!"

Stone Boy did not speak right away. Then he asked Tô, "Didn't you ask the birds to help find Mother? I am sure they heard you. They will try to do what you asked. But how can they find someone they never have seen? You and I must go ourselves and look for her."

Tô cocked her head, "How? Where? We don't have any idea where she is!"

"No, but we must look for her everywhere. Please trust me. I know we will find her. We cannot sit here forever waiting for her to come back."

Tô knew that her friend was right. They had to climb mountains and cross rivers. If one month was not enough, they had to look for two months. If one year was not enough, they had to look for two, three, or even four years. They had to find her. Tô knew that once they found Mother, everything would be all right again.

Without Mother, yesterday and today were filled with fear and worry. Once Mother was found, the gunmen would stop shooting, the children would stop being hurt, and the destruction of villages would cease. She was convinced that they had only one task—to go everywhere and look for Mother. She asked Stone Boy, "When should we start?"

"Right now. Remember the little fishes that survived and returned to the stream. Now we must go and find our ma."

Tô and Stone Boy walked up the hill to their small house. Tô filled a large cotton bag with food and cooking utensils, and Stone Boy swung it over his shoulder. Tô put on the old raincoat her father used to wear, and she hung her flute across her back. Pushing the front door closed, the two children left to find their mother.

∞

First Tô and Stone Boy went to the Upper Village. At the school gate, they asked several people if they had seen Mrs. Ba

Ty, but none of them had. They walked to the Lower Village and saw soldiers standing guard in several places. Stone Boy described to Tô how there were embers and smoldering ash where houses had stood. It was a village of desolation, and people were cleaning up the terrible mess. They asked if anyone had seen their mother, but no one had. They walked around the outlying areas of the village, but had no luck, so they continued walking.

As long as the road stretched out in front of them, they walked on, not knowing where the next village might be. They climbed several hills and walked through small woods, but they could not see even one hut. It was getting dark. After crossing a bamboo bridge, they stopped for a few moments to rest their legs, cooling their feet in the stream. Tô asked Stone Boy to find three stones. She set her cooking pot on them, built a fire, and cooked some rice in the pot they had brought with them.

The moon, barely a sliver, hung in the vast, dark sky. For Tô, it was no problem to eat in the dark. She and Stone Boy were famished, and they ate the whole pot of rice. Stone Boy walked to the stream and brought back water for drinking and washing, and they lay down close to one another under Father's raincoat.

They woke up as the sun was warming the chilly air, and went down to the stream to wash their faces before setting off again to search for Mother. Tô walked close to Stone Boy, holding his arm. After crossing thick undergrowth, they expected to see hamlets or at least a few houses, but the dense jungle trail stretched endlessly in front of them. At nightfall, Tô proposed that they stop and make camp at a place where she heard the sound of running water. While she cooked a pot of rice, Stone Boy found a good place surrounded by trees and bushes to sleep. He broke a number of thorny branches and placed them around the spot for protection.

During the night, Tô heard the crackling of a large fire. She reached out for Stone Boy, but he was already awake, watching something. Stone Boy held Tô's hand firmly and whispered, "Keep still. There are hundreds of men with guns around a campfire near the stream. They just finished cooking rice and are about to eat it."

Tô and Stone Boy listened as the men sang strange songs with powerful rhythms that sounded like ocean waves breaking on a rocky shore. Tô sensed in their songs a force, as if they were about to stampede forward and crush everything in their way.

The group sang other songs which sounded gentler. Stone Boy watched as some men stood up and told stories, and he noticed that everyone in the group was beginning to feel more relaxed. One man, wearing green palm leaves in his hair, stood up. He held a long cane like a lance in his right hand and a flaming stick in his left. Swinging the flame in front of him, he sang:

> Our beautiful, precious land—
> I'll do my duty here.
> Three years as a soldier—
> On guard at dawn, in the office at night,
> This is my fate, so why should I complain?
>
> O soldiers, let us cry our hearts out to the bamboo
> and *wu-tung* trees.
> Our suffering is like salt in an open wound.

Tô was moved by this strange, poignant song. She thought of her own father as a soldier in the jungle with scarcely enough food to eat, sleeping on hard ground, exposed to the rains, without his family to care for him when he was ill. Tô realized that these men were the same as her father. They were singing vigorously now, but soon they would be brought down by jungle illnesses, bullets, or bombs. They would lie on the ground like the little dead bird with its head twisted upon its chest, its legs and claws crumpled under its belly. This soldier's song was much closer to the ones Tô composed on her flute. It was sorrowful, and it spoke of longing and resignation. The earlier soldiers' songs were forceful, like the wind and the rain in a great storm. Tô wondered how these men could have such different voices and feelings.

When the man ended his song, there was no applause, just a long silence. One man spoke up and criticized the singer, and then the group returned to patriotic songs, infused with fight and courage. They sang for a while, and fell silent. Stone Boy and Tô could hear nothing but the occasional crackling of the big fire going out. They stayed very still and soon fell asleep.

The two children awoke to find that the strangers had gone without leaving any traces, not even ash or coal from the fire. Stone Boy and Tô started out again. They walked all day before emerging from the forest. By the time they reached a small village, night had already begun to fall. The village was surrounded by a strong, high fence of sharpened bamboo stakes, and watchtowers dotted the area. Stone Boy and Tô decided to spend the night under one of the thatched roofs of the market so that they would not have to go far to inquire about Mother in the morning.

In the middle of the night, Stone Boy and Tô woke up to the explosion of bombs. Guns blazed, and someone sounded a brass bell as an alarm. Occasionally, the gunfire became intense, and a flare burst in the sky, sending light into every corner. Bombs brought down the central roof of the market. Loose tiles and debris whizzed toward the thatched roof where Stone Boy and Tô sat. Children and adults screamed, and soldiers shouted angrily. Houses caught on fire. People ran to alert one another to put out the fires in the midst of the fighting. The attackers broke through the line of defense, yelling "Forward! Forward!" and the shooting intensified. Stone Boy kept getting up, but Tô struggled to keep him down as bullets whizzed by their heads. But Stone Boy was strong and eager to help the others. Tô lay trembling like a small frightened bird. Houses were burning, people were dying, and men on opposing sides were on a murderous rampage. Before Tô knew it, the words "Ma! Ma!" escaped from her lips. Then, without fear of being hit by a bullet, she sat up and screamed at the top of her lungs.

When Tô stopped screaming, she could not believe her ears—Stone Boy was singing. He had gone into the open marketplace and started singing. She shouted, "Lie down, Stone Boy, please!" But he did not hear her. His voice rang louder and louder, and Tô heard the wind rise and flutter. The sound of the forest far away blended in with his voice. Stone Boy stood fearlessly, as if he were on a tranquil hillside. Tô felt all her sorrow and fear melt, and she began to accompany him on her flute. The sound of wings beating signaled to her that the birds had come again and were circling above.

The battle subsided. The shooting became less intense, and the screams and shouts quieted. The sound of Tô's flute rose up, and it wept over the fate of the woodcutters forced to become soldiers who never came back from the war. Her music mourned for the firewood-sellers who lost their children during a battle; for small boys and girls who wandered homeless; for soldiers who died in utter loneliness in remote mountain passes; for old women and babies who had been hit by stray bullets and bled to death unattended. Heaven and Earth heard these cries, and all the birds in the forest listened. Children and grownups, and even the soldiers who had just been shooting each other, were now holding their guns down and listening. Tô was begging for help from Heaven, from Earth, and from all living creatures. As her music quieted, Stone Boy's voice rose again. In his voice there was a deep faith in the interconnectedness and love among all beings, which soothed all pains like a spring breeze. It was autumn dew cooling the fire of hatred, the miraculous water that brought forth young buds on dying trees.

The guns were silent now. Even the wind had quieted. The birds were flying away. Tô and Stone Boy held hands in silence. In the east, there was a hint of dawn.

∞

Life returned slowly to the village. Several men appeared with torches blazing in the thick, white mist. People called out to their loved ones. The dead were being carted away. Rebuilding had already started. Reinforcement for the next attack was being planned, and a request for help was put through to the district headquarters.

A detachment of men on patrol saw Stone Boy and Tô and, since they were unknown to the local people, they were arrested. A few military and civilian men suspected they were enemy scouts and threatened to shoot them on the spot. Stone Boy looked deeply at them, bewildered. He did not know what those words—scouts, couriers, spies—meant. But Tô was terrified. She burst out crying and proceeded to tell the men everything that had happened. The men did not believe her, but rather than having them shot, the commander ordered that they be brought to the district headquarters and turned over to the civilian authorities.

At noon, army trucks took them to the police station of the district's capital. They were given some food and nothing but a blanket and a straw mat to spend the night. Three days went by until they were taken to the provincial capital and placed in the Juvenile Reform Center.

The center was a large tract of land dotted with long, low buildings and surrounded by high walls studded with glass shards. Stone Boy and Tô were brought to a room with an interrogator and a typist. Tô said right away that she was Hoang Thi Tô, nine years old, in the fifth grade, and daughter of Mr.

and Mrs. Ty, woodcutters from the Upper Village, An Lac District. She said that Stone Boy was her brother, twelve years old, but he was not going to any school, for he had to stay home and help their widowed mother. Then she declared proudly that their father had given his life to his country.

The interrogator asked Stone Boy to tell him all he knew about the attack at Phuoc Binh four days ago, and, yes, to tell him honestly whether he was working for the rebels. Stone Boy did exactly as he was asked, relating all the details of their search to find their mother, leading up to their arrest. When Stone Boy told the interrogator about the men with guns on the bank of the stream, Tô could sense the interrogator's suspicion. Indeed, he sat silently for a long moment and then ordered Stone Boy to be taken to Camp A and Tô to Camp D. The tall, thin secretary took Tô's hand and told Stone Boy to follow them. Though they were to be kept in separate camps, she said they could see one another twice a day, after lunch and after supper. She added that they could always ask permission to visit at other times as well.

Although Tô was allowed to participate in all activities at Camp D's school, she could not see what was written on the blackboard, nor read the books. When it came to things that did not require eyesight, however, she was fine. After only five days, she was able to make her way around the reform center without a guide. And her roommate Lê, though a sharp and tough girl, liked her very much.

Stone Boy could not keep up in his school. He asked for permission to go to Tô's class and sit next to her. After mealtimes, she would teach him the basics of reading, and in less than a week, he was able to read and write simple sentences. Then Tô showed him arithmetic, and in just one day, he learned addition, subtraction, multiplication, and division.

Most of the children at the center were friendly, except for a few tough ones whose joy came from bullying and beating up others. Even Stone Boy was roughed up once by two older boys because he smiled when they tried to intimidate him. Though his face was bloodied, Stone Boy did not fight back. Tô happened to be there, and she ran to get help. When the authorities arrived, Stone Boy had collapsed onto the dirt floor and was bleeding profusely. He was taken to the infirmary, and Tô asked for permission to sit with him. From that day on, the others began to call Stone Boy "the dumb one," because he did not fight back when he was beaten. And Tô, of course, was called "the blind one."

By the end of that year, Stone Boy was released from the reform center and placed in the School for Wards of the State because of his exemplary conduct and excellent school work. Tô was transferred to the School for the Blind at Bien Hoa. They were in a panic when they were told of their new destinations. They both thought that, once separated, they would never be able to find Mother. But the decision had been made. They would be allowed to correspond, and once in a while Stone Boy would be permitted to visit Tô at the School for the Blind.

∞

One night, Tô was awakened by gunshot in the distance, and she was filled with sorrow. She had just dreamed that Stone Boy was back, and they were walking side by side. It was now more than six months since she had heard from him. She had lost him the same way that she had lost her ma.

While Stone Boy was a ward of the state, Tô received four letters from him, which she kept in a tin can among her clothes. Once in a while, she would ask a young woman who worked at the school to read them to her. As soon as his letters stopped coming, Tô asked the School's administration to make inquiries about him. They reported that Stone Boy had been transferred to the reform center in Vung-Tau because of misconduct.

Tô could not believe that Stone Boy would do anything wrong. She had never known anyone kinder or gentler. But he was never afraid of anyone, not even those in power. Perhaps if she had been with him, this would not have happened, she thought. How could a little blind girl ever find the two persons dearest to her in the world?

During the first few months at the School for the Blind, Tô learned to read Braille. As her fingers moved along the stiff sheets of paper with dots of varying patterns, images materialized in her mind, and a smile came to her lips. It was a pity there were not many of these books available. She learned to write letters with a stylus and a Braille typewriter.

Tô learned weaving and sewing, and she was a member of the school's musical group because she played the flute so well. However, the school only allowed her to play nice folk songs —songs about the beauty of rural life in peaceful times. She was not happy about this restriction and, instead, she played tunes that expressed her pain and hope, and the suffering and aspirations of thousands of children like her. She found it hard to understand why adults tried to hide the truth. Everywhere she and Stone Boy had gone, they had witnessed unfathomable suffering. At Têt New Year, when everyone expected life in the cities to be peaceful and happy, there was the most terrifying destruction of all. Even in Saigon, entire neighborhoods of houses were destroyed, and putrefying corpses littered the streets. There were so many deaths that bulldozers had to be used to push the bodies into common graves. Hospitals overflowed with wounded adults and children. Even at Bien Hoa, Tô's school was shelled and several of her classmates were killed. This was the reality, yet everyone went on pretending nothing of any great consequence was happening.

Just the day before, as the school bus stopped in front of the city hospital, she had heard a small girl singing a song by T.C. Son:

I weep for the clouds asleep in the mountains.
I weep for the trees on the rolling hills.
I weep for my brothers, whose blood is running dry.
I weep for our homeland, drenched with tears.
I weep for the birds that have left the forest.
I weep for the nights of funerals and wakes.
I weep for my sisters, whose fate is sorrow.
I weep for my teardrops, which have no name.

Tô could tell that the girl was about her own age and that she, too, was blind. Tô guessed that the person accompanying her on the zither was her father, who had been handicapped by the war. He probably has no other means of livelihood than to take his child to sing in the streets, Tô thought. As the little girl sang, Tô could hear the blind child's clarity about what was happening around her. It made Tô wonder for what purpose adults had eyes.

Just a day or two earlier, Tô had had a strange dream about wandering with Stone Boy in search of Mother. It was a hot summer morning, and they were standing on a hill with seven or eight suns in the sky, and a moon and stars, too! She could not believe it—suns and stars at once! It was joyous, like a festival.

Suddenly, there were explosions, and the suns began to collapse and disintegrate as they landed. The sky went dark, and the moon and stars disappeared. Cries of anguish could be heard from every direction, and she knew that these terrible things were happening because she had lost her mother. She knew that if she could find Mother, the suns would come back bright and hot in the sky, and the moon and stars would reappear too. She staggered in the dark, listening to cries of thousands of motherless children.

Then Stone Boy appeared out of nowhere with a sunflower in his hand—a big sunflower, as big as a Bien Hoa grapefruit, and filled with light—which he held up like a lamp to guide their way. Tô and Stone Boy went into villages and hamlets buried deep in darkness. At each place, Stone Boy raised his sunflower and sang. Once, they stopped in front of a row of houses crowded together, which appeared like a mountain, silent and cool in the dark night. Stone Boy raised his sunflower and sang. After a long while, a window opened, emitting a pale light. Dark figures gesturing to Stone Boy and Tô appeared at more and more windows. The children heard the growling of fierce wild animals. As the growling became louder and nearer, Tô took Stone Boy's hand, and they ran away.

The scene changed from a village to a deep forest. Stone Boy shone his luminous sunflower on every bush, tree, and stone. Then they were at the bottom of the ocean in the Kingdom of Waters, looking at every fish and blade of seaweed in the light of the flower. Tô and Stone Boy went everywhere, looking deeply at things. They met a very old man with snow-white hair, who handed Stone Boy something big and round like a pumpkin. It shimmered like mother-of-pearl and he called it the sun of the Sea Palace. They could borrow it, he told them, and return to land to look for their mother. As Tô reached for the sparkling object, she woke up.

She tried to go back to sleep to continue the dream, but the sound of distant gunshot disturbed her. She sat up and opened her window. The cool air rushed in and refreshed her. She reached along the edge of her bed and found her flute. Raising it to her lips, she began to play very softly.

Tô played for a long time until she heard something besides her own music. It was the golden bird, with whom she had "conversed" for nine days in the forest. Tô was overjoyed, as the bird told her that Stone Boy had arrived. She raised her flute and, by her music, asked the bird to confirm what she had understood. Yes, the bird was telling her that Stone Boy had returned. She put a jacket over her shoulders and, with flute in hand, opened the door and walked out into the yard. The golden bird hovered directly above her. Reaching the gate, she pulled back the latch, pushed it open, and walked out. Then she heard someone calling her name.

She turned. It was Stone Boy. He rushed to her and held her in his arms. Tô stood still and wept softly. Then they heard the bird crying in the sky, and Stone Boy told her, "Let's go now, before daylight." He took her hand, and the two children followed along the wall surrounding the school to find their way out of town. All the while, the golden bird hovered above them, pointing the way.

Tô wiped her eyes and asked, "Where are we going now, Stone Boy?" Though only nine months had passed, Stone Boy seemed nine years older, and Tô was confident he would know the answer to her question.

"We'll get out of town first. Then we can try to find our way back to Dai Lao Forest. We must go back to our house and see whether Mother has come home. Then I must return to the mountain. I have been away for twelve moons now, you know."

"But how do you know which way to go? Home is so far away. We'll get lost."

"Don't worry, Tô. The golden bird will show us the way. He has been with me all the way from the mountains of Lang Son. He helped me find you, didn't he?"

Yes, Stone Boy had come to her all the way from the forests and mountains of the north. She was delirious with joy. If he had been able to find her, he would be able to find Mother, she thought.

Tô recalled the dream she had had the night before in which the white-bearded old man gave them a sun, as big as a pumpkin, shimmering like mother-of-pearl. She told Stone Boy about her dream, saying that perhaps the dream was a premonition of what was to come. She held Stone Boy's arm and walked close to him, and he listened to her every word. He asked her to tell him all that had happened since the day she was sent away to the School for the Blind at Bien Hoa. He listened in silence, except for occasional questions to clarify details. Soon they were outside the town and heading deeper and deeper into a rubber tree forest. They walked all day with just two short rests. The golden bird fluttered overhead and faithfully accompanied them. Upon arriving at a manmade canal, they found an abandoned canoe and made it into a shelter for the night.

Tô and Stone Boy walked on for days, toward the northwest. They crossed a forest of banana trees, full of ripe, succulent fruit, which they ate, along with fresh water from a nearby stream. Passing through a forest of bamboo trees, they broke some shoots and roasted them on a fire of dry bamboo leaves. They foraged in the jungle for days until they reached the clearing where months before they had seen soldiers camping on the bank of a stream, singing around a fire. Tô still remembered the man's sorrowful song about soldiers guarding lonely outposts far away from home.

During these days of walking, Stone Boy told Tô about his time at the School for Wards of the State. He had made friends with many other students whose fathers or brothers had died in battle. They formed a singing group to express their yearning for peace, and their songs touched everyone deeply, adults and children alike. Soon, however—perhaps the audiences' responses were too enthusiastic—the school's administration started dictating which songs could be sung. Stone Boy and his friends refused to sing these new songs. Threats and punishments, then special favors and coaxing, could not sway them. Finally the school expelled Stone Boy, whom they considered the instigator, and they sent him to a very strict cadet school at Vung Tau.

At the cadet school, Stone Boy met many like-minded boys. One day, he and a group of his friends presented a petition to the school which stated that, instead of preparing to become fighters, they wanted to be trained as social workers. They could help villagers rebuild their homes, till the fields, and become part of the nationwide movement working for an early end to the war. The fact that students at a school for cadets should engage in such "subversive" activities was enough to create quite a stir, not only within the school itself, but also in higher places. Stone Boy was charged with "propaganda for the enemy" and taken away to Chi Hoa Prison.

In prison, Stone Boy saw a number of Buddhist monks whose arms were in shackles. When he asked them what they had done, they told him that they had publicly called on both sides to cease fire and discuss peaceful reconciliation, and for this they were imprisoned. During Stone Boy's second week at Chi Hoa, three hundred monks and nearly two hundred other prisoners began a hunger strike. One night Stone Boy was brutally awakened and brought to a room. He was accused of inciting the monks, through his songs, to go on a strike. Stone Boy was shackled and taken to a camp in central Vietnam for political prisoners.

In the camp, Stone Boy met a very eccentric Taoist monk, whose hair was so long it covered both his ears. He was thin, even frail, but his eyes were sharp and brilliant. His brown peasant suit, after many washings, was the color of pale dirt. This unusual man always kept with him a cage containing a cat and two mice. It never ceased to amaze people that the cat never harmed the mice.

The old monk told Stone Boy that he had gone with his cage to the provincial headquarters and asked for an audience with the commander. When he was denied entrance, he sat down at the main gate and refused to leave. People stopped and stared, and the old monk was only too happy to explain to anyone willing to listen, "I'm here to tell the government that if a cat can live in peace with two mice, why can't we human beings live in peace together? We must stop killing one another today and start rebuilding our homeland."

Some people were moved to tears, but others railed at him, calling him stupid and naive. "No cat and mice can live together," they said. "This monk is crazy. Let them put him away." And, indeed, the old monk ended up in prison.

Now he looked at Stone Boy and pointed at his cage, "See, over a month they have been together and the cat has not eaten the mice, has it?"

Stone Boy enjoyed hearing the old monk tell stories. He said he had gone all over the villages in the east and collected bullets and bomb shrapnel to cast a big bell. Every night he would stay up late and invite the bell to sound in a slow, solemn manner. He had hoped that the sound of the bell would reach the hearts of people and wake them up to the reality of the choice they were facing. He told Stone Boy, "By making those pieces of metal into a temple bell, I helped them follow the peaceful way of a Buddha." Stone Boy was delighted by the image of deadly pieces of metal following the way of the Buddha, though he knew that such remarks could only confirm the suspicion that the old monk was indeed crazy.

The old monk and Stone Boy became close friends. At one point, they joined hundreds of other prisoners on a hunger strike. After a week, they were all taken to Quang Tri, the northernmost province of the South, and ordered to walk north onto a bridge of Ben Hai, the river that separated North and South Vietnam. A southern officer, in a camouflage suit, said to them as they were leaving, "Go on! Over there you'll have plenty of chances for hunger strikes."

As they reached the other end of the bridge, they were warmly greeted by the authorities and people of the North. When they were asked why they were expelled from the South, the old monk and Stone Boy told the simple truth, which everyone seemed pleased to hear. Later, in private, an official told Stone

Boy that he should say that people in the South were leading a miserable existence, and that people in the North should send their young men south to save their fellow countrymen, and that the foreign soldiers must be forced out of the country.

Stone Boy listened carefully, but he knew they were not speaking the truth. Yes, in the South there were people who exploited others and profited from the war while thousands of soldiers and civilians were dying every day. It was true that the authorities in the South did everything in their power to hide the truth about the war and to crush anyone who had the courage to call for negotiations for an end to this fratricide. But the people in the South also suffered immeasurably because of the soldiers who came down from the North. Millions of people lost their homes, their loved ones, and even their own lives because of this clash between brothers. The real pain was shared by people of the same race and same history who were unable to sit down and resolve their differences. This was the real cause of the suffering, not this or that exploitative foreign power, even though the guns and bullets both sides were using to destroy each other were brought by outsiders. After the authorities departed, Stone Boy revealed his thoughts about the war to the old Taoist monk. The old monk nodded in accord.

During the following days, the monk and Stone Boy went into hamlets and villages and visited with the ordinary country people of the North. Everywhere they went, they saw people living in poverty, though there was not as much destruction as they had seen in the South. There seemed to be only the very old and the very young in the hamlets. The able-bodied were all in the armed forces.

When the people heard Stone Boy talk about the real situation in the south, they realized they had been deceived. They trusted that their sons and their brothers had gone south to fight foreign invaders. They had no idea that brothers were killing brothers. After discussing the situation among themselves, the villagers decided to go to the provincial committee and demand that their sons be allowed to come home. Old ladies wept openly and hugged Stone Boy, telling him that their sons had been killed in battle, they knew not where. The local cadres reported this to their higher-ups, and the old monk and Stone Boy were separated and taken away. The Taoist monk held Stone Boy's hand in his and laughed heartily. He recited a short poem—witty, ironic, and delightful—about being constant and courageous, and keeping a sense of humor in the face of adversity.

Stone Boy was taken to a reeducation camp, where he had to do strenuous physical labor with little food or sleep. Absolute obedience was the rule. During study periods, he was only permitted to listen and remember what he was told, and he was not allowed to speak up or present anything of his own that ran counter to the official line. Stone Boy was shocked to find out that in the North there was as much cover-up of the truth as in the South. Perhaps the official lies were even more complete and the discipline more harsh in the North. He realized, too, that even if he were permitted to speak up, it would have been to no avail. People at the "citizens' meetings," convened by the authorities themselves, raised their hands or brought them down like automatons. They had been trained to do so for a long time. He saw, too, that while they moved their arms up or down—to applaud or condemn this or that—their faces were impassive, betraying no emotion whatsoever, only resignation and acceptance.

One day, during a "political study session" in which the air was stifling like the sky before a summer storm, Stone Boy began to sing. Everyone turned toward him and stopped listening to the formal speaker. At first the speaker was infuriated, but after a while, the song entered him also, and he sat down with bent head, listening along with everyone else.

Stone Boy was transferred to another reeducation camp. His punishment was to walk from Ha Tinh to a camp in the harsh mountain region of Lang Son Province, where inmates were deprived of even the most basic health care and nutrition, and where many became partially paralyzed, blind, or gangrenous because of neglect.

One day, while Stone Boy was cutting wood in the forest under the watchful eye of a cadre, he felt an urge to return to his mountain home. Suddenly, a high mountain appeared against the deep, blue sky. Huge boulders formed a stony point that jutted out from the mountain. Every night, dew would collect in a crevice the size of a sunflower. One sip of this miraculous water, and the pain, thirst, and torments of a thousand lives would dissolve.

Stone Boy thought that if Tô could climb up that mountain, take a sip of that water, and wash her eyes with it, she would be able to see again. As Stone Boy thought this, he began to sing. The cadre looked at him in disbelief and suddenly, from all corners of the forest, came the sound of wings beating. Birds filled the sky. Then Stone Boy heard the cries of the golden bird. He raised his voice and asked the bird to lead him to his friend Tô.

Stone Boy and the golden bird took two weeks to reach Bien Hoa. As they approached the School for the Blind, Stone Boy heard the familiar sound of Tô's flute. When Tô walked through the gate, Stone Boy told her about the crevice in the rock filled with the miraculous dew that could heal her eyes. As Tô felt a great hope rise within her, she realized that the water had already begun to have its healing effect.

Tô and Stone Boy chatted so excitedly that they reached the Upper Village without even knowing it. Their old village looked very dilapidated and vacant. Stone Boy could see that the war had not spared even this humble corner. He identified Tô's old house and cried with joy. Tô raised her hand to her chest and felt her heart beat wildly. She asked him, "Is it still standing, Stone Boy? Do you think Ma is in there?"

Stone Boy could see that the house was intact, but there was no one in sight. They crossed the stream and followed the path up the hillside. Stone Boy pushed back the bamboo door and led her inside. Now Tô no longer needed a guide, for she knew every inch of that little house. She went straight to the kitchen, then to the water basin in the back, then finally to the vegetable patch. But everywhere she went, she felt only voidness. It was obvious that her mother had never come back from the marketplace since that Wednesday many months ago. Overcome with grief, Tô went out and sat on the doorstep.

Stone Boy asked her to walk with him to the stream. He reminded Tô that they had freed two fishes there—one orange and the other silver. "You know, they started their journey the same day we did. I wonder whether they have found their mother. If so, we might see them here again."

Tô could see, in her mind's eye, the two tiny fishes swimming together. She hoped that they had not been separated from each other during their search for their mother. If they had been, she hoped they would be reunited as she and Stone Boy were now. A smile formed on her lips as she remembered how the two fishes had been as small as two fingers. A year had now passed; they must be as big as her hand!

∞

Stone Boy and Tô spent the night in the little house. The next morning, they got up early and walked toward the Dai Lao Forest, from which they could walk to the summit of the mountain. The path became steeper and steeper until Stone Boy could no longer see the golden bird, but he did not need a guide anymore. It became increasingly difficult to climb, especially for Tô, but they continued. After three arduous days, as dusk fell, they reached the base of the summit.

"Only a little way further, Tô. But let's rest here," he said, leading her to a large, flat rock and inviting her to sit down.

When Stone Boy saw that Tô's brow was drenched with sweat, he picked up a large leaf and fanned her with it. Tô sat and breathed deeply for a while and began to feel rested and happy. She realized that the air around her was extraordinarily clean and cool. Tô noticed a fragrance and wondered whether it was of plants and flowers, or of the sky and clouds themselves. She felt a lightness, a floating sensation. This was the land of Stone Boy's birth.

She asked him, "Are there any houses up here, Stone Boy? You will take me to your house, won't you? To meet your father and mother? They'll be so glad to see you again."

Stone Boy remembered how he had found it difficult to say anything the first time Tô and her mother asked him about his home and family. They thought it was too painful for him to talk about the parents he had lost, and they did not persist. But now, Stone Boy thought, he must tell the truth. He put down the big leaf and told Tô, "This is where I come from. That's all I know. I don't have a father and a mother the way you did. There are no houses up here. I was born a long time ago. It is possible that since I was born, the full moon has gone over the summit of this mountain one thousand times, or perhaps ten thousand times. I sit here days and nights listening only to the songs of the sky, the clouds, the rain, the wind, the flowers, and the birds. Though no one has taught me, I know how to sing."

"But every child has a father and a mother. You must have parents. Who are they?"

"As I said, I do not know. Perhaps Heaven and Earth gave me birth. Or perhaps the stones brought me here. But look, Tô, I do have a mother! My mother is Mrs. Ba Tỵ, your mother, your loving, wonderful ma. You and I, we are Ma's children. We just spent a year looking for her!"

A tear pearled on Tô's eyelashes. She realized that Stone Boy was right. When Mother gave birth to her, she also gave birth to Heaven and Earth, houses and trees. Were there no Mother, how could there be forests, fields, grass, and flowers? Without Mother, how could there be Stone Boy himself? Now it seemed obvious to Tô that Stone Boy had indeed come into this world thanks to her mother. Even the two little fishes had been given birth by Mother, so they too were now looking for her. Without lifting her head, Tô said, "Stone Boy, brother, do you think we'll ever find Ma?"

"Yes, of course I do. We'll find her. She cannot be dead and gone and lost forever. She has given birth to Heaven and Earth, forests and fields. If they are still here, so is she. There is only one thing that we must do, and that is to find her. Once we have found her, everything will be all right. Once we have found her, people will no longer kill one another, villages will no longer be destroyed, and children will no longer be lost. I am looking for Mother. You are looking for Mother. The two little fishes are looking for her, too. Even the old Taoist monk is looking for her. And I think she, too, is looking for us. Yes, Tô, don't you think so? Ma cannot be dead and gone forever. One day we will find her." Tô did not speak. Ever since she had come to know Stone Boy, she had always believed what he said. And he was speaking to her again.

"I used to sit up here and listen to the sound of your flute wafting up from the forest below. I could hear you as well as if you were sitting next to me. I heard your music, and I knew you were in pain. That was why I came down from the mountain. I came down and sang for you, and served as your eyes, your guide. We were two persons, yet we walked together and became one person. In truth, you and I are one, because I am within you and you are within me. You may not see this now, but one day you will. And once you have understood this, wherever you go in this world, you will see that I am with you.

"Look, the moon is almost perfectly round tonight. This is the full moon day of the fourth month. Last year on this day, I came down the mountain. Are you rested now? It is just a short walk from here to the top." Tô stood up. Stone Boy offered his arm, and the two children walked under the bright moonlight.

A short time later, they reached the summit. Stone Boy found a place for Tô to sit with her back against a flat rock. It was perfectly still. Tô felt as if the entire forest were very far away, and that the flat rock was a small island surrounded by the vast ocean. The wind blew softly and brushed against Tô's face, making her cheeks cool, almost cold. The dew was falling. Tô heard Stone Boy's approaching footsteps, then his voice.

"We've got to wait until midnight for enough dew to collect...." Stone Boy interrupted himself and went back to sit next to Tô, saying, "The moon is very bright, but down below the mist obscures everything. There is mist up here, too, but it's very light and we can still see the stars. Time has flown, hasn't it? Twelve full moons like this since I left my mountain!"

Putting his hand on Tô's shoulder, he continued, "Tomorrow, we can follow the direction of the rising sun to return home. You will want to stop at the stream and see if the little fishes have come back, won't you? What are you thinking, Tô?"

Tô replied, "I am thinking about the dream I had the night you came to the School for the Blind. You were holding a big sunflower that emitted a pale light, just bright enough for us to see our way ahead. Yes, I was able to see as if I were not blind at all. O, Brother Stone Boy, I am no longer a blind girl with you next to me. You *are* my eyes."

The moon was directly above the children. It was midnight, and very still. Stone Boy went to look at the stone hollow.

"Tô, it is full of dew now."

Stone Boy returned to help Tô make her way slowly up the treacherous path to the summit. When they reached it, Stone Boy explained, "This is miraculous dew, my sister. I will scoop it up for you to drink and wash your eyes. You will feel better than you ever have before. You'll be able to go for months without food or water, and your body will be healthy and your mind clear. This dew will give you back your eyesight."

Stone Boy carefully cupped his hands and filled them with the miraculous dew. It seemed to Tô as if time had paused, as if above her the moon and the stars were watching her in great solemnity. The old man with the white beard, whom Tô had met in the Kingdom of Waters, was standing next to Stone Boy, about to hand her a big sunflower. Tô knelt down on the stone, and her knees began to shake lightly. Stone Boy brought his hands to her lips, and she drank the dew with utmost respect. Tô felt transformed, and a sense of ease welled up in her and spread throughout her body. She breathed long, deep breaths, and she felt all her fears, worries, and pain dissolve. Again and again, Stone Boy cupped his hands and scooped up the precious dew to wash Tô's eyes.

Then he led her to a big flat rock, and as she lay down, he placed his jacket over her and said, "Cover your forehead. You can go to sleep now. I am right here."

Tô lay very still and listened to the stillness that surrounded her. She again felt as if she were on a small island adrift in the ocean. The wind rustled far away. She heard an occasional drop of dew falling to the ground, and she was aware of Stone Boy's regular and light breathing. She said to herself she ought to go to sleep, too, but she went on listening to Stone Boy's breathing, which seemed to merge with the breathing of the gentle wind.

∞

Tô awoke to the sound of birds singing. She brought one hand to her eyes, and was struck by a strange yet familiar impression. It was the sunlight! She was no longer blind. Tô put her hands over her eyes, the light was so glaring, but she tried to see between her fingers. Here and there, she could see the stones, the sky. A moment later, she dropped her hands from her face.

The first thing she saw was an immense rock, three or four times as large as her parents' house. It was standing upright against the vast, clear blue, cloudless sky, which spread over and beyond the summit, and curved down on all sides of the mountain. She stood on a lone island.

Tô turned around and saw that the forest and the mountains below were still bathed in the morning mist. The immensity and depth made her feel she had escaped an existence full of suffering and sorrow.

She looked around but did not see Stone Boy. She called his name, and the sound of her voice rolled into space, touching the trees, the mist, the stones, and echoing back to her. There was still no response. She called his name again with all her strength, but no one replied.

Tô began to panic. She climbed up the nearest rock and looked in the direction of the rising sun. There was no sign of anyone. Then her eyes caught a vision at the very top of the highest peak, which took her breath away. The rock had the shape, the form, the bearing that was Stone Boy's. Yes, it *was* Stone Boy, and he was waving to her.

How strange, for when she was blind she had never seen Stone Boy; yet she recognized him in the shape of the rock. It was an image she had previously formed while listening to the sound of his voice and feeling the lines and shapes of his face. Now, for the first time, perhaps the only time, she could see him with her own eyes.

Tô rubbed her eyelids and looked again. The stony figure was no longer waving to her. Though it still resembled Stone Boy, he had gone back to where he had come from. He had again become stone.

"Days and nights, I sit on the summit of the mountain and listen to the songs of the sky, the clouds, the rain, the wind, the flowers, and the birds. Though no one has taught me, I know how to sing." Now Tô understood what Stone Boy had said the day before. "I was born a long time ago…Since I was born, the full moon has gone over the summit of this mountain one thousand times, perhaps ten thousand times."

"Stone Boy has left me all alone in the world," she thought. "He came to be with me—why didn't he stay with me forever?"

"In truth, you and I are one, because I am within you, and you are within me. You do not see this now, but one day soon you will understand. And once you understand this, wherever you go in this world, you will see that I am with you."

Tô bent down and wept, for she was, after all, only a child. She cried until the sun rose and hung above her head. She had no doubt now that Stone Boy had left her forever. He never really loved her, she thought. Her own mother had left her. And now even Stone Boy had left her. Alone, how could she ever find her ma?

She suddenly wished she were blind again so that Stone Boy would be with her, talk to her, and let her touch his hands and face. With tears in her eyes, she brought her flute to her lips and poured all her pain into her music. Even the clouds flying past the sides of the mountain stopped and gathered around. The golden bird returned and began to sing. Tô stopped playing and listened. Though it was a bird's song, she knew what it was saying to her:

> Do you remember the day
> our Mother first brought me here?
> Through the five rivers, I have come to you.
> But one day, when you no longer see me,
> smile, and quietly look for me
> in all the things that come and go.

You will find that I am
that which never comes
and never goes.
I am that reality beyond time,
beyond perception.

Tô listened to the golden bird's song, and she knew these were Stone Boy's own words. Though she did not understand the meaning, she tried to inscribe them in her mind and heart, so that she would never forget them. She raised her flute and played, asking the bird why Stone Boy had gone away. But the bird only sang the same song again.

Tô knew the bird had one message to tell her. There was no way she could learn anything more. Slowly, she put down her flute. Without Stone Boy, how could she go down the mountain alone? Then a light flashed through her mind. Now, she said to herself, I have regained my eyesight, so I can go down the mountain by myself. Only the day before, she recalled, she had said to Stone Boy, "Brother, when you are with me, I am no longer blind. You are my eyes." Stone Boy would always be present for Tô now that she could see.

She understood what Stone Boy had said to her. "In truth, you and I are one, because I am within you, and you are within me. You may not see this now, but one day soon you will. Once you understand this, you will see that I am present with you wherever you go."

A warm teardrop rolled down her cheek, soothing her heart full of sorrow. No wonder Stone Boy had told her, "Tomorrow, we will follow the direction of the rising sun and return home." "Of course Stone Boy is with me," she thought.

Tô raised her head and looked at the sky, the clouds, the rocks, and the trees. She knew that Stone Boy was also looking at them, seeing them, and transmitting their images to her eyes. The sounds of trees and the wind were his voice. She had only to listen, and she could hear him. From then on, she knew that not only was Stone Boy within her, but he was present everywhere.

The rocky peak on the mountaintop was indeed Stone Boy. No, Tô was not going down the mountain now. She wanted to stay here for the rest of the day. There was time, for now she had faith in what Stone Boy had told her. Her ma was alive, and she would find her. She would go—not alone, for Stone Boy would be with her—and they would find Mother, just as the two little fishes had done, just as the old monk had done. Tô was sure that the day when she found Mother would be a day all wars would stop—people would stop killing one another, destroying each other's houses, and causing so many children to wander around like stray animals.

Tô wanted to show Stone Boy that she truly understood what he had taught her, so she raised her flute to her lips. Sky and clouds, mountain and trees, settled down in peace and listened to her song.

∞

A Lone Pink Fish

A LONE PINK fish swims quickly in the South China Sea. The waves reflect the glint of her bright, sunlit scales as she rises to the surface. Fishing boats seldom encounter this fish. Her secret is well kept. In fact, only one person knows her mission, and that is a young Vietnamese woman named Dao.

Dao is nineteen and, together with the young man she loved and forty-two others, she left Vietnam on a small boat. On their way past Quai Island, off the Thai coast, they were attacked by pirates who stole everything they had and raped all the women aboard. Dao was violated by three of them, one after another. The men aboard tried desperately to protect the women, but they were no match for the pirates who beat and bound them. Dao's fiancé endured this fate. Terrified, Dao kicked and screamed. When she scratched her third attacker, he grabbed her by the leg and hurled her into the sea. Her cries, along with her body, were swallowed up by the ocean, and she lost consciousness. But Dao did not drown. She was rescued by the pink fish, who carried her to a sandy beach on a tiny, deserted island.

When Dao regained consciousness, she noticed that her body was badly bruised, and it took all of her strength just to sit up. Waves lapped onto the shore close to her feet. She struggled to stand and then staggered toward some boulders that offered shade. Heaving a sigh, she collapsed against one of the boulders and marveled that she was still alive.

Slowly she recalled all that had happened. She cradled her head in her arms and dared not look out at the sea for fear the pirates were still there. But no, the terrifying scene of the previous day had passed. When she finally lifted her head, she saw only the vast, endless sea. As she thought of the pirates' cruelties, tears streamed down her cheeks. She looked down at her aching body. Not a shred of clothing remained. Ashamed, she covered her breasts with her arms and looked up again. Sunlight shimmered on the sea. The deep blue sky was cloudless. There was no sign of any vessel. No black dot was visible in any direction.

Dao thought of Dat, the young man she loved, and she agonized that he must have been beaten and killed by the pirates. Wrapping her arms around herself and gasping for air, Dao sobbed. Her arms went limp, and she fell to the ground. Feeling her strength seep away, Dao was sure that she would cease breathing and die alone on the deserted island. But to her surprise, her breathing regained an even rhythm, and she fell into a deep sleep. She did not wake until the radiant moon shone in the vast sky.

∞

Dao felt a small hand touch her forehead. A young girl, ten or eleven years old, wearing a pink shirt and frayed white pants, was standing above her. She had bright black eyes and hair that brushed her shoulders.

"Who are you? Why are you here at this hour?" Dao asked anxiously.

Calmly the child answered, "My name is Hong. I arrived as the sun was setting."

The young girl reached over and pulled some clothes off a branch, and handed them to Dao. "Put these on so you won't get cold, elder sister, and then we can talk. It's already getting misty, and look, you're shivering."

Dazed and bewildered, Dao took a pair of Vietnamese pants and a blouse still fragrant with camphor. As Dao buttoned her blouse, she wondered, "Who is this child alone at night on this island? Is this a ghost come to haunt me?"

As this doubt crossed Dao's mind, the child spoke, "I'm not a ghost, elder sister. I'm a real person. I was born in Vinh Long, where my parents were merchants for almost twenty years. Come, sit down and eat some of these crackers while we talk."

As Dao sat beside her, Hong opened a large tin canister and took out a plastic bag filled with crackers. She tore the bag open with her teeth, and handed two crackers to Dao. Dao's stomach rumbled. She hadn't eaten a thing in nearly two days. The crackers were the kind on which she and her friends had always spread sweetened condensed milk. Each cracker was four fingers wide. After eating one, Dao asked, "Where did you get these?"

Hong laughed, "This is one of several tins a Danish ship threw into the sea. Go ahead and eat another while I tell you about it. You see, today there was a refugee boat that ran out of food and drinking water. The boat's motor had died. Most of the eighty-four people aboard were children. A ship bearing the French flag approached. The refugees waved their shirts and cried for help, but the French captain pretended not to see them. Several hours later, a British ship passed by, but they, too, pretended not to see the refugees. Just before sundown, a ship flying the Danish flag came near. Hearing the cries for help, the ship circled the refugee boat three times. They did not want to take the refugees aboard, but they did drop down two barrels of water and ten canisters of crackers. Seven tins fell onto the boat and three fell into the sea. This canister is one of those."

Dao asked, "Did the boat meet any ship after that? And did they finally make it to shore? Were you one of those aboard? Where are the others? Did the boat sink and everyone else drown?"

"You ask so many questions I feel dizzy. No, I was not aboard that boat. And it has not sunk yet. In fact, right now the northeasterly wind is blowing it toward Thailand. I think they will make it safely to shore."

Hong's face grew sad. Dao wanted to ask Hong more, but she hesitated. How does this young child know so much? And how extraordinary is her calm, mature bearing and manner of speaking. A normal ten-year-old, lost on a deserted island, far from her family, would never speak so serenely and matter-of-factly. It would seem more natural for such a young child to cling to me as an older sister and cry out for her mother. Yet here she is taking care of me as though she were the elder sister, giving me clothes to wear and food to eat. Perhaps I'm dreaming, thought Dao, and she bit her lip until it drew blood.

Just then, Hong raised one finger and gestured to Dao, "Listen, I think I hear running water. Maybe we can find fresh water to drink. Please stay here while I look."

Hong skipped lightly over the rocks and vanished among the dark shadows of the jungle trees. Waiting for Hong to return, Dao reached into the bag for two more crackers and ate them slowly. Hong returned holding a large leaf folded into a cup brimming with clear water.

"This water is fresh. Here, drink some."

Hong lifted the leaf cup to Dao's lips. The sweet water refreshed Dao all the way down to her stomach.

"Go ahead, drink it all. I've already had some."

Dao emptied the leaf cup and thanked Hong.

Hong told her, "Near the spring there is an enclosure sheltered from the wind where we can sleep. It's too cold to stay here, and the tide might come in during the night and take us out to sea."

Hong put the crackers back into the tin and handed it to Dao. She lifted the bag of clothes and proceeded down a rocky path leading to the spring. The moonlight shone brilliantly over the whole island.

At one place near the spring, Hong waited for Dao to sit down and then she spoke, "We were lucky to find water. With our tin of Danish crackers, we'll be fine for at least a couple of weeks. We can also look for fruit and edible plants. We must keep a lookout for any refugee boat that might pass by so we can signal them to rescue us. I scavenged a bundle of clothes while you were sleeping. I thought the shirt and pants would fit you, so I hung them up on that tree branch to dry. We can dry out the other clothes to use as blankets. Now, if you're not too tired, elder sister, tell me your story."

Dao told Hong how she had become a boat refugee. In 1976, her father, a writer, was sent to a reeducation camp in the northern highlands of Vietnam. Two years passed before Dao's mother could save enough money to visit him. She found him thin and wasted and deeply depressed. He urged his wife to take their children and escape to another country, but Dao's mother refused to abandon her husband and told her friends, "There is a saying, 'As long as there is water, a harvest is possible.' Just so, as long as my husband is alive, I will wait for him."

Afterwards, she and her mother could only afford to send him a letter, a small packet of sugar, and a bottle of salt once every three months. Sometimes six or seven months would pass with no news from him.

Life grew harsher with each passing day. Dao and her sixteen-year-old brother tried their best to help their mother earn a living as a vendor. But they could not make enough money to feed the family.

Dao had a friend named Nguyen, whose family was also poor, but they managed well, thanks to relatives overseas who sent them packages every two months. The parcels contained cigarettes, canned butter, and antibiotics, which they could sell to buy rice and other necessities.

When Dao's fiancé suggested that they try to escape by boat, Dao could not make up her mind. She did not fear for her own life, but she was afraid her mother could not survive without her. One night, her mother held her close and, weeping, urged Dao to go. Dao left everything she owned with her mother. All she took with her was her high school diploma and the clothes she had on. She stayed up late with her brother the night before she left and asked him to take care of the family.

"As soon as I reach Malaysia," she said, "I'll send you a telegram."

But the engine of their boat broke down in the middle of the sea, and they were tossed about for sixteen days and nights, leaving them prey to an attack by sea pirates. Images of the rapes, beatings, and violence loomed up in Dao's mind, and she covered her face. Tears fell like rain as she contemplated Dat's suffering, and her own, as well as the suffering of everyone aboard. She cried for her mother, her brother, and the man she loved. In desperation, she screamed, "I will beat my head against these rocks until I kill myself!"

Hong was listening quietly, now and then squeezing Dao's hand in her own, but she did not interrupt her. When Dao jumped up to bash her head against the rocks, Hong held her with such unusual strength that Dao could not move, and she fell to her knees. Though the night air was chilly, Dao was covered with sweat. Hong gently helped her onto the grass and used her sleeve to wipe the perspiration from Dao's forehead.

She waited until Dao's pain eased before saying softly, "Dao, please think of your parents, your brothers, and your sisters before you destroy yourself. They would suffer all their lives thinking you had drowned at sea. You have a good chance of being rescued by another refugee boat and making it to land, where you will be able to find work and help your family. Just knowing that you reached shore safely will give your parents happiness the rest of their lives. And the other people aboard your

boat also have a good chance of reaching shore safely. The pirates left after they threw you overboard. I saw your boat being carried by the waves toward the southwest. In just a few days,
it will probably reach Malaysia. Dat is still alive, and you may
meet him again."

Dao clutched Hong's arm. "Are you sure? Are you sure Dat
is still alive? How could you have seen his boat? Where were
you? What boat were you on? Where are your parents?"

Hong said, "I promise to tell you everything tomorrow. My
story is like yours. But it's very late, and we should sleep so we
can get up early and look for boats. Please lie down. You can
use the root of this tree as a pillow."

Dao joined her palms and said, "I pray with all my heart that
Dat is still alive." She paused and, with an agonized expression,
continued, "But little sister, my body is spoiled now. I am no
longer worthy of Dat. It's horribly unjust how a woman pre-
serves herself carefully for her future husband, and then in seconds everything is ruined by a pirate. There is nothing left for
me to live for."

Dao wept bitterly. Slowly, Hong spoke, "Many people live
not for pleasure, but for responsibility and love. Living for responsibility and love can be a source of great happiness, elder
sister."

In her misery, Dao could not grasp the deep meaning of
Hong's words. But because they were unusual words to come
from one so young, Dao listened attentively, somewhat awe-
struck, as Hong continued, "Who knows how many people have
drowned and had their flesh ripped and devoured by sharks? But
the ocean is not the only place where sharks are found, elder
sister. There are sharks on land who devour flesh and bones in
order to survive. Pirates are a kind of shark. Perhaps because they
suffer on land from other sharks, they in turn become sharks
on the sea. Sharks swimming in the sea have devoured tens of

thousands of our people. Sharks on boats have attacked tens of thousands more. You were attacked by three such sharks.

"You endured one part of our people's great sufferings. Who among us has not been wounded? Who among us has been able to keep our body and spirit intact? In my eyes, you are still pure and chaste, Dao. The pirates attacked you and forced themselves upon you, but they could not really take anything from you. You never consented to give your body to them. You bear no blame. Your wounds will heal one day, like the wounds of someone who has survived a shark attack. It is essential that you not allow your wounds to become infected with poison. Wounds can poison your spirit as well as your body. In ten days or so, you will make it to shore, and there you can find a doctor who can prevent the poison from infecting your body. But no doctor can heal the wounds of your spirit. That is up to you."

Each of Hong's words touched Dao's heart. Her tears flowed, and she felt lighter inside. After a few moments, Hong said, "When I was still in Vietnam, my grandmother used to chant the *Heart of Perfect Understanding Sutra*. I didn't understand the words, but whenever I heard them, I felt refreshed inside. You are so tired and sad. Let me chant the sutra for you."

Hong began to chant without waiting for Dao to respond. As Dao listened, she felt the pain within her subside. Tears as sweet as dew rolled down her cheeks. Hong had not yet finished chanting the sutra a fourth time when Dao fell into a deep sleep. She did not stir again until the sun rose.

When Dao opened her eyes, Hong was not there. Guessing that Hong had gone off exploring, Dao washed her face in the spring water and rinsed the salt from her hair. Then she climbed onto a large boulder and looked out in all directions. Sunlight poured across the sea and lit up the small island. There was not a cloud in sight. A sudden pain in her stomach reminded Dao of her hunger, and she walked back to get a cracker from the tin. She took small bites and chewed slowly and carefully. The cracker was fragrant and buttery, truly delicious. She only ate one, for fear they would not last, and she scooped up a handful of water and drank until her stomach was full.

Then she opened the bundle of clothes and saw a purple blouse, a sweater the color of milk, a large yellow towel, and a child's shirt the shade of incense smoke. "This will fit Hong," she thought, as she carried the shirt and other things back to the spring to wash them. After rinsing the salt from the clothes, she wrung them out and lay them on the rocks to dry. Hong still had not returned. Dao called Hong's name, but there was no response. "Where could she be?" Dao worried. She followed the stream up to the top of the island, stepping carefully on patches of grass and smooth stones to protect her tender bare feet.

The island was densely covered with wild, tropical plants. Dao picked a leaf from a guava tree and crushed it in her fingers to smell its pungent fragrance. She felt as if she had just met an old friend. She remembered her grandmother's guava tree in Can Tho. As a child, Dao had often climbed it and sat among the branches eating the fruit and smelling the leaves. Her grandmother used to scold her, "Girls do not climb trees!" Dao never could understand this admonition, and so she continued to climb trees, but in secret.

Climbing along the guava branches was always great fun, as the flexible branches never broke. Her brother once fell when a plumeria branch cracked. Dao knew that the plumeria branches were brittle, so she never climbed on them, even though the flowers were so fragrant. Besides, the plumeria tree was right in front of the house, and she did not want to be caught climbing trees.

Dao was happy to see a familiar guava tree in a place so strange to her. Although there were only a few fruits, and they were out of reach and not yet ripe, she longed to have a taste. First she looked around to make sure no one was watching. How funny, she thought, to worry about being caught climbing a tree on a deserted island! She grabbed a branch to climb up, but her strength failed her. So she broke off a low, dry branch, pulled down one of the higher branches with it, and plucked one unripe fruit. It was quite sour, but the familiar taste filled her heart with joy. She had been separated from her homeland only two weeks and from the people on her boat merely a day, but she felt cut off from everything she had ever known.

Thanks to this guava tree, she realized that she was still standing on the familiar green Earth. Dao looked ahead, out over the sea. The sun was to her left, so she must have come from the east. She must not be too far from the coast of Thailand. Dat's boat was drifting toward Malaysia. She believed everything Hong had told her, as if Hong possessed a special knowledge. How strange this child was who acted and spoke like an adult! The more Dao thought about it, the stranger it seemed. Many changes had taken place in Dao's heart since yesterday, and they were all thanks to this little girl. If Hong had not been present, Dao probably would have thrown herself against the rocks and ended her life. How could a ten-year-old, eleven at most, speak with such authority? "You've endured one part of our people's great sufferings. Who among us has not been wounded? Who among us has been able to keep wholly intact our body and spirit? In my eyes you are still pure and chaste. The pirates attacked you, but they could not really take anything away from you. Your wounds (are) like the wounds of someone who has survived an attacked by a shark."

These words, containing such deep understanding, soothed the pain in Dao's heart. A ten-year-old girl had taught her more in one day than she had learned in all her years of school.

But who was Hong, and why did she refuse to answer Dao's questions about how she had made it alone to the island with a tin of crackers and a bundle of clothes? How did she know Dat's boat was being blown toward the southwest? And how could a ten-year-old be so much more serene and wise than a nineteen-year-old like herself? Was Hong a supernatural being? Dao shivered at the thought, even as the warm sunlight streamed down across her face.

She went back to see if the clothes and tin of crackers were indeed real. Were they only sticks and stones a ghost had transformed to trick her? No, Hong could not be a ghost. Dao had as proof the very clothes she was wearing, which Hong had given her the day before. Dao remembered clearly that she had awakened without a stitch of clothing on, and she could see the clothes she had just rinsed drying in the sun. Dao gathered the dry clothes and folded them neatly. "No, Hong couldn't be a ghost," Dao thought. "But where was she now? Why hadn't she returned?" Dao climbed up on a high rock for a better view, when she heard Hong's laughter coming from along the shore. Then she saw Hong coming up from the water, yet her clothes were perfectly dry.

Without dwelling on this strange fact, Dao was elated, and all her worries vanished the moment she heard Hong's childish laughter—bright and clear. Dao called, "Where were you? It's past noon. I've been looking everywhere for you!"

Hong stood beside Dao and pointed to the black clouds gathering. "There's going to be a storm, elder sister. We'd better find shelter."

Hong led Dao toward the huge boulders, and they found a large, dry cave. "Sit here, elder sister. I'll go back and get our crackers and clothes."

Dao brushed away the pebbles on the cave floor and cleared a place to sit. She leaned back against the rock wall. Outside, the sky grew very dark. Large raindrops fell as though someone were hurling down heavy stones from above. Lightning flashed across the sky, followed by an explosive clap of thunder so loud it seemed immediately overhead. When Hong returned, Dao hugged her close and brushed the rain from her hair and shirt. The young girl let Dao take care of her. The rain outside rushed down like a waterfall, but the two girls stayed safe and dry inside their cave. They both were thinking about how rough and choppy the ocean must be in the storm. Slowly Hong opened her eyes and said, "When the sea is like this, many refugee boats sink."

Dao listened solemnly. In her mind, she could see boats filled with frightened men, women, and children, tossed about by monstrous waves; arms waving frantically, terrified cries lost in the howling wind; bodies sinking beneath the water where sharks circled. Trembling, she felt as if her heart were being squeezed by a cruel hand, and she asked herself why her people had had to endure such suffering day after day for more than fifty years. She looked at Hong and saw the child's cheeks stained with tears. Seeing Hong weep made her own pain subside, and she felt the cruel hand release its grip on her heart. She wiped Hong's tears away with her shirt sleeve, and the two girls sat quietly together, as dark clouds raced across the sky and the wind howled. Lying in Dao's arms, Hong closed her eyes and slept. Her breathing grew light and even. Dao felt as though she were holding everything she had ever loved.

The rain continued until late into the afternoon. Finally, the clouds passed, the sky grew quiet, and the sun began to shine. The island looked refreshed. Dao and Hong helped each other up onto a large boulder and looked out across the horizon. There was no sign of any boat. Dao pulled Hong down onto the rock and asked her to tell her story.

Hong looked troubled for a moment and then replied, "I'll tell you my whole story, but only if you let me tell it in two parts—part now and the rest tomorrow. Do you agree?"

Dao nodded in assent. After a moment of silence, Hong began:

"When I was a baby, my world was only as big as my mother's arms. Safe in that world, I felt secure and peaceful. I did not

know that beyond those protective arms lay a universe of violence and storms. My mother kept that world from my view
so that I might enjoy endless peace and safety. But recently I
have seen the world outside.

"Back in Vinh Long, my parents had an ice store and a small
grocery. They were good, generous people, well loved by their
customers and employees. My parents also tended a fruit orchard
of more than 500 mango, longan, and durian trees. But my father was killed by a soldier's stray bullet, and our grocery store
was destroyed by bombs. Mother was two months pregnant
when Father was killed, and soon afterwards she gave birth to
a beautiful boy. My little brother, named Bich, looked exactly
like my father. Mother and I cherished Bich. When the Pro-
visional Government of South Vietnam came to power, my
mother decided to return to the countryside. I started attend-
ing the village school, and every afternoon Mother would carry
Bich to meet me at school. Then we would stroll among the
mango and longan trees.

"Mother gave the ice store and all her money to the local officials for the state. She wanted only to retain the fruit orchard,
as we could easily support ourselves selling the fruit. In the past,
Father had always contributed money to the Revolution from
the profits of the ice business and grocery. Even after giving two
businesses to the state, Mother intended to continue support-
ing the Revolution each year by giving twenty percent of all she
earned from the orchard.

"One day Mother invited a local party cadre to dinner, and
she outlined her plan of support. But the cadre, an old friend,
advised her to uproot the fruit trees and plant rice instead.
Mother was shocked. It had taken ten years to establish the orchard, and she could not believe he wanted her to uproot the
trees. But the cadre said that the country needed rice much more
than the luxury of fresh fruit. He warned that her taxes would
be increased considerably, and that the money she made sell-

ing fruit would not be enough to pay taxes, much less feed her family or contribute twenty percent to the state. However, he advised, if she cultivated rice, she could expect much lighter taxes. After years of experience, Mother felt she knew best how to earn a living. To clear the fruit trees for rice seemed preposterous. Mother refused to believe the cadre's words. It was only later, when a government inspector informed her how much tax would be levied on each fruit tree, that mother understood.

"A great resistance welled up inside her and, instead of agreeing to clear the trees, she gave the orchard to the government. My grandmother had died, so we no longer had a country refuge. We went to live with an old and dear friend of Mother's in the village, whose husband had been sent to a reeducation camp. This woman had to sell everything she could in order to support her three children. We were given a room in her house, and Mother made porridge to sell every day at the market.

"There were no men in the house to help support us. Mother and her friend tried to manage, but it was simply impossible to earn enough to feed two adults and five children. Little by little, we sold all our possessions. Each night, we held each other tight and tried desperately to fall asleep and forget our hunger.

"One day, Mr. Bay Nhieu, whom we called Uncle, came to see us. He suggested that we try to escape from the country by boat, even though we did not know anyone overseas. Uncle Bay Nhieu was from our village, and my parents had helped him many times in the past. His two sons were about to be drafted to fight in Cambodia, where many young men were dying, and he was most anxious to help them escape. Uncle had a boat with provisions ready to go, and two other families were going with him and his sons. They had all contributed money to pay for gasoline, motor oil, and food for the ten days they expected to be at sea. There were still three places on the boat, and he wanted Mother, Bich, and me to join them.

"Mother did not consider herself a political refugee. She only knew that it had become impossible to survive in her own country, and she must leave if her children were to live. She had heard that refugees were often taken aboard foreign ships and resettled in that ship's home country. Just as Uncle Bay Nhieu's sons had no choice, Mother, too, had no choice but to leave.

"After thinking it over for three days, Mother agreed to go with Uncle Bay. She made arrangements to take Bich and me and follow Uncle into the countryside. I didn't take anything with me. I wore my prettiest blouse, white satin pants frayed at the edges, and a pair of rubber thongs. We walked through the jungle in two groups. The small children were sedated with sleeping pills to prevent them from fussing or crying and possibly alerting the government cadres. We walked nearly two days and nights before reaching the spot where Uncle Bay had hidden the boat.

"As soon as we set sail, we saw four government fishing boats, so we turned back quickly to avoid being seen. The next night, all was clear and we made it away safely. By morning we had reached international waters, and we thought we had reached freedom. Little did we know this was only the beginning of a nightmare of terror.

"We sailed for just one day before the motor stopped, and we were helplessly tossed about by the waves, unable to control our boat's direction. Everyone prayed that a foreign ship would appear and rescue us, but four days passed with no other ship in sight. We did not even know that we were in the Gulf of Thailand."

Having recounted that much, Hong looked at Dao and asked, "Did your boat meet any foreign ships, elder sister?"

Dao nodded, "Yes, we met a Russian liner, two ships from Panama, an Australian ship, one from Singapore, and one American ship. And when they saw our boat, each of them went right by, as if we were invisible. How could they be so merciless? My mother used to tell me that it brought much merit to be able to save a human life. I'm not sure about merit, but I know it must bring great joy to save another human being. Yet those ships didn't seem to consider us any more important than ants. It was horrible."

Hong responded, "In the beginning, a lot of ships rescued boat people, elder sister. But they found that once they had taken the refugees aboard, no country was willing to accept them, not even temporarily. The refugee camps in Malaysia, Indonesia, and Thailand exist only because the United Nations High Commission on Refugees intervened. These countries actually did not want to let refugees in, and they secretly order their marine police to pull refugee boats back out to sea whenever they can get away with it. Many, many boats are forced to wander on the open sea until they finally sink in a storm. No one knows how many boats have sunk at sea."

Dao's eyes opened wide, "How do you know all this? Have you read these things in a newspaper?"

Hong's eyes filled with sadness. "I know because I know, elder sister. I don't read any newspapers. Singapore is one of the most ruthless ports of all. Some refugees who have arrived in Singapore have sunk their boats to avoid being dragged back out to sea. But after that, many have been arrested and taken somewhere—no one knows where. If a journalist, an embassy, or a United Nations representative knows about them, the government of Singapore cannot mistreat them. In time, the refugees may even be accepted by some Western embassy for immigration to a new country. But if no one knows about them, they will probably remain in prison until they die.

"The Malaysian police often try to intimidate boats by firing at them. Sometimes the bullets seriously damage the boat or wound people aboard. Once, I watched two boats carrying sixty refugees each land on Malaysian shore about ten miles north of Mersing. The refugees, including many children, stood on the sand and begged to be allowed in, but the Malaysian police forced them back onto their boats. They cried and pleaded, but the police said they did not have the authority to let them stay. The refugees told the police that their boats were damaged and could not possibly sail again. But the police found someone to repair them.

"Four hours later, they were forced back onto their boats and pushed out to sea. Almost immediately, one of the boats was struck by a huge wave and it capsized. The passengers on the other boat witnessed this tragic scene. The captain decided to take them back to shore, even at the risk of being shot. They landed and immediately destroyed the boat. The bewildered police decided to house the refugees temporarily in an abandoned barracks. The women and children could not stop crying. The men silently stared into space, refusing to eat or drink, even the provisions that the villagers spontaneously brought them.

"Only two men aboard the sunken boat survived. They swam for five hours before being picked up by a Malaysian fishing boat. But when they were brought to shore, they were taken somewhere by the police and never seen again. The police threatened the passengers from the other boat that they would be sent back out to sea on an old boat if they mentioned the incident to anyone. No one knows what happened to those two men. Maybe they were killed to keep the incident hidden from the international press. Not a week passes without an incident like this, elder sister."

Hong spoke as though she had seen it all herself. Dao watched Hong's face become profoundly sad, yet calm. Dao could not explain why, but she believed everything Hong told her, even though it was impossible that a small girl could know so much. But her incredulity was secondary to the pain in her heart. Dao recalled the miseries her own boat had suffered after the engine failed—the thirst, the hunger, the pirates, and all the unspeakably horrible details. But now she was aware of the tragic plight of all her people. How many had perished at sea, she did not dare guess. But she knew it was many, many. Unable to survive in their own homeland, they had fled on boats only to be shot, raped, and robbed, until at last they drowned in the sea. Dao lay her head on Hong's shoulder and wept streams of tears. The sun had set, and the evening wind grew chilly. At last Hong stood up, and holding a cracker and some spring water, offered Dao some nourishment.

Late that night, Dao tossed and turned. All she could think of was Dat's boat. Where had the waves carried it? Was there any food or water aboard? If the boat reached Malaysia, would they be allowed to enter a refugee camp, or would the police drag them back out to sea to sink? If Dat died, Dao did not want to live. But then she remembered Hong saying that she must live for her mother, brothers, and sisters. Dao whispered, "Dear mother, I will not die. I will live for you and my brothers and sisters." Her tears fell like rain.

Hearing Dao weep, Hong awoke and moved toward her. As if she could feel the sadness in Dao's heart, Hong said, "Many boat people have landed near the refugee camps and been admitted. Don't worry. Though Dat and the others have no more water or food, they will surely be able to hold out for a few more days. And if they meet a kind fisherman, their boat may be pulled to a safe shore."

"But one does not often meet such good fortune. Hong, I'm afraid."

"Don't be. You yourself were thrown overboard by a pirate, and yet here you are alive. Strange and wondrous events take place all the time. Just a few months ago, seven young people left Vietnam in a rowboat and rowed all the way to Thailand, where they were admitted to the Songkhla Camp. One family with two young children escaped on a tiny boat just seven yards long. They were shot at by the authorities as they left the port of Rach Gia. The husband was hit in the chest, but they sailed full speed to escape. He died two days later, but his wife and their two young children struggled for seven days and nights and finally made it to the coast of Thailand. Many sinking boats have been rescued by passing fishermen. The universe is filled with marvels that most of us never see or hear about, elder sister.

"But enough, it's late and we need to sleep. Tomorrow I will tell the rest of my story. Now I will recite the *Heart of Perfect Understanding Sutra*, and then let us go to sleep. I hope you sleep peacefully."

Hong recited in the way she had heard her grandmother:

> *The Bodhisattva, Avalokita, while moving in the deep course of perfect understanding, shed light on the five skandhas, and found them equally empty. After this penetration, he overcame all pain.*

The soft sounds of her chanting were like raindrops falling gently on flowers. Dao lay quietly and allowed the words of the sutra to fill her heart and mind. Soon she dreamed she saw a refreshing stream of water running through a field dotted with many yellow and violet flowers.

∞

It was Dao's third day on the island. When she awoke, Hong was already gone. "This little girl certainly likes to do her exploring early," thought Dao. She went to the spring to wash her face and change into the violet blouse from the duffel bag. She washed her other blouse and spread it on the rocks to dry. Though she waited a long time, Hong did not return. Dao took two crackers to eat and some spring water to drink, and then she wandered up the stream, hoping to find Hong.

When Dao came to the guava tree she'd discovered the day before, she stopped to pick another fruit. Even though it was still so sour it made her cringe, she relished it. She noticed dandelion greens nearby and picked a large bunch to take back. A little farther upstream she found a handful of chicory and wild watercress, and she picked a handful of each.

Dao returned to the small rock enclosure where she and Hong had spent the night, but Hong had still not returned. Dao thought, "How strange that she disappears every morning." She called Hong's name over and over until she was hoarse, but there was no answer.

Dao began to worry that Hong had really lost her way this time, as unlikely as that seemed. The more Dao thought about Hong, the more she marveled, "Sometimes when she speaks, she sounds like a great master teaching. She comforts me like a mother and seems to know everything that happens at sea. In fact, she speaks as though she has witnessed it all herself."

Around two in the afternoon, dark clouds gathered and the sky grew turbulent. A great storm was breaking, and Dao crouched beneath the rock ledge, picturing Hong somewhere on the island getting drenched like a wet mouse. Her worry grew as the downpour continued. Finally, in the early evening, the rain stopped.

When the sky turned to a dusky violet, Dao's worry increased. Then, at last, Hong returned. She came up from the beach, her hair and clothes again not at all wet, not even a drop. Overjoyed, Dao called her and raced to the beach to hug her as tightly as she could. Hong let Dao hold her for a long time before gently moving out from Dao's arms. Then Hong spoke, "I've got good news, elder sister. Dat's boat has reached shore!"

"What? What did you say? Dat's boat has made it? Really?" Dao asked in a frenzy, not even stopping to wonder how Hong could know such a thing.

"Dat's boat met a Malaysian fishing boat, which pulled them to nearby Bidong Island. Everyone was allowed to disembark and enter the refugee camp there. I told you we shouldn't give up hope!"

Dao hastily asked, "Is it really true, little sister? Oh, I'm so happy! Now I'm sure I can go on living! And how is Dat? Was he hurt badly? Are his wounds infected? Is his life in danger?"

Hong shook her head. "Dat is fine. A doctor checked him and all the others. He wasn't hurt badly. Some of the other refugees rinsed his wounds with ginger and water. But he is suffering because he thinks you drowned."

"Oh, Hong, I feel so sorry for him. How can we let him know I'm still alive?"

"There is no way yet, elder sister. When you reach the other shore, you can write him, but we aren't there yet. We just have to wait. I'm not sure how long."

"What if I die on this island and never see him again?"

"There you go again," Hong admonished her, "letting despair take hold of you. You just received wonderful news. Why spoil it with such a terrible thought?"

"I am foolish. Please forgive me. I believe that we will be rescued. But Hong, how did you know about Dat? Where have you been all day? I have been worrying about you."

Hong took Dao's hand gently and led her to some rocks, where they sat down. "I promised to tell the rest of my story today. Every story is both sad and happy. I know you've been wondering how someone as young as I can know so much, even about things that happen far away. Listen, yesterday I said that there are strange and wondrous things we rarely see or hear, but that does not make them impossible. I am the ten-year-old child Hong, but I am also a fish…You look surprised. Please smile, Dao…Okay, now I can continue telling you the rest of my story.

"After our boat reached international waters, it sailed swiftly for one day. On the second day, our engine failed. Uncle Bay revved the motor again and again, but it just would not start. From then on, our boat was tossed about on the sea. We did not encounter a single boat for four days. On the sixth day, a storm came up, and we were thrown relentlessly by the wind and the waves. We came so close to capsizing that we dropped all our possessions overboard to lighten the load, even our food and water supplies. By dawn, the storm had calmed, but we were all so exhausted, hungry, and thirsty, that we could not move. As the sun rose, it became hot as an oven, and our parched throats burned without relief. Uncle Bay told us to save our urine to drink, and we did so. At night, the air grew deathly cold. After days of exposure to the elements, most of us became ill.

"My little brother, Bich, caught a fever. Without medicine or water, he died the same day. Mother clutched his body in her arms and refused to let go. She wanted to weep, but she had no tears left. All the while, the water was seeping in the many holes in our boat. The men took turns bailing it out until they became too weak to continue. Only Uncle Bay had the stamina to keep the boat from capsizing.

"The next day, Uncle Bay told Mother that Bich would have to be buried at sea. She refused, but finally, when his little corpse began to smell, she had to agree. All of us recited the *Heart Sutra*. Then Uncle Bay began to chant the Buddha's name, and the rest of us joined him. As we recited the Buddha's name, Uncle Bay gently removed Bich from Mother's arms, leaned over, laid the child's body on the face of the ocean, and released him. Brother's body quickly sank beneath the waves, and Mother wailed. We chanted the Buddha's name ever more loudly, trying to absorb her tragic cries. When the chanting stopped, Mother collapsed.

"That evening a pirate ship attacked us. They caught our boat with a metal hook and pulled up alongside us. There were twelve of them, armed with sharp knives and clubs. We didn't dare resist. In fact, none of us had the strength to fight back. The pirates robbed what we had left, including any clothes on our bodies worth anything. One pirate approached Mother to see if she had a necklace hidden beneath her blouse. I shouted, "Don't touch my mother!" but he ignored my cries. He grabbed Mother's blouse and began to rip it open. With all my strength, I hurled myself at him and grabbed his leg to try to make him fall. But I was so weak, he just straightened out his leg and kicked me over the side of the boat. I heard Mother screaming as if possessed by demons, but there was nothing I could do.

"I don't know if it was because of some magical power, but I did not drown. Instead, I found myself swimming and breathing like a fish. After the pirates had grabbed everything they possibly could, they rammed their ship into ours and broke it in two. Water rushed in, but everyone was too weak to move. Heartwrenching cries rose as our boat slowly sank. The pirates revved their engines and sped away.

"I had become a fish about the size of a young girl. But by the time I realized that I could rescue people, Mother and all the others had disappeared. I dove deep to look for Mother, but all I saw was the fathomless water. I swam around that spot for a week, but there was no sign of Mother. Had she been devoured by a shark? Or had she turned into a fish, too? If Mother was a fish, was she nearby looking for me? I resolved to swim the entire Gulf of Siam searching for Mother.

"Every day I swam quite far, and on full moon nights I returned to the spot where our boat had sunk, in hope of finding Mother. For more than a year, I looked for her every day. Because I swam all over the Gulf of Siam, I encountered many refugee boats. Whenever I saw a sinking boat, I tried to save at least one person, usually a small child. I carried the child on my back with its head above the water until we got to a sandy beach. I swam near the coasts of Thailand, Malaysia, and Indonesia, because it was easier to help victims who were already near a shore. Some refugees thought I might be a magic fish, so they followed me. From time to time, I was able to help boats avoid hidden rocks, or show them places where there were no police. Other refugees raised their knives to kill and eat me in order to appease their terrible hunger, but when I saw someone draw his knife, I dove deep beneath the water, and the boat lost its guide. I wasn't angry at those who wanted to kill me, because I understood how hungry they were.

"One full moon night in April, I rescued a fourteen-year-old boy and carried him to shore near the port of Kota Baru. I was afraid that the water might carry him back out to sea during the night, so I wiggled up along the sand to push him beyond the water's reach. Then, how marvelous! I turned into a girl again, wearing the same pink shirt, frayed white satin pants, and rubber thongs as before.

"I danced with joy beneath the April moonlight. I called out, 'Ma!' and found that I still had my same voice. Ecstatic, I called my brother's name, 'Bich!' I chanted the *Heart Sutra* just like my grandmother used to every day. I realized that although I was still a fish, I was also a ten-year-old girl.

"I knew that I was on the coast of Malaysia, after crossing the Gulf of Siam without a boat. I knew I could stay on land, but I wanted to return to the sea to look for my mother and to save children from the sinking refugee boats.

"The boy was not yet conscious, but his chest rose and fell evenly. Confident that he was breathing, I knelt down, kissed him lightly on the forehead, and ran back to the water. When I jumped back into the sea, I became a bright pink fish sparkling in the moonlit water.

"From then on, I went ashore often, either to carry someone to safety or to mingle with the refugees in the camps to find out about their situations. Everyone assumed I was the daughter of some family in the camp waiting to resettle in another country. But I never stayed in a refugee camp longer than a morning or an afternoon. I spent most of my time looking for Mother and searching for ships to rescue at sea.

"I ate nothing but seaweed, and grew very strong. I could swim an entire day without feeling tired and carry a person on my back for fifteen nautical miles. The day the pirates attacked your boat, Dao, I was there and saw the whole scene. It was less than two miles from where my own boat had sunk. When you were thrown into the sea, I swam beneath you and carried you toward this island. After pushing you ashore, I went back and discovered that the pirates had left, and that northeasterly winds were blowing your boat toward Trengganu. I hoped that your boat would drift to a fishing area north of Kuala Trengganu, and that one of the fishing boats there would tow your boat to shore in southern Thailand or northern Malaysia, to a place like Patthani, Songkhla, Kota Baru, or Trengganu.

"The next morning, I pushed one of the tins of crackers that had been tossed from the Danish ship all the way to this island. Then I returned to sea, and swam that entire day, but there were no other chances to rescue anyone. That evening I carried back a bag of clothing that I found bobbing near the wreckage of a boat destroyed in a bad storm. When I got back to the island, I saw that you were still sleeping, so I opened the clothes bag, wrung out a shirt, and hung it on a branch to dry. The moon had just risen. I sat beside you and placed my hand lightly on your forehead to see if you had a fever, and it was then that you awoke."

Dao grasped Hong's arm to feel that the child before her was a real child of flesh and blood. Hong's clear and innocent eyes looked at Dao as though amused. Dao hugged Hong and cried, "How wondrous, Hong!" The marvelous reality before Dao's eyes was almost too good to be true. And yet, her own joy and gratitude verified the unmistakable wondrousness of Hong's real presence. As if she could read Dao's thoughts, Hong laughed and said, "When you see Dat again, will you see how wondrous he is, too? And will you believe he is real?"

Dao felt as if she had awakened from a long sleep. To see Dat again, to hold his hand, would indeed be a miracle. She imagined embracing him and exclaiming, "How wondrous!" just as she had with Hong. Dao remembered seeing how the guava tree the day before had felt like a miracle. She smiled, thinking about how these seemingly ordinary events allowed her to see the world of the present moment in a bright, new way. Suddenly she could even appreciate the small details of her life on this deserted island. Now Hong was telling her that she could continue to live in appreciation of so many precious gifts of the universe.

Dao had spent many hours with Dat, sitting with him, looking into his eyes, being held in his arms, but she had never really thought of him as miraculous. Dao had taken everything in her life for granted—Dat, her family, the sun, the clouds, the trees...Now, for the first time, she realized how truly wondrous all these things were. Everything was infinitely precious, just like the child Hong sitting before her.

Dao asked Hong more about Dat's boat. Hong explained how she had swum beside the boat until it met a Malaysian fisherman, who pulled it to Bidong Island, just beyond the town of Kuala Trengganu. Hong had gone ashore and seen Dat and the others admitted into the camp.

"I am sure a boat will soon pass by here," Hong assured Dao, "and you will be rescued." Before they went to sleep, Hong promised Dao that early the next morning she could watch her dive into the water and turn into a fish.

∞

While morning mist hung in the air, Dao watched Hong go down to the water and wade in up to her chest. She held her palms together, bowed her head, and dived into the water. For an instant, Dao saw the shape of a pink fish waving its tail, creating a froth of bubbles behind it. And then Hong was gone.

Dao looked out over the sea, her heart filled with sadness and love. The ocean had closed over so many of her people, yet beneath that same ocean swam a lone pink fish full of love.

Dao felt sad that Hong would probably never find her mother, and joyful for all Hong had done to help her people. Dao resolved that once she found refuge, she too would work with all her energy to help those in need. Hong had warned Dao about the many hardships that awaited her in the refuge camp, but Dao was not afraid. Knowing that Hong was in the Gulf of Thailand was a great comfort and inspiration to her. Dao would work to overcome difficulties and be worthy of Hong's faith and courage.

All day long Dao sat on the sand knowing Hong was somewhere out at sea. When the sky was twinkling with stars, Dao heard Hong's voice and saw her friend, luminous in the starlight, stepping along the sand toward her. Overjoyed, Dao stood up to greet Hong. Hong took Dao's hand, and they walked up the island. Dao offered Hong some crackers and spring water. Hong did not eat the crackers but drank the clear water.

Hong recounted her day's discoveries. A refugee boat had sunk near Narathiwat, and of four hundred persons aboard, nearly one hundred had drowned. When Hong arrived, she saw pieces of the boat floating on the waves, including a plank on which was painted the boat's number, "LA1945." One of the surviving passengers described how they had encountered rough seas as soon as they had left Vietnamese waters. Their boat was thrown about for five days and nights. On the sixth night, a huge storm struck, and waves roared against the boat's little cabin and left a gaping hole for water to gush through the hull. Everyone thought their hour of death had come, but thanks to swift hands and an excellent captain, they were able to keep afloat. They struggled that night and all the next day. Around six in the evening, they spotted the coast of Thailand and steered the boat toward it. Night descended. The boat could no longer hold them, and their only chance of living lay in their ability to swim to shore. Ninety-seven people lost their lives. The day dawned on women weeping for their husbands, mothers for their children, brothers for sisters. Grief wailed up and down the beach. Local brigands stole their money and possessions. At last, the Thai police put the refugees on a truck and took them to the refugee camp at Songkhla.

Hong told Dao about a refugee boat that had come to shore near Patthani. It carried only thirty people who had left Vietnam from the port of Ca Mau. Throughout their first two days and nights, they sailed with ease, but on the third day, as they neared Thai waters just twenty miles from Cut Island, they were attacked. Pirates disguised as fishermen stole their clothing and belongings. The women were all raped twice. After the pirates left, the boat continued to seek a way to shore. The following day the same pirates returned. They checked to make sure that they had not missed anything, and then they raped the women again. Having endured two brutal attacks, the boat people still managed to make it to shore several times, but each time they were towed back to sea by marine police.

Two days later, they were attacked by three pirate boats at once. The pirates were furious because there was nothing to steal, so they shot two of the refugee men and threw their bodies into the sea. They threw four others overboard for nearby sharks to attack. Of these, one young man managed to escape. He swam far out, grabbed hold of a barrel that someone had thrown overboard, and then hid behind it. The pirates rammed their vessels against the refugee boat. Four terrified children grabbed floatable plastic containers and jumped into the water. The boat was gashed open, and the pirates left, confident the boat would soon sink. But the boat did not sink. The children were pulled out of the water, and the boat continued to float on the sea for

three more days and nights. During that time, they were attacked twice more by different pirates. These pirates grabbed
their few remaining clothes and raped the women, but they did
not kill anyone. Finally on the morning of the next day, the boat
was given permission to come ashore, and the police took them
to Songkhla. The youngest woman on the boat was sixteen years
old. She had been raped twelve times and appeared to have lost
her mind.

Listening to Hong, Dao could not hold back her tears. Who
knew how many cruelties were committed each day? Her shoulders shook. She could no longer hold back the flood of anguish
inside her. She would never be able to understand how people
could be so cruel to one another. Perhaps the end of the world
was at hand? She cried for a long time, so long that when she
stopped, the moon was shining brightly overhead. She saw
Hong sitting quietly beneath the moonlight like a bronze statue.
Hong said softly, "I wanted to let you cry so you could ease your
pain. Go now and wash your face at the spring. It will refresh
you. We can chant the sutra before we sleep. It's already very
late and tomorrow I must be off early."

∞

It was Dao's fifth day on the island. She knew it would be
dark before Hong returned, and so she did not worry while she
waited. She looked out over the sea for any boats that might
pass near the island. Following Hong's advice, she tied a shirt
onto a stick, so she could run down to the shore and wave it if
she spotted a boat. But Dao did not see one boat the entire day.

When Hong returned, she told Dao of the many refugee
boats she had seen in the vicinity. Every boat that had neared
shore had been threatened by police gunfire or been tugged back
to international waters. Hong encountered one boat with a broken motor floating aimlessly beyond Patthani. There were fifty

people aboard, all dead except for one man who was barely breathing. They had run out of food and water.

Hong also saw a Thai fishing boat pull a refugee boat toward Songkhla. Because the fisherman was afraid of being caught by the police for aiding refugees, he cut the rope that attached the two boats before reaching shore. The refugee boat was trying to make it ashore when a pirate boat came alongside. These pirates took all their jewelry, money, and good clothes, but did not rape any of the women. The refugee boat finally made it to shore, and the refugees were accepted into the Songkhla Refugee Camp.

Hong smiled as she told Dao about a strange boat she had encountered many times in the Gulf. It was a Thai fishing boat called the Shantisuk. Hong noticed all kinds of fishing gear aboard, including spear guns for large fish, but not once had she seen the eight "fishermen" aboard do any fishing. Hong had seen them give refugees food, fresh water, gasoline, and sea maps that pointed out dangerous hidden rocks as well as the locations of refugee camps. Hong followed the Shantisuk once to the port of Patthani. Anchored among the other fishing boats, it did not stand out at all.

Hong admired the quiet mission of this vessel and began paying more attention to it. Though there were only eight people aboard, they spoke to each other in four different languages— Thai, French, English, and Vietnamese. Four of them were Vietnamese, three Thai, and one French. Hong swam right beside the boat and floated near the surface in order to hear their conversations.

It appeared that everyone aboard was vegetarian. One morning Hong saw the Vietnamese woman toss back into the water some flying fish that had jumped onto the boat during the night. She also saw the woman release some live fish that she had bought from a small fishing boat near shore. Hong noticed that the woman even spoke to these fish, and she was very moved and felt a special kinship with her. Several times the woman had noticed Hong and called the others to come look at her.

Knowing that these people would not harm her, Hong swam unafraid alongside their boat. By listening to their conversations, she soon understood why their rescue mission had to be carried out in secret. The governments of Thailand, Singapore, Malaysia, and Indonesia did not want to accept refugees on their shores, and they resented any efforts to save refugees at sea. These governments preferred to let refugees die at sea, rather than subject their countries to the economic and political problems of accepting refugees. The Shantisuk had to pose as a fishing boat in order to save people. The Thais aboard, including a young monk from the countryside, disagreed with their country's heartless policy. All eight of them were disciples of a spiritual master who lived in a small hermitage on the mountain peak, Doi Suthep, in northern Thailand.

The Vietnamese aboard the Shantisuk had become citizens of other countries. As Vietnamese nationals, they could not have obtained the necessary documents to allow them to enter Thailand, Malaysia, Singapore, and Indonesia. The Frenchman aboard, named Jean-Paul, had once been a sailor off the coast of Brittany in France. He could sit in meditation as well as Hong's grandmother, and once Hong had watched him sitting in the full lotus position at the boat's helm.

Hong knew they kept many dried foods aboard, including packets of instant noodles, of which Jean-Paul was especially fond. Even though the Shantisuk was disguised as a fishing boat, it had been attacked once by pirates in Thai waters. The pirate vessel was equipped with radar and could travel at great speed with an eight-hundred horsepower engine. They threatened those aboard at gunpoint and took their money and food supplies. They did not search for jewelry or gold, as they knew it was not a refugee boat, and they left the men and the woman

unharmed. Everyone sat quietly and let the pirates take whatever they wanted.

After this attack, Captain Luc suggested that they buy a gun
for self-defense. This stirred a debate which lasted several days
and nights. Hong listened and understood their difficult situation. Luc's suggestion was rejected by several on board. As disciples of a pacifist monk, they did not want to use weapons to
protect themselves. But Luc said, "Having a gun does not mean
we are going to kill anyone." In the past, Luc had been a good
marksman, and he felt sure they could use a gun to fire into
the air or hit something small on the pirates' boat in order to
scare off the pirates. The woman aboard smiled and remarked
that it was only when one's spirit was weak that one thought
about guns. If their motivation was to help people, they would
be protected. "Before we left the mountain," she said, "Master
told us we must respect the sacredness of life and use only love
to respond to hatred and violence. He told us we were not to
harm even a fish in the sea."

Luc countered, "A gun is only an outer form. The essential
thing is how we use it. We could use the gun in a completely
nonviolent way. I'm sure the Master would agree with me."

In the midst of these debates, however, their most pressing
concern was that they had been discovered by pirates to be foreign fishermen. The pirates were from Mahachai, located in the
Samu Sakorn district, a place of ill repute much like Cau Muoi
in Vietnam.

"If the Mahachai pirates wish to harass us, we will not be able
to go on with our project. We are all grown people, and we have
to make our own decisions. We cannot go running back to the
mountain with every problem to ask the Master's advice," said
Luc. And so the discussion continued.

For some time after that, Hong did not encounter the Shantisuk. But just the day before, Hong had seen it near the northern shore of Malaysia and heard several things about their

dealings with pirates that were most heartening. In Mahachai, Luc had managed to make friends with the leader of the pirates who had attacked them—a man named Tana, or Tan for short, who was well-accomplished in the martial arts. Luc had gone on his own into Mahachai to seek out Tan. Tan's followers were taken aback by the grim expression of resolve on Luc's face as he approached Tan, especially after Luc threw one of them to the ground when he tried to bar his path. When Luc demanded Tan's whereabouts, several pirates jumped up to warn Tan of his arrival. Tan invited Luc into his home and asked him to sit down. Then suddenly, Tan struck at Luc with a karate blow. Luc reacted quickly, moving out of the way to avoid being struck, and then calmly sat back down. Tan grabbed a sharp knife from the table and made a menacing stab at Luc. Luc did not try to grab the knife but only leaned far enough to avoid Tan's thrust. After a second thrust, Tan did not test Luc anymore, but accepted him as a brother, praising his bravery and skill.

Tan was in need of a good marksman and invited Luc to join his band of pirates. He also promised he would order his followers to return everything they had stolen from the Shantisuk. Tan still believed that Luc's boat was only a fishing vessel. He suggested Luc sell the Shantisuk and become the captain of an eight-hundred horsepower boat equipped with radar.

Luc did not dare reject Tan's offer outright, but answered that he needed some time to think it over and discuss it with his friends. Luc also said he needed a gun for self-defense against the pirates. Tan said he knew some police and could arrange to provide Luc with a gun permit. How strange, thought Luc, that Tan should have so much authority. Luc got the permit within an hour, but because his friends still refused to have a gun aboard the Shantisuk, he did not buy one.

Luc's boat was not harassed again by Tan's men, but other pirates still posed a threat, among them a group based in Trad. The Shantisuk's policy, the wisest one possible in Hong's mind, was to race away full speed whenever they encountered a pirate vessel. But those aboard feared that many of the pirate vessels had radar and guns, and could travel much faster. Before there were refugees in the area, pirates had attacked Malaysian and Thai fishing boats, sometimes killing the fishermen aboard after robbing them. The Thai marine police had often sent out patrols, but were unable to destroy the pirates' hold. Recently, an entire patrol led by a Thai police captain had been killed by pirates near Ko Kut Island—the same location where the Shantisuk had almost been robbed.

Having set sail from Trad one night, the Shantisuk was navigating toward Ko Chang and Ko Kut Islands when Luc spotted two vessels. Thanks to his keen observation, Luc guessed their ill intentions when they were still five hundred yards away. The channel was quite narrow, and they knew they could not possibly avoid the pirates if they continued on course. Jean-Paul observed that the boats signaled one another by flashing lights, even though there was still enough daylight to see. To find out whether they were pirates or not, Luc steered toward the right to see what they would do. After exchanging another flashing light signal, the two boats also veered to the right, attempting to block the Shantisuk. Hong, who was close by, began to worry. Suddenly, the Shantisuk veered around and fled full speed back toward Trad, where many other boats were still anchored. At three the next morning, the Shantisuk set sail with a host of other fishing boats to avoid being attacked. From then on, the Shantisuk no longer sailed around Trad.

For some time now, pirates had been doing whatever they pleased and no one could control them. Word had spread like wildfire when pirates first found gold on the refugee boats. Soon pirates had staked out territories at sea where they could attack refugee boats, especially in the vicinity of Ko Kut and Ko Chang, where the greatest number of refugee boats passed. Every day the numbers of pirates increased, due to poverty and hardship.

Many were not "professionals" in that they did not own guns, but instead carried knives, hammers, and clubs. The Thai authorities were aware of the pirates' activities, but because they did not want any more refugees to come ashore, they ignored the cruel goings-on. Yet even if the authorities had wanted to control the piracy, it was unlikely they could have done so.

One day when the Shantisuk was docked at Chantaburi, a Thai man approached Luc and suggested they use the dinghy to search for gold at sea. When Luc asked where gold was to be found, the fellow replied he knew of some buried on a small island near Ko Kut. After questioning him carefully, Luc learned that the man was the sole survivor of a band of eighteen pirates who had robbed four refugee boats near Ko Kut and buried the bounty on a nearby small island. Soon after, they were attacked by another band of pirates for crossing into their territory, and they had all been killed except for him. Now he wanted Luc to accompany him to the island to claim the gold. Luc refused, saying he did not have the courage. Hong knew that the real reason was that Luc had not come to the Gulf of Siam for gold.

Hong told Dao that the refugees' greatest danger was the pirates. Piracy had grown so widespread that nearly every refugee boat was attacked at least once. Some had been attacked more than ten times. The average was three or four. Some pirates were ruthlessly savage. Others pitied the refugees after robbing them and agreed to pull them closer to shore. Some pirates, after robbing and raping the boat people, killed everyone aboard and sank the boat. Others took only money and clothes, but did not touch the women.

Dao trembled as she listened to Hong. She felt her courage seep away. But Hong assured her she would seek every means possible to help Dao get to the other shore without encountering any more pirates. That night Dao asked Hong to teach her the *Heart of Perfect Understanding Sutra*. She knew the sutra would help her find serenity and strengthen her spirit. Sad for her fate and for the fate of all her people, Dao's tears fell even in her sleep.

∞

When she awoke, Dao knew that Hong had already gone to sea. She walked to the spring to wash, and then ate one cracker to ease her hunger and drank more spring water. Dao climbed up on a large boulder in the shade and tried to sit in meditation. She had never meditated before, but she imitated the crossed-legged position and kept her back straight. She had once heard someone say that breathing was the most important part of meditation, so she began to take long and quiet breaths, relaxing her face in a slight smile. After fifteen minutes, Dao felt relaxed, refreshed, and quite stable both physically and spiritually.

Dao began to recite the *Heart Sutra*. After chanting it several times, she smiled when she realized she was imitating Hong's voice. She did not understand the meaning of the sutra's words, but their sounds were joyous and comforting. She was especially struck by one section:

> *Hear, Shariputra, all dharmas are marked with emptiness; they are neither produced nor destroyed, neither defiled nor immaculate, neither increasing nor decreasing. Therefore, in emptiness there is neither form, nor feeling, nor perception, nor mental formations, nor consciousness.*

It seemed to her that if she repeated this a thousand times, she might understand the deep meaning of the sutra. These words were at once as gentle as floating clouds and as explosive as thunder. Dao knew they contained something very important, though she could not penetrate their meaning. At the same time, she knew she understood something, though she was not sure exactly what. She only knew that she was drawn to those words.

Dao stopped chanting when she saw that Hong had returned much earlier than usual. The sun was poised straight above. Dao ran to meet Hong, and led Hong to a shady place while she ran to fetch some water. After drinking, Hong looked at Dao and said, "Elder sister, get ready to cross to the other shore this afternoon."

Before Dao could ask anything, Hong continued, "A refugee boat will pass by here in about three hours. You have plenty of time to get ready. Take all the crackers and the duffel bag of clothes. When the boat approaches, tell them to come ashore to refill their water containers. I'll catch their attention to be sure they see you and come to pick you up."

Dao grasped Hong's arm. "Will you come with me? I'm so afraid."

Hong smiled and said, "Why should I cross to the other side? I need to remain here. I must continue looking for my mother and helping refugees in trouble. Today is the Thai New Year and everyone is at home celebrating. There isn't a pirate vessel in sight, not even a fishing boat. Let's go down to the beach and I'll trace in the sand the route from here to Ko Kut Island, from Ko Kut to Ko Chang Island, and from Ko Chang Island to the Leam Sing district in the province of Chanthaburi. The local villagers in that area take refugees ashore and give them food, water, and medicine. By tomorrow the police will escort you and the others to the Leam Sing refugee camp."

Hong led Dao down to the beach. With her finger, she traced in the sand a map of the Gulf of Thailand, explaining every detail to Dao. Hong carefully pointed out the spots where hidden rocks lay, and she warned Dao how to look carefully at the sea surface and veer away from places where the waves indicated the presence of large, submerged rocks. Hong taught Dao how to tell directions by the sun and stars and by the locations of

Ko Kut and Ko Chang Islands. Then she erased the map and asked Dao to draw it, saying aloud all that Hong had told her. Hong repeated all the things that Dao had not yet fully grasped.

When they were finished, she asked Dao, "Do you know anyone in Europe, Australia, or America?"

"Yes, I have an uncle in France."

Hong advised, "When you get into Leam Sing camp, write a letter to your uncle immediately. Ask the Reverend Doug Kellum, who visits Leam Sing camp every week and helps the refugees, to mail it for you in Chanthaburi. Ask your uncle to send a telegram to Dat at the Pulau Bidong refugee camp in Malaysia, just off the coast from Kuala Trengganu, telling him that you are still alive and in the Leam Sing camp. You can also write to Dat yourself. Tell the United Nations representative that you have an uncle in France and that you want to file a request to be resettled there. Dat plans to request to go to France as well, doesn't he? Remind him he needs to request specifically to go to France. And when you get to the camp, please don't forget to make sure you are seen by a doctor. Tell him privately you do not want any scars from the pirates remaining in your body or your spirit."

Looking up, Dao saw two shining tears in Hong's eyes. She hugged Hong tightly. "I'll do just as you say, little sister. Will I ever see you again?"

Moving gently from Dao's arms, Hong led Dao to sit on a boulder in the cool shade. She said, "I might have a chance to see you again, but I'm not sure. So for now, let's consider this our last afternoon together. Listen, elder sister, refugees are now coming out in such great numbers that all the neighboring countries have agreed to take strong measures to refuse them entry. They are carefully policing their beaches to prevent refugees from coming ashore. But that's not all. They are also planning to organize anti-refugee demonstrations to support their practice of forcing refugees back on boats and towing them out to international waters. If they carry out such a plan, our people will all die. I hope that international opinion will prevent it. But once you get to the refugee camp, you must warn our people so they can prepare to defend themselves. Work together and devise ways to prevent such actions from taking place. Even at night, you must be on guard and ready to resist. If you are ordered back onto your boat, refuse to go, even if they thrust their guns at your chest. In the event you see they mean to carry out their threats of violence, you must find some way to sink or destroy all the boats remaining on shore outside the refugee camp.

"Life in the refugee camp you are about to enter is very difficult, just as in the other camps of Songkhla, Pulau Bidong, Pulau Tengah, Pulau Pinang, and many others in this region. You will have to remain there for four, six, or even eight months. If you can, elder sister, as a special favor to me, please give all your energy to those people suffering in the camp."

Hong looked up and laughed, though her eyes were still moist with tears. "I have some good news. Captain Luc went to meet Tan again, and this time he told Tan the whole truth about the Shantisuk. He said, 'Knights never oppress others. You might temporarily steal gold from the rich to help those who are hungry, but you never have the right to kill or rape. Your followers must never sully your good name.' Luc was very courageous, and Tan promised he would give such an order to his followers.

"But, elder sister, there are hundreds of pirate bands on the sea. Perhaps the few followers of Tan won't threaten the lives and welfare of refugees, but what about all the others? The Shantisuk itself is being threatened by other bands of pirates. I'm afraid that one day soon they will not be able to sail anymore. I'm afraid for their lives. Perhaps the master on Doi Suthep mountain will call them back because of the dangers at sea. But, look, in the distance, your boat is approaching! Get the branch with the shirt and we'll go down to the shore."

On the eastern horizon, Dao saw a black dot. Each minute it grew larger until finally she could see clearly that it was a refugee boat. Hong said, "Wait for them to come a little closer and then wave the shirt. Don't tell anyone aboard about me, okay? I'll swim out and catch their attention so that they see your signal for help. Remember, do as I've told you, and especially remember to destroy your boat as soon as you get to shore."

Hong hugged Dao tightly. Then, just like a child, she let go of Dao and ran toward the water. She dove into the sea and swam out until Dao could no longer see her. Dao waved the shirt on the stick back and forth. She walked forward until the water rose up to her knees, all the while waving her flag. The boat saw her signal, and the pilot altered his course, steering in the direction of the island.

∞

The Moon Bamboo

IT WAS LATE afternoon by the time Mia finished gathering the last bundle of bamboo shoots. She lifted it to her shoulder and walked along the path leading out of the bamboo grove. Her two cousins, Chanh and Cam, sat beneath the banyan tree on the hill, leisurely combing each other's hair as they waited for Mia. When they finally saw her coming, they dusted off their clothes, lifted their own bundles onto their shoulders, and joined Mia for the walk home.

Since early that morning, Mia had worked very hard. Chanh and Cam had picked just a few shoots when they abandoned their work for the cool shade of the tree. Mia, careful to choose only the youngest, most tender shoots, finished filling her cousins' bundles before she filled her own. She knew she would be beaten by her aunt if she picked any shoots that were not tender and sweet.

From the day Mia was orphaned and taken in by her mother's sister, she had endured abuse and cruelty. Because Mia was more beautiful than her older cousins, they were jealous of her; they always managed to get her into trouble with their mother, even though she usually did their work for them.

When the three girls reached a grove of sim trees bordering a spring, they put down their bundles and rested. Chanh declared she was hungry and wanted a piece of sim fruit. The girls gaily picked some fruit, and lay on the grass enjoying its sweet and sour taste. Before long, the moon rose in the sky, and Mia urged her cousins to return home, but they ignored her. Cam wanted to swim in the cool spring, so the three girls undressed and plunged into the refreshing water, giggling and shouting as they splashed each other.

Suddenly, Mia heard the sound of someone softly clearing his throat. She turned around but saw no one. Certain that the sound had come from a man and not from either of her cousins, she looked up and was startled to see on the moon a young farmer leaning on his hoe, looking down and smiling at her. Mia felt extremely embarrassed, and she dunked down into the water, as Chanh and Cam continued to play, unaware of the observer. When some passing clouds covered the moon, Mia ran out of the water and hurriedly put on her clothes. Chanh and Cam, thinking that Mia no longer wanted to swim, called, "Come on, Mia! Swim some more! Why are you in such a rush to get home?"

Without responding, Mia lifted her head. The soft, radiant light of the moon shone through the parting clouds, and the three girls all saw the young farmer. But he was not looking at Chanh or Cam. His gaze was only for Mia, who was trying to hide beneath the leafy branches of a tree. Her cousins resented the special attention Mia was receiving, and they did all they could to distract the young man, to no avail. A moment later, dense clouds covered the moon again, and the two cousins, angry and disappointed, climbed onto the bank, got dressed, and picked up their bamboo shoots. On the way home, neither Chanh nor Cam spoke one word to Mia. That night the moon did not show its face again.

Mia's aunt scolded her for returning home so late and for picking such tough bamboo. In fact, all the bamboo she had picked was tender and young, perfect for eating. The tough bamboo shoots had been picked by her negligent cousins. But they feigned ignorance and Mia took the blame. Of course, returning late had not been Mia's idea, either, as they well knew.

More than likely, Mia's aunt also realized this, but she had fallen into the habit of blaming Mia for all her own troubles.

The next evening, the villagers organized a full moon celebration, but Mia was not allowed to go. As a ploy to prevent Mia from getting all the attention from the fellow on the moon, Chanh and Cam told their mother that Mia should remain at home to guard the pigs from thieves. They also hid Mia's one decent set of clothes in the rice barrel, for they knew she would not dare to venture out in her tattered house clothes.

The steady beat of the village drums resounded all night, echoing Mia's own anxious heart. There were so few full moon celebrations in a year, so few nights of song and dance, and she could not be there to share in the fun. To ease her disappointment, Mia gazed at the moon from the porch. Without a cloud in sight, the moon shone brilliantly. But tonight there was no sign of the young farmer hoeing his fields. Didn't he know a celebration was taking place on earth below? The bright moonlight and the steady pounding of the drums made Mia's disappointment unbearable. She resolved she would attend the celebration despite her aunt's orders. But when she went inside to change, she could not find her good clothes anywhere. She knew her cousins must have hidden them. In vain, she searched everywhere and then she sat down to reflect on her situation.

She thought about how her aunt and cousins had treated her the past years. She remembered the times that she had gone hungry, the beatings and cursings she'd endured. Chanh and Cam had a new set of clothes sewn every year. Mia had not had anything new for three years, and now even her one very worn set of nice clothes had been hidden. The more she thought about her situation, the more resentment flooded her heart. "How can they be so cruel?" she thought. "I never do them any harm, and they always hurt me." So she decided to run away. Taking only her personal knife, she stepped outside and latched the door behind her. Alone, she entered the forest to start a new life.

Late that night when Chanh, Cam, and the aunt returned home, they could not find Mia anywhere. They guessed she had sneaked out to the full moon celebration even in her tattered clothes, and the aunt declared she would beat Mia in the morning for daring to disobey her. But Mia did not return the next day. Chanh had to carry the water from the well, do all the cooking, and sweep the house. Cam had to gather duckweed from the marsh and cook bran porridge for the pigs. They cursed Mia as they worked. If Mia had been there, they would never have dirtied their hands with such tasks. Several days passed, and still there was no sign of Mia. They knew she had run away. Without Mia, housework came to a standstill, and her aunt and cousins realized how much they depended on her. Chanh and Cam were only willing to do the most basic tasks, such as carrying water from the well and cooking meals. They neglected all other chores such as straightening the house, sweeping and scrubbing, tending the garden, and feeding the livestock. News of Mia's disappearance spread quickly. The villagers knew very well it was because of the cruel way she had been treated by her aunt.

In the village there was a young fellow named Tao, who was both kind and industrious. He was in love with Mia, and his mother had asked the aunt for Mia's hand in marriage to her son. But the aunt had replied that she must find husbands for Chanh and Cam first. She suggested that Tao marry Chanh, but he flatly refused. Mia knew about all this. She knew Tao loved her, and it was true that she had feelings for him. But she had not yet given much thought to marriage.

One morning, Tao went by the aunt's house to inquire about Mia's disappearance, and he found the aunt hiring men to search for Mia in the forest. Carrying bows and arrows and long knives, they looked more prepared to go on a hunt for wild animals than to seek a young girl. Tao joined them, but after three days of searching, they found no sign of Mia. They concluded she had been swallowed alive by a boa constrictor or devoured by a tiger, bone and all. Tao returned home with a heavy heart. He could not eat for three days.

Of course, the aunt's regrets were no more than the regrets one might feel in losing an excellent maid. Seeing the demise of her household, she began to scold and scream at Chanh and Cam, and the atmosphere in their home grew increasingly unbearable.

∞

One day while gathering wild figs in the forest, Mia heard a group of men approaching. She quickly looked for a place to hide and found a hollow in a tree just large enough for her. As she sat concealed from view, she listened to the men's conversation and learned that they had been hired by her aunt to find her. She knew that if she were returned to her aunt, she would surely be beaten. She sat perfectly still.

After a moment, one fellow said, "We've looked everywhere. Most likely she's been eaten by a tiger. Let's return home."

Mia waited until the men were far out of reach before she dared breathe normally again. Cautiously she climbed out of the tree, shuddering about what might have happened if they had found her.

Mia knew that from that time on, no one would look for her again. Relieved, she cut leaves and branches and built a small hut. She knew the forest well and had no difficulty finding edible fruits and wild greens to eat. She was fortunate not to encounter any poisonous snakes. She often met rabbits and deer, but she had no desire to hunt them for food.

One day while gathering bamboo shoots, Mia came across a tender pink shoot, smooth as agate and fragrant as magnolia and orange blossoms. Using her knife, she dug up the young plant, careful not to damage the roots, and carried it gently back to plant by her hut. Mia watered the sprout every day and was delighted to see how quickly it grew into a firm bamboo tree with an emerald green trunk and smooth, shiny leaves. She continued to tend it affectionately and, before long, the young bamboo tree had grown three times higher than the roof of her hut.

One night, so hot and humid that it was difficult to fall asleep, Mia decided to refresh herself by bathing in a cool stream nearby. Moonlight illuminated the forest. Splashing herself, Mia remembered the night long ago when she and her cousins had paused to swim. Mia lifted her face to the moon and gasped when she saw the young farmer hoeing his fields. He looked down and smiled at her.

Shy and embarrassed, Mia sank beneath the water, leaving only her nose and eyes peeking above the surface. A moment later, clouds drifted by and covered the moon. Mia dashed from the water, dressed, and ran back to the hut. The moon did not reveal itself again that night. Black clouds tumbled across the sky and a great storm broke. All night the rains pounded.

When the first rays of dawn appeared, Mia was awakened by the sound of rushing water overflowing the stream's banks. Water poured down from the mountain and rushed around Mia's hut. The wind howled. When Mia looked outside, all she could see was the flash of white water. She did not know what to do to save herself. Water rushed into the hut and rose to her ankles and then to her knees. Panic-stricken, she ran outside and clung to the bamboo tree.

She began to climb the tree. When she was high as the roof of her hut, Mia looked out over the forest. All she could see was a great curtain of silver rain. As the flood waters rose, she climbed even higher, her arms and legs clinging to the bamboo tree. The tree stood straight and solid as the rising waters dashed against it. Continuing up, Mia soon found herself higher than the highest trees in the forest. It began to feel as if the bamboo tree itself was also stretching upward, its green leaves appearing and disappearing in the torrents of rain.

A mighty gust of wind came up and caused the bamboo to lean all the way over to Mia's old village, until it poised exactly above her aunt's house. Mia looked at the house, set among areca trees, which were shaking wildly in the wind, and knew she could jump down onto the roof if she wished. But she had not forgotten the years of abuse she suffered at the hands of her aunt and cousins. She hesitated. Should she jump to safety? No, she would rather die than return to her old life. At that moment, the bamboo righted itself and stretched all the way to the Moon. When she saw the Moon's surface only a few yards away, Mia summoned her remaining strength and climbed the last bit of tree. She reached out and placed her foot upon the Moon.

The Moon's unfamiliar surface seemed enormous. The rocks, soil, and sand were golden yellow, unlike the brown, red, and black hues Mia knew on Earth. She saw before her fields of a curious sort of rice, odd vegetable gardens, and small villages in the distance. The houses had many windows and were more solidly constructed than the thatch and palm leaf homes Mia knew.

Hearing a bird sing, Mia looked up. She had never seen such a colorful bird before! And the branch on which it perched was smooth as stone, unlike any branch she knew. Mia was met by one surprise after another. She followed a path that wound alongside a field and discovered it led to a small, tidy house. She hesitated before the gate.

Mia was startled by the familiar sound of a man softly clearing his throat. She turned around, and there before her stood the very young farmer she had seen while she bathed in pools on Earth. His hoe was propped over his shoulder, and he smiled like someone who had just discovered gold.

Mia felt too timid to speak, but she knew she couldn't just stand there. After all, she had made the decision herself to come to the Moon. Taking a breath to calm herself, she asked, "Is this your home?"

The young farmer nodded. "And are you an Earth woman who has just arrived on the Moon?"

His language was foreign to her ears, yet somehow Mia understood him. She nodded and said, "There was a flood on Earth so I climbed up here. I'll return home after a few days."

The young man invited Mia into his home and brought her a refreshing drink. They sat and talked for a long time. Mia learned that his name was Dan and he lived alone. His parents had both passed away and his two younger sisters were married and living in distant villages. Dan owned and tended several acres of land that grew a strange, rice-like grain, a kind of sweet potato, and fruit trees. He tended all his land by himself.

Shyly, Mia said, "This isn't the first time I've seen you."

Dan smiled. "And this isn't the first time I've seen you. The first time was when you were out gathering bamboo shoots with two other girls. The three of you swam in a spring. Then I saw you again, alone in the forest, several times—building a hut, tending a young bamboo tree, gathering wild fruit and greens. I saw you again last night, bathing alone."

Mia remembered the night before, when the moon had shone brightly. She lowered her head. Seeing her tattered clothes, she felt ashamed and placed her hand over the tears in the cloth that revealed her skin.

Dan said gently, "Please don't worry about that, Miss Mia." He went into the back room and offered her a set of clothes that had belonged to his youngest sister. Mia hesitated, but then accepted them. Dan showed her to the bedroom and left her there alone, closing the door behind him. Mia removed her old clothes, still damp from the rain. She held up the strange clothes Dan had given her. Only after several attempts did she figure out the proper way to wear them.

She stepped outside and asked Dan if she could wash her own clothes so that when she returned to Earth she could return his sister's things. Dan led her to a clear stream and waited as she rinsed out her old clothes. Together they returned to his house, and he prepared a meal for her. He served the food on an unusual platter without any chopsticks. Mia felt awkward as she watched Dan in order to learn how to eat the food. After dinner, Dan asked her about her life on Earth, and he listened intently while she told him everything. Learning about her situation, the affection and love he already felt for her grew even deeper. When she had finished speaking, he asked her if she would become his wife.

"Together we could tend these acres of land, Mia. There's plenty to eat here. Why should you return to Earth where your aunt and cousins only abuse you? You cannot live forever in the forest eating nothing but fruit and wild greens. Eventually you will grow ill and die."

Mia thought about it for just a short while. "Yes," she decided, "I will become your wife."

Mia learned Dan's language and before long she could converse fluently with her husband and the other villagers. She quickly learned how to tend the fields on the Moon. In no time at all, the two of them created a happy and secure life together. Mia gave birth to two children. She named her first-born son Summer, and her daughter Spring, after the seasons of their birth.

∞

One day Mia's aunt wandered deep into the forest with her two daughters to gather bamboo shoots. By chance, she discovered an abandoned hut and immediately guessed it had belonged to Mia, and that she might still be alive. When she saw the bamboo tree rising to the Moon, she was certain Mia had climbed to the Moon and was now living there. She wanted to go up herself to persuade Mia to return, but she was far too stout to make such a climb, and her two daughters were too frail and lazy.

It was early in the morning and the moon had not yet set. Looking up at the white globe, Mia's aunt could barely discern the uppermost leaves of the bamboo tree fluttering against the Moon's surface. Looking even more carefully, she suddenly caught a vague glimpse of Mia working among the fields on the Moon. "She's still an industrious worker," thought the aunt. "Since the day she left, I've realized what an asset she was."

The aunt plotted how she could entice Mia to return to Earth. She called her daughters to walk home, and a sinister smile formed on her lips as she went over the plan in her mind.

The following day when the aunt went to market, she informed all her friends that any fellow who could climb to the Moon and bring back Mia could have her for his wife. By evening, all the young men in the surrounding villages had heard about the offer. There were many young men who had hoped to marry Mia, but who had been thwarted because the aunt had wished to find husbands for Chanh and Cam first. This was their chance. They gathered at the aunt's house, sixteen in all. Among them was the kind and attractive Tao.

The aunt led them to the bamboo tree in the forest next to Mia's hut, which now leaned over to one side and was missing most of its thatch. The bamboo tree, however, still stood straight and tall, its trunk glistening like emerald and its uppermost leaves piercing the clouds.

"How can we be sure this bamboo tree really reaches all the way to the Moon?" asked one fellow. It was a cloudy day and no one could see the Moon.

The aunt replied, "Believe me, I saw Mia with my own eyes working in a rice field up there. Whoever makes it to the Moon, tell Mia how much I miss her. Tell her that if she returns, I will always love her and I will never beat her or yell at her again."

The first fellow nodded and grabbed hold of the tree to begin his climb. But the bamboo trunk was unusually smooth and the branches were far apart. He climbed only five or six lengths before he slipped straight back down. Undaunted, he spat on his hands, and made a second attempt. But still he could make no progress.

The others, anxious to prove their strength, met with no better success, even though they each tried two or three times. When it was Tao's turn, he gave his best effort, but like all the others, he came right back down the slippery trunk. One fellow, growing suspicious, asked aloud, "That bamboo is so smooth. How could Mia ever have made it to the Moon?" Tao had been asking himself the same question. Most of them suspected that Mia had never climbed to the Moon. They thought this whole event must have been a scheme by the aunt to make them forget Mia once and for all and turn their attentions to Chanh and Cam. Angry and disgusted, they left, swearing they would never speak to the conniving aunt again.

But Tao truly believed Mia had gone to the Moon. He left with the others, but he returned to Mia's abandoned hut the next morning, determined to climb the bamboo tree. He brought with him a sharp knife and a gourd filled with fresh water, and he began to climb up as far as he could without slipping. Then he took out his knife and cut a small notch in the tree, just large enough to provide a grip for his foot. It worked! He cut more notches, and as he ascended higher and higher, the cuts he had made below were already healing on the amazingly healthy tree. By noon, he had climbed more than half a mile. He reached for the gourd and took a long drink to quench his thirst. He knew he had to ration his water wisely, because he still had a long way to climb. He continued up carefully, stopping occasionally to catch his breath. He no longer dared look below, for fear the height would make him dizzy. In this way, Tao climbed for two days and two nights.

On the morning of the third day, when the sun had just risen, Tao heard a bird singing above his head. He looked up and saw that the Moon was no more than ten yards away. Bamboo leaves fluttered above him and he felt a sudden surge of strength. In the space of just three breaths, Tao was on the Moon. Clinging to a bamboo branch, he lowered his feet to the surface.

Because his climb had been far more arduous than Mia's, Tao did not notice much of the Moon scenery. He simply followed the path before him. It was, of course, the very path that led to Dan's house. When he reached the house, there was no one in sight. After waiting a while to see if someone would appear, Tao walked out into the fields, and suddenly, he caught sight of Mia working in a patch of what appeared to be melons. He hid behind some bushes, cupped his hands around his mouth, and made a cry like a cuckoo.

Mia was startled. She stopped what she was doing and stared straight ahead. For five years, she had not heard that familiar sound. Excitedly, she began to search for the bird. Tao made another call and Mia found him. He stood up to greet her. It was the first time she had seen someone from Earth since she had arrived, and here was the very Earth person for whom she had always felt the most affection. Overjoyed, she asked Tao when he had arrived. They sat and talked on the edge of the rice field, and Mia told him how homesick the cuckoo's call had made her feel.

After a long conversation, Tao learned that Mia was already married. His heart sank, but he made a great effort not to show his disappointment. He asked Mia about life on the Moon, about Moon customs, clothes, and food. In turn, Mia asked Tao how life had been on Earth.

"During these past years, there have not been any more floods. The harvests have been plentiful. You should return to Earth to live, Mia. Life here is too strange. Surely you cannot be truly happy?"

"Am I happy?" Mia asked herself. For five years she had lived in peace. Kind and gentle Dan had never spoken an angry word to her. They had prospered by their hard work, and they had never known want or hunger. Summer, her four-year-old son, and Spring, her three-year-old daughter, were darling, bright children. She had only to recall what life had been like with her aunt to know that her Moon life was indeed a happier one. She answered, "Tao, I've found peace here. I cannot return to Earth. If I did, I would surely encounter my aunt again, and I suffered enough with that family. Besides, I have a husband and children here. How could I ever leave them to return to Earth?"

Knowing he could not possibly persuade Mia to abandon her life on the Moon, Tao talked instead about Earth activities. He described the cheerful days when young men and women sang songs back and forth as they harvested the rice. He described how they gathered on the village courtyard at evening to thresh the rice beneath the golden harvest moon, while carrying on lively, flirtatious conversations. Mia's eyes grew bright.

Seeing her homesickness grow, Tao continued to describe other familiar scenes on Earth—swimming in the fresh, cool springs; mornings spent gathering sim fruit; full moon nights of song and dance; and the first warm days of spring gathering the plum and peach blossoms that perfumed the mountain forests. He reminded her of special foods like the New Year's earthcakes, sweet rice with mung beans, steamed coconut cakes, candied tamarind, stewed bananas, red beans with rice dumplings and coconut milk, salted fish stewed with greens, sour soup, sweet mung bean soup. The mention of these made Mia's mouth water. It had been such a long time since she had enjoyed their tastes.

"You don't wish to return to live on Earth, and I won't try to persuade you," said Tao. "But why don't you come to visit for a few days?"

Mia's eyes shined at the idea. She thought there could be no harm if she went for just a brief visit. Dan had taken the children to their aunt's, and they would not be home until nightfall. Mia answered, "A few days would be too long, my friend.

It would never do for my husband and children to return home and find me gone. I will come only for the afternoon. I must return here by nightfall."

Mia recalled from that day long ago that climbing to the Moon takes about three hours. She did not realize that the tree had sprung up at a terrific speed while she herself climbed only a few hours. Tao knew that the slide down would be quick enough, but that climbing back up might take more than two days and nights. But he said nothing. His only thought was to find a way to get Mia back to Earth.

They walked together to the bamboo tree. Tao told Mia to grab hold of a branch, wrap her legs around the tree, and slide down. Mia did as she was told and slid rather quickly. Tao waited until she had gone a good distance, and then he grabbed hold of the tree. In his right hand he held his knife. Every few feet, he reached up and cut off a section of bamboo, which fell randomly to the ground below, without Mia's notice. When she finally reached the Earth, the sun was directly overhead. She let go of the tree and saw her old hut, now in ruins.

Mia was still looking around when Tao arrived. He said, "If we return to your old hamlet, we may meet your aunt. Let's go instead to the highland village. No one there knows you." So they walked together in the direction of the highland village.

Mia was delighted to see jack fruit, bananas, sandalwood, and other trees she knew so well. As they emerged from the other side of the forest, she felt a great joy walking alongside fields of sweet potatoes and green rice. This marvelous earth was Mia's own homeland. A grasshopper jumped near her foot. Laughing like a small child, she chased it and tried to catch it in her cupped hand. When they came to a fruit orchard, Mia picked a guava leaf and crushed it in her hand to enjoy its wondrous fragrance. She did the same with a lemon leaf, and felt her whole being refreshed.

After passing a grove of green bamboo, they reached the out-skirts of the highland village. Two young girls drawing water at the well stared at Mia's strange clothes. Feeling self-conscious, Mia walked by quickly. Beyond the well, a woman vendor was selling red beans with rice dumplings and coconut milk. Mia's eyes sparkled. Tao bought her two bowls of the sweet treat. It had been so long since Mia had tasted food so delicious, she easily ate both bowls.

Tao and Mia saw the village children flying a kite. Mia asked if they could follow the children, and she watched with delight as one boy lifted the kite and ran, while another held the string and chased after him. When they had picked up speed, the boy with the kite released it to the wind, and it flew higher and higher as he unwound more and more of the string.

As she watched the kite soar, Mia's thoughts turned to the Moon. It was already late afternoon, and Dan and the children would be home. Soon Mia said to Tao, "I must return now. Please take me back to the bamboo tree." Tao did not answer. Guessing that he wanted to persuade her to remain on Earth for a few more days, Mia said, "I can't possibly stay any longer, Tao. Dan and the children will be waiting for me. I'll come back to visit again when I have a chance."

Tao remained silent. His expression was a strange mixture of regret and fear. Despite Mia's pleas, he did not move from where he sat. Exasperated, Mia stood up and said, "Very well, if you won't take me back to the tree, I'll go by myself." Hastily, she walked back in the direction of her abandoned hut, and Tao ran after her. Mia slowed her pace to allow him to catch up and then quickened her steps again. They reached her old hut just as dark-ness was beginning to settle on the forest. The moon had risen. Mia put her arms around the tree and said farewell to Tao.

She had just begun to climb when Tao finally spoke, "Mia, it is no longer possible for you to return to the Moon." Before she could question him, Mia noticed the sections of bamboo trunk strewn about the forest floor. Looking up, she discovered with a shock that the tree rose no more than twenty or thirty feet. "Tao, what happened? The tree has been chopped down!" she exclaimed.

Mia grew even more frightened when she saw Tao cover his face with his hands without answering her. She grabbed his shoulders and cried, "Did you chop down the tree, Tao? Answer me! Did you chop it down?"

Mia began to sob so violently that her eyes turned red and her hair fell in tangles across her face. She beat her hands against her chest and then pounded Tao's shoulders. She screamed in his ear, "Tell me! Are you deaf? Why did you chop it down?"

"Because I love you too much," was Tao's only reply. He again covered his face with his hands in an expression of terrible remorse.

"Love me? You say you love me and yet you destroyed the only way I have to return to my husband and children? Tao! How could you have done this to me?"

The whole forest trembled with Mia's sobs. The moon shone so brilliantly that when Mia looked up, she could not make out anything at all. Knowing that her husband and children were waiting for her made her tears fall like rain. Mia cried for seven days and nights. She did not eat or sleep. Silently, Tao cut bamboo branches to repair the roof of her old hut to protect her from the sun and rain. He brought fruit for her to eat and water for her to drink, but she would have none of it. When her throat grew unbearably parched, she ran alone to the spring and scooped up a handful of water to drink. She rinsed her face and sat quietly by the spring for a long time. But thoughts of her husband and children soon brought back her tears. She was beyond comfort.

Tao made Mia some rice porridge, but when he offered it, she pushed his hand away. He placed the bowl beside her sleeping mat, but two days passed and Mia still had not touched the porridge. He made a fresh bowl and offered it to her, and again she pushed his hand away. But this time he did not put the bowl down. He continued to hold it before her. When his right hand grew weary, he switched the bowl to his left. He spent the entire night sitting before her, switching the bowl back and forth in his hands. At daybreak, unable to stand it any longer, Mia grabbed the bowl and placed it by her sleeping mat. But she did not eat any of the porridge.

Tao spent the day in the forest chopping wood to build furniture for the hut. When he returned in the evening, he was overjoyed to see an empty bowl beside Mia's mat. The fruit he had placed in the same spot was also gone. At last Mia had eaten. Tao gently placed his hand on her shoulder, but she pushed it away.

Tao was not disheartened, for he knew that Mia had wept all her tears and he must only be patient. Quietly, he repaired the thatched roof and transformed the hut into a comfortable home. One day he took courage again and placed his hand on Mia's shoulder. This time Mia did not push his hand away. She had forgiven him, and she had become resigned to her circumstances.

Tao cleared a section of forest and planted rice and corn. Together he and Mia started a new life. Sometimes they went to the highland market to sell firewood in order to buy sugar and salt, but Mia never returned to her own village for fear of meeting her aunt. Whenever she thought of her husband and children alone on the Moon, she covered her face and wept. On full moon nights, she sat alone and gazed at the Moon. But no matter how hard she looked, she never saw Dan, Summer, or Spring.

At the year's end, Tao suggested they pack their possessions and move to the highland village. He hoped that village life with its bustling market and friendly neighbors might help Mia think less often of her old family. They moved, and Tao wasted no time planting rice fields and fruit orchards. Mia took up the craft of weaving.

In the autumn of the following year, on the full moon of the eighth month, Mia gave birth to a lovely baby girl. They named her Autumn. With little Autumn to care for, Mia's spirits brightened. It was as though her heart put forth new roots, which went deep into the heart of the Earth. This renewed connection to her homeland made Mia's eyes and hair shine again. One day Mia sang this lullaby to Autumn:

> Making soup with young bamboo shoots
> and small fishes of the mountain spring,
> From now on, Mother must change sadness to joy,
> O my beloved child.

Mia's garden was fragrant with the mint and coriander she had planted. The vines which climbed the trellis were heavy with melons and squash.

∞

With Spring in his right arm and Summer in his left, Dan entered the house and cheerfully called out, "We're home!" But the house was strangely cold and empty. Startled, Dan put the children down and went outside to look for Mia. She was nowhere in sight. Ghostly shadows flitted across the empty wheat fields. Dan walked to the melon field and found Mia's footprints along with some the size of a man's. Anxiously, Dan ran toward the bamboo tree. It was no longer there. Though he peered far below, there was no sign of fluttering leaves. He knew the tree had been chopped down.

Dan returned to the house. He gathered his children in his arms and wept. The house was dark. No one had lit the lamps or cooked a meal. His house was as cold as a coffin. Spring and

Summer both called out, "Mama!" Dan went to the kitchen to find some leftovers for his children to eat.

Days passed and Mia did not return. Dan did his best to care for the children and to keep on living as before, but it was difficult. He thought it would have been better if Mia had never come to the Moon, than to come and then abandon them. He felt as though Mia had taken the meaning of life with her. Though he often looked down to Earth while hoeing his fields, he never saw Mia. "Why did you leave us, Mia?" was his constant thought.

That year, the Moon suffered a terrible drought. Without rain, Dan's harvest was a failure. The children still cried constantly for their mother. Dan cried, too, when he tried to console them. One day when he returned from working in the fields, he could not find either of the children. Dan looked everywhere, until finally he knelt down by the spot where they often sat huddled together, crying for their mother, and there he found a large puddle of water. Dan understood that his children had cried until they turned into a puddle of tears. He touched the water with his finger and placed it on his tongue. The salty taste told him that truly these were his children's tears. Unable to contain his pain, he began to weep until he, too, was transformed into a stream of tears that joined the tears of his children. The heat of the sun caused the large puddle of tears to evaporate and form a small gathering of clouds, which traveled on the wind and wandered back and forth over the Earth's surface, as if searching for something. The clouds wandered until one day they came to pause over Mia's backyard.

It was an oppressively hot, humid day. Tao and Autumn had gone to the market. Mia had waited in vain all day for the clouds to burst into rain and offer some relief. She decided to draw cool water from the well behind the house in order to take a shower. Around the well Mia had planted a dark green hedge of hibiscus dotted with flowers the color of bright flames. She undressed and splashed herself with buckets of cool water. She was startled by the rumble of nearby thunder. She looked up and saw a formation of clouds hovering above her. Of course, Mia did not know that these clouds were her husband and children from the Moon. Still, she could not help staring at them.

The clouds recognized Mia and instantly burst into streams of rain that cascaded over her. The raindrops were warm and comforting on Mia's skin. As the water touched her skin, it began to assume shapes. In an instant, Dan and the two children materialized before Mia's eyes. Mia was ecstatic. She embraced Summer and Spring and then turned to Dan, her heart overflowing with happiness. She did not need to know how they made it to Earth. They were beside her!

Mia got dressed and led Dan and the children into the house. Dan spoke first, "Why did you leave us, Mia? Didn't you love us anymore?"

Her eyes clouded with tears as she answered, "Of course I loved you. I was homesick for the earth and intended to visit for only a few hours. But the bamboo tree was chopped down. I cried without stopping for many days. All these years I have longed for you and the children. I never meant to abandon you."

Mia recounted every detail of what had happened. When she finished speaking, Dan said, "Well, now that we have found you, we can return to the Moon together." He did not know how they would do so, but with Mia back, he was sure they could find a way.

Mia hesitated. On the Moon she would have Dan, Spring, and Summer. But she would lose Autumn and Tao. Nearly three years of life with Tao had bonded her to him. If she returned to the Moon, she would surely miss him, and she knew she would long terribly for Autumn. "On earth I miss the Moon, I long for Dan, Spring, and Summer. On the Moon I would long for Tao and Autumn. What should I do?"

At just that moment, Mia heard Autumn's laughter coming from the front gate. Tao had returned from the market. Panic-stricken, Mia gasped in terror. Not knowing which family to choose, she grabbed a knife from a corner of the room and plunged it into her head.

It was the exact moment of noon, and the sun was poised directly above them. Unknown to them all, Mia had plunged the knife into her head at a most sacred and magical moment, and something most wondrous occurred. The knife, as if it had a will of its own, proceeded to cleanly cut through Mia's head, neck, and body, dividing Mia into two identical and whole Mias. The only thing distinguishing them from the original Mia was their smaller size. One Mia, whose hand still held the knife, said to the other Mia, "Sister, you take Dan and find a way to return to the Moon. I'll stay here."

Moon Mia picked up her two children and walked with Dan out the back door. Everything happened so quickly that Dan forgot to say farewell to the other Mia. They walked past the well and followed the path by the rice field.

Meanwhile, Tao and Autumn entered by the front door. "Anyone home? We're back from the market," called Tao. He saw Mia sitting by the loom, busily weaving. She did not return his greeting. He gazed at her strangely and then lifted her to her feet. He looked into her eyes and uttered, "How strange indeed, Mia! I recognize your face and body, but why are you so small today?" Mia replied, "Because this is only half of me. The other half has returned with Dan to the Moon."

∞

Moon Mia led Dan and the two children beyond Tao's fields to the outskirts of the village, in order to avoid being seen by anyone. She did not know where to take them, when she suddenly remembered her old house in the forest which Tao had rebuilt. Since Tao and Mia had gone to live in the highland village, no one had tended either the house or the field. She led Dan and the children to her old home in the forest.

Much had fallen into disrepair, but together Dan and Mia fixed up the house and recultivated the fields. In time, they sowed rice, corn, and other vegetables, and raised some chickens. Summer and Spring wandered freely among the forest hills, and their mother taught them which fruits were good to eat.

Mia showed Dan the stream where long ago he had smiled at her. They sat on a large rock by the stream and watched the moon rise. Mia asked Dan what had happened on the Moon since the day she had returned to Earth. He told her everything, careful not to leave out any detail. He told her how they had cried so hard that they had turned into a great puddle of tears. He mused, "Perhaps the ocean itself is salty from the tears people have shed. Throughout the ages, who can say how many wives have been separated from their husbands, children torn from their parents, brothers and sisters forced to part—none of them knowing if they would ever see each other again. Now we are together and I will never allow us to be separated."

Tears fell from Mia's eyes as she and Dan sat bathed by the light of the moon. They both gazed at the Moon. After a long moment, Mia noticed that tears glistened on Dan's eyelashes. She knew he missed the Moon, just as she had once missed the Earth. She remembered how she felt when she had first returned, how smelling the guava and lemon leaves had filled her heart with an immense love for her homeland. She remembered how precious it had been to hear a buffalo boy's song, watch children fly a kite, gather tamarind fruit, and taste familiar foods again. Now it was the same for Dan. He missed his life on the Moon—its homes, fields, foods, birdsongs, plants, and the way people conversed with each other.

Mia felt greater love for Dan than she ever had before. She placed her hand on his shoulder and said, "I know how much you miss home. Everything is strange to you-—the food, the animals, the language—but you have me and the children. Now we know that we will never be apart." Mia paused for a moment, and then continued, "You and the children were not able to live without me, but now we are together. Be patient and find happiness here. Who knows? Some day we may find a way to return to the Moon."

Dan looked at her and asked, "If we are able to return to the Moon, will you still long for the Earth? Will you leave us as you did before?" Mia took Dan's hand and answered with all her heart, "No, never. I have lived on the Earth and I have lived on the Moon. Half of me will always remain on the Earth, and half of me will be free to live on the Moon. You know, when I returned to Earth, I missed my life on the Moon. I was homesick, not just for you and the children, but also for the trees and grass, the birds and streams, and the food you taught me to cook."

Dan was filled with happiness to hear Mia speak her heart's truth. Together they stood and walked back to the house. They covered the children, who were already asleep, with a light mat, and then lay down to sleep themselves.

∞

Earth Mia lived happily with Tao and Autumn. Though she was Earth Mia, she was no different from Moon Mia. She was neither younger nor smaller. Her heart filled with warm affection, and she smiled whenever she thought of Moon Mia. She was at ease, knowing that her identical half was caring for Dan and the children. She knew they would have happiness with Moon Mia by their side. Whatever she could do, Moon Mia could do as well. She even believed that Moon Mia had returned to the Moon with Dan, Summer, and Spring, though how, she could not guess. She smiled whenever she thought of her old house on the Moon with its many windows and solid walls, and the fields of curious rice and melons. It was true, the Moon did not resemble the earth at all.

Earth Mia regained her original size in just three days, thanks to a sudden increase in appetite. She thought of herself as a plant from which a cutting has been made to start a new plant. The new plant continued the life of the original plant, in putting forth buds, leaves, flowers, and fruit—two plants but also one. One plant became two and could just as easily become five or ten new plants.

Mia found herself smiling as she remembered her mother, who had been so beautiful. Once she had happened upon her mother massaging her grandmother's head with balm to ease a headache. Mia remembered grabbing hold of her mother's sleeve to play. Suddenly a hissing sound of boiling water came from the kitchen. Mia's mother cried, "Oh dear, the soup is boiling over!" She put down the massage balm, removed Mia's hand from her sleeve, and started to run to the kitchen, just as her husband called, "Dear, come quick, I can't open the stable door without help!" Mia's mother stood between the kitchen and the front door, torn between reducing the fire on the stove and running to assist her husband. She turned to Mia and exclaimed, "If I only had four arms I could cook the soup, massage your grandmother's forehead, open the stable door with your father, and keep you from running out to the pond! But I only have two arms!"

Mia had thought, at the time, how strange a person with four arms would look. But a few days later, her mother took her to a temple where she saw a Buddha with many arms, each holding something different—a pen, a lotus flower, a flute—to perform a different task. Mia's mother told her it was Kwan Yin Bodhisattva, who had a thousand arms to perform a thousand deeds, and a thousand eyes to see a thousand things. Mia's mother had only wished for four arms. Mia wondered if that was why her mother came to offer incense to Kwan Yin.

But in truth, Mia's mother did not really need four arms. With only two, she cared for Mia's grandmother, assisted her husband, cared for Mia, managed the household tasks, and worked in the garden. She was as talented as Kwan Yin. It was sad she passed away early, leaving Mia to fall into the hands of her cruel aunt.

As Mia sat weaving cloth at her loom, her thoughts drifted back to the day Dan came to plead with her to return to the Moon. She remembered that fateful moment she heard Tao returning from the market while Dan stood before her. She remembered the terrible panic and anguish in her heart. If it had not been for a sacred moment in time, she would now be dead, leaving both families to suffer.

Mia knew other village women who expressed the desire to turn into four or five persons—one to care for their own parents, one to care for their husband's parents, one to care for their husband and children, another to cook the meals and tend the garden. Mia wished everyone could divide themselves as she had, like a plant that puts forth shoots to create new plants.

∞

Dan transformed the forest house into a spacious, comfortable home. The rice and corn plants in their fields grew green and healthy. Dan became accustomed to eating Earth foods such as boiled corn, fish cake, manioc soup, and salted fish. When he told Mia that he found these dishes as delicious as his favorite Moon foods, her face broke into a smile.

With Dan and the two children beside her, Mia felt as though she possessed the Moon, and she no longer missed or longed for it. But she knew that, though Dan had found happiness on the Earth, his happiness was incomplete. Unlike Mia, he still distinguished between the Moon and the Earth. She had told him that if she returned to the Moon she would no longer miss the Earth. She was able to say that because, for her, the Earth was no longer the Earth, and the Moon was no longer the Moon. Both Earth and Moon lived in her own heart, and Mia was at peace. She hoped to share that peace with her husband and children, but she knew that Spring, Summer, and their father, having been born on the Moon, missed their old life.

One day while returning with water from the well, Mia heard Spring calling, "Mother, Mother! Come and see this strange plant!" Mia put down her carrying pole and asked, "Where, my daughter?"

Spring tugged at her sleeve and led her to the edge of the garden. "It's so strange, Mother. I saw a new little bamboo shoot, as rosy as a jewel and fragrant as an orange blossom!"

"Where was it, child?"

While Spring pointed to the place, Mia realized she was looking at the roots of the old bamboo tree. The trunk of the old tree had long since died, and Mia had never imagined a new shoot would sprout by its side. She told Spring to run and find Dan. When he arrived from the fields carrying a pole heavily laden with pumpkins, Mia showed him the bamboo shoot.

"Look, Dan, this old tree is the very one that once rose to the Moon, the one on which I climbed to the Moon, the one which was later chopped down. It has given forth a new little sprout. This sprout will become a mighty tree just like its parent. We shall be able to return to the Moon!"

Dan understood. His shining eyes warmed Mia's heart. When Summer and Spring heard they would be able to return to the Moon, they clapped their hands with joy. Mia had never seen her husband and children so happy.

"Summer," she said, "give me a watering can. Dan, bring me a bucket of water. We must water this bamboo shoot so it can quickly grow into a tree."

From that moment on, not a day passed that they did not carefully tend their bamboo tree, their source of hope.

Peony Blossoms

TANH RANG THE bell and waited for his nephew, Thi, to come to the gate and greet him. Thi was a pale, delicate eight-year-old, whose large black eyes revealed how very much he loved his uncle. Each Saturday he would firmly take hold of Uncle Tanh's hand and lead him into the garden, where they would spend more than half an hour wandering among the cool shade trees. Thi would ask questions on every subject imaginable.

Thi's family lived in an elegant house surrounded by six acres of land. They were fortunate, as it was difficult to find such a lovely place so close to Montpellier, an industrial city in the south of France. Doan, Thi's father, worked for the Institute of Physics Research and taught at the University of Montpellier.

But on that Saturday it was Tuyet, Thi's mother, who met Tanh at the gate. "Your little nephew has been sick in bed since yesterday," Tuyet told him, with a touch of worry in her voice.

Sister and brother followed the white gravel walkway toward the house. They went into Thi's room, and saw that the boy's eyes were closed. "He must be asleep,' Tuyet said. "Otherwise he would have opened his eyes and smiled at his dear Uncle." She placed her hand gently on his forehead, lifted the cotton blanket over his chest, and turned to Tanh, "Yes, he's finally dozed off. Let's sit in the living room."

Tuyet told her brother about Thi's illness. The day before, Thi had complained of a headache. Tuyet gave him a sugar-coated aspirin and coaxed him into drinking a glass of milk. At lunchtime, the boy did not eat at all, and he began to run a fever, so Tuyet phoned Dr. Peltier. At three in the afternoon, the doctor came and diagnosed the symptoms as nothing more than a common cold. He left Thi another bottle of sugarcoated pills. At six, Thi seemed better, and he ate a few spoonfuls of soup. But by nine o'clock, his forehead was hot as an ember. Thi's parents took his temperature: it was 104 degrees Fahrenheit. In a panic, Tuyet phoned Dr. Peltier, who came and again reassured Tuyet that it was not particularly serious. "Let him sleep through the night," he said, "and tomorrow he will be fine." The doctor promised to return the next day. That night, Thi did not sleep at all, and his mother could not sleep either. She wanted to phone the doctor but, reluctant to impose again, she decided to wait. "He will be back tomorrow," she consoled herself. But it was not until moments before Tanh arrived that the boy finally fell asleep.

Tanh listened attentively, and told his sister, "I am sure our dear Thi will be fine. It is probably a flu or something. Let's not worry." And he asked her if she had any news from friends and family back home in Vietnam.

Half an hour later they were still talking when the boy's father, Doan, emerged from his study. He walked past his wife directly to Tanh, and, holding his brother-in-law's arm, he said, "I hope you will stay for lunch. I have a meeting at the university this afternoon, and your sister is so worried about her little rascal, I'd be more comfortable if you stayed with her." Tanh agreed, and Doan quickly prepared to go.

Tuyet said, "I'm so glad you'll be staying. Let me see what we've got for lunch."

"Take your time, there's no hurry," her brother replied. "I'll be out in the garden."

Doan's garden was large and well-tended. It was early May, and the leaves were young and green. The linden trees, in particular, were bursting with new growth. "In a couple of weeks,"

Tanh thought, "I can come and pick the blossoms for tea." Tanh loved linden tea. It refreshed him and helped him relax after long hours at work on his paintings. He thought, "How funny. The Chinese call lindens *bodhi* trees, and their blossoms, *bodhi* flowers, flowers of awakening." Then he walked to the wooden bench below the large chestnut tree. The straight branches, loaded with blossoms, reminded Tanh of the candlesticks in Buddhist temples.

Tanh knew that if Thi were present, the boy would be asking dozens of questions, including many Tanh would not be able to answer. One time, Thi pointed to a spot on the chestnut tree and asked what color it was. It was a patch of moss somewhere between green and purple, certainly not any kind of blue. Tanh did not know what to call it, so he answered, "It's just that color!" The boy understood, and was satisfied.

Tanh felt very close to Thi. He had often used that color, himself, in his paintings. In fact, Tanh was so familiar with it that he never felt the need to name it. Similarly, names were not important in the manner of greeting people in Vietnam. If you met someone and smiled, or held their hand, that was enough. It was more important to remember the person than his name or position.

Tanh remembered with delight another incident that made him feel close to his nephew. Tuyet had given Thi a peach and, rather than eat it, Thi studied it and held it against his cheek. Tuyet told him, "Uncle Tanh brought us plenty of peaches, so you eat this one and have another one later." Thi shook his head to say he did not want another peach.

When Tanh later reminded him of the exchange, Thi told him, "When I looked at that peach, I realized it was a miraculous creation. How many months it must have taken for its mother, the tree, to create it! How many brothers and sisters it must have! I held it against my cheek and enjoyed its friendship." Thi had treated the peach as a being worthy of his full attention, not just as something to ingest. When he ended up biting into the fruit and swallowing it, his uncle had teased, "There goes your 'friend'!" Thi had laughed too when he saw his uncle laughing.

The warmth expressed between uncle and nephew was not often the case between father and son. Doan was immersed in his teaching and research, and rarely had time for even a walk in the garden with Thi. He was certainly a kind, considerate man, but physics was his passion, and he was always absorbed in it. Doan, preoccupied with mathematical determinants, was worlds away from his son's broad face and bright eyes. He could use mathematics to describe the physical laws which control the reflection and travel of light, but he could not see the simple yearnings of his little boy.

Now Thi was ill, and Tanh sat alone beneath the chestnut tree. He thought about the gap between Doan's world of elementary particles and Thi's world of feelings and sensations. Tanh understood Doan's love of physics and math. As an artist, he knew that both science and art can engage one so completely that one overlooks the details of everyday life. Although he could not converse with his brother-in-law in technical language, Tanh understood that the world of elementary particles could be more real to Doan than the world of the senses was for his nephew and himself.

Once, while they were having coffee together, Tanh chided Doan, "You know, it's possible that your subatomic world is only a world of ghosts."

Doan laughed. "Yes, sometimes I think so too. But those ghosts are real, and that is why I spend so much time looking for them. You know, atoms and electrons do not occupy specific locations in space and time. As we approach them, they flee. What we think of as solid or permanent simply does not exist in the subatomic world."

"Then it must be easier to demonstrate interconnectedness and impermanence in that world than in everyday life."

Doan nodded. "Yes, of course. Look for yourself. In the world of our senses, a cup of coffee is a cup of coffee. It cannot be both a cup of coffee and a glass of wine. Tanh is Tanh. You cannot be at the same time Tanh and Doan. But in the world of elementary particles, electrons can appear as either particles or waves. Are they two things at the same time? This gives scientists headaches!"

"I see. So you scientists have given up?"

"No. We recognize them as both one thing and two things, and we call them 'wavicles,' which means both wave and particle. We know that we cannot adopt the images of ordinary life to describe the entities of the subatomic world. After all, how can we call an electron solid or permanent when it is only movement? How can we follow it on even one trajectory? We cannot 'recognize' an electron because we cannot grasp its 'identity.' We can see the difference between Tanh and Doan—each of us can have a separate I.D. card—but we cannot distinguish between two electrons."

As Doan explained how elementary particles do not have separate 'selves,' Tanh remembered reading that they do not even act according to the rules of cause and effect or the laws of statistics. He sympathized with scientists working to rid themselves of the most common assumptions about life. Ultimately, they would even have to go beyond even the scientific method itself! With what mind could they then enter the world of elementary particles?

Tanh always enjoyed his conversations with Doan, as he found his brother-in-law to be remarkably broadminded and intelligent. They often stayed up until three in the morning discussing science, art, and even Buddhist philosophy.

Tuyet came out to the garden and found her brother sitting under the chestnut tree. "Thi is awake and wants to see you," she said. "He looks much better. Can you sit with him while I finish preparing lunch? And please do stay for dinner as well."

"I'd be happy to," he said, as they walked back to the house together.

As soon as his uncle appeared, Thi stretched out his arms to embrace him. "Because you are sick, I had to go to the garden all by myself," Tanh said, lifting the boy above him.

Thi's eyes brightened as he thought about the garden. "Next week, I'll walk with you. The shiny, green peony buds have blossomed into beautiful flowers. Did you see them?"

"No, I didn't. I only walked as far as the chestnut tree. I'll wait until next week and we can see them together. Did you know that peonies are *maudon* in Vietnamese?"

Thi's French was much better than his Vietnamese. Sometimes, Tanh spoke to him in French with the sort of intimacy children enjoy, but he made it a point to keep him from forgetting his Vietnamese. Tanh was patient, and Tuyet was always happy to see her brother and her son speaking together in her native tongue. His uncle always had the impression that when Thi spoke French, he was not the same child as when he spoke Vietnamese. It was as if he had two souls, one for each language. Tanh smiled to himself, for he remembered the conversation with Doan about the two different natures of an electron.

After a short conversation, Tanh left Thi's bedroom and went to the kitchen. Tuyet asked her brother about his art. "I haven't painted for months. Some big change is going on in me. I have been watching it closely, and I don't want to interfere with it."

Tuyet often worried about her brother's ability to support himself. She knew that he was an artist with integrity, who did not spend time developing styles to please wealthy patrons. Tanh believed that an artist needed only a few lines, shapes, and colors to make a painting, just as a writer needs only a few words to create a good poem. Once Tanh knew clearly what he wanted to express in his art, it came forth easily.

But there were times when he would not even touch his brushes, for he knew that the seed within him was not yet ripe. The true work of an artist, Tanh believed, always began with awareness of his deepest inner turmoil. He needed to continuously observe it with great care and acceptance. Only after such feelings completed their cycle and became transformed could they express themselves in a painting. At such times, an artist needed only to hold his brush, and the form and style would manifest. Mixing colors and handling brushes were secondary to the vital technique of stopping, observing, and entering life itself. For Tanh, the practice of art lay in nurturing his inner life and being attentive to small changes, not in acquiring technical or stylistic originality.

Tanh never regarded fallow periods as a waste of time. If he did not have paintings for sale, he was content to work as a housepainter. He told Tuyet many times, "Don't worry. Before I go broke, I will ask you for a little rice."

Tuyet would always tell him, "Heavens. I would like nothing better than for you to eat with us every day! Thi especially would love it. In fact, why don't you move in with us? We have plenty of room. We could turn the basement into a studio. Why must you pay rent when you could be so comfortable here?"

Tanh looked at his sister and smiled. "It's really quite pleasant at home. I'm used to it, my rent is reasonable, and I enjoy traveling between our two places."

"You are so stubborn, my dear brother! But I won't insist. I think you like your privacy too much. Now let me serve our lunch."

Tanh woke suddenly at two in the morning. He had had a strange dream, and his forehead was wet with perspiration. He reached for a washcloth and wiped the moisture. Then he lay on his back, his arms and legs outstretched, and began a slow, deep breathing exercise to help regain calmness in body and mind.

In the dream, Tanh had been holding little Thi's hand, and they were wandering together in a forest filled with beautiful trees and wildflowers. They were breaking small twigs and gathering leaves to build a small "palace," when suddenly the sky darkened and they could not even see each other's faces.

Tanh called out for Thi, but there was no reply. He reached out, groping in the darkness. Even the trees and bushes seemed to have disappeared. He reached for the ground, but it had become a kind of liquid, and he lost his balance and fell. Struggling in what seemed like water, he felt something and grasped it. It was Thi's arm. The two of them managed to float and tread water for a long time. Finally they reached a tree and climbed up onto it. By then, it was daylight, and they saw that the forest had disappeared.

Tanh took Thi's hand, and they ran across vast, empty stretches of land bristling with sharp rocks, glass shards, and clumps of burned-out, blackened trees. Overhead, a storm was approaching and Tanh could hear a screaming crowd angrily pursuing them. He looked for a safe shelter but there was only emptiness and destruction around them. Tanh and Thi realized it was useless to run any farther, and they stood still, ready to face their pursuers. The screams stopped, and the gathering storm froze in stillness.

At this point, Tanh awoke. He knew he had to continue concentrating on his gentle, deep breathing, in order to invite a thought that could help him understand the dream. He did not want to use reason to arrive at an explanation, for he felt that his intuition could offer him a much deeper understanding. A long while passed, and no insight arose, but Tanh did feel refreshed from the breathing exercise. He stood up, walked slowly to the bathroom, and turned on the shower. The fine jets of warm water soothed him. After a few minutes, he turned off the water, dried himself carefully, and put on some comfortable clothes.

In his study, Tanh lit a stick of fragrant incense and sat down cross-legged on a folded blanket on the floor. Sitting meditation was an important part of his work. As always, he focused his mind on his breathing. About twenty minutes later, he let go of conscious deep breathing and allowed his mind to go wherever it wanted, continuing to watch it, much as a buffalo boy watches his herd roaming freely in a grassy field.

Tanh began to see images of himself in the village along the river bank where he had grown up. It was a small village crossed by the Hau Giang River in the province of Long Xuyen. Rich, immense rice fields flourished along both sides of the river. As a child, Tanh had run barefoot with his friends on the dikes of those rice fields, digging for earthworms, catching fish, setting shrimp traps, and hunting for black crickets. What had become of those friends? Some had died on battlefields, others were in "reeducation" camps, and others, he had learned, had simply vanished without a trace. He knew that Que, his closest friend in grade school, had been killed in the Battle of Pleime. "His body must be one with the earth by now," Tanh thought. Many boys of the younger generation had been killed by bullets and bombs. His own nephew Thi was more fortunate. Although both his parents were Vietnamese, he was born in France. His collective karma was linked with other Vietnamese children, but his personal karma set him apart, providing him with advantages that children in Vietnam couldn't even imagine.

Ever since Tanh had arrived in France, whenever he saw children playing in a schoolyard or on a sidewalk, his thoughts always went back to the children of Vietnam. Tanh had held in his arms many little bodies torn apart by bullets or bomb shrapnel, and many times he had had to bury them with his own hands. As a member of the ambulance team of the Buddhist Youth Association, Tanh had braved many dangers to help wounded, helpless civilians.

Tanh could never forget holding the limp body of a four-year-old girl, her head twisted to one side, her hair matted with blood. He didn't have time to shed even a single tear for her, as hundreds of others were in great need, crying out for help from him and his comrades. He only had two or three seconds to look at that young girl, but they were seconds he could never forget. Tanh felt torn apart inside. The more pain and suffering he saw, the deeper the roots of his being went down into the soil of his homeland.

It was now four years since he had boarded the plane which took him to Paris for the "Family Reunification Program." How could he have left Vietnam? Not for his own future. Not for his art. Certainly not for a comfortable existence. Was it for freedom? Would personal freedom for someone whose life had such deep links with the soil of his homeland be possible? Tanh shook his head in doubt. He did not want to think any further.

His friend Que—even his bones must have disintegrated by now. And True, his elder brother, had been a communications officer in the South Vietnamese Army when he was lost in action in 1972, and his remains still had not been found. Truc's bones, too, must have become soil somewhere in the mountains along the Laotian border. And the little girl who had died in his arms—had her little bones gone back to the earth of her people? Tanh could still recall the precise location of her small grave within the burial compound of the Congregation of Binh Dinh Province. Had her flesh become soil yet? He had buried her with neither casket nor ritual. He did not know her name, or her family. All he could do, pushing earth back into the hole in the ground, was to say the name of Amidha Buddha over and over again.

Tanh's parents were killed when a bomb destroyed their home in Long Xuyen. He was nineteen at the time. Several years later, he went back to his village and sat on the mound of bricks, tiles, plaster, and wood where his ancestral house had stood. Sitting there, he caught sight of one tiny wildflower with five purple petals growing through a crack in the stone, and its fragile beauty touched him deeply. He realized that the flower did not mind the destruction at all. Here was life in all its power and wonder springing forth in the midst of chaos, hatred, and death.

The delicate flower called out to Tanh and told him that although the reality of life is suffering, suffering is not enough. Nothing exists forever; everything is interconnected. Life is the ceaseless movement of creation and destruction. Tanh realized that joy and pain, far from being in conflict with one another, are complementary in the same way as creation and destruction.

The wildflower helped Tanh understand the teachings of Toan, the elderly sculptor under whom he studied at the Art Institute. Toan, when holding a chisel and a mallet, or manipulating clay, looked like an ancient priest performing a sacred ritual.

He was at once gentle and powerful, graceful yet solemn. He did not produce much, but whatever art he did create was rich and vigorous.

Once he took Tanh to the An Quang Pagoda to show him his sculpture of Manjushri, the Bodhisattva of Great Understanding. After that, Tanh frequently returned to An Quang to see his teacher's work. Looking at the statue, Tanh knew that no artist could have carved such a beautiful figure without having suffered and loved to such a great extent.

Here was the face of a being who had a deep knowledge of all existence. Facing the wooden Bodhisattva's carved eyes, one could not avoid noticing the true nature of all joy and pain. Viewers were opened by Manjushri's gaze, just as flowers open their petals to the sun for illumination. His eyes looked at the beholder, not with a look that probed or judged, but with one that understood and calmed.

It was the look of compassion, confirmed by the smile on Manjushri's face. Only one who had known the deepest pain could smile so gently, and look on the world with such compassionate eyes. The Bodhisattva's posture and the position of his hands were those of a sympathetic human being, not of a supernatural god. Toan's figure communicated that a human being, once he or she becomes deeply human, can become a Buddha. The Bodhisattva sat perfectly still, fearless and complete, but not at all remote.

Tanh had visited Toan often, and had begun to learn to sit in meditation. "Sitting," Toan told him, "is a way to help artistic inspiration ripen before it transforms into a work of art." Toan also helped Tanh understand the relationship between his homeland, Vietnam, and himself, an artist: "Every nation and its people go through times of glory, as well as times of suffering. An artist, by expressing his own hopes and pains, can speak for a nation, because the artist's sentiments are so deeply resonant with those of his people." Tanh had not fully understood Toan's words until he saw the wildflower springing up amidst the rubble of the war.

Often Tanh looked at his nephew Thi and thought, "Here is a child born and raised in a country without war, a child well loved and cared for by his parents and other adults around him, and provided for with many material comforts." Then he thought of the children whose bodies were mangled by bombs and bullets, and children who wandered about cold and hungry, lost in a world of hatred.

He recalled the dream that had awakened him during the night. He was holding Thi's hand, and they were running, while a storm was about to break. Tanh realized that his running expressed his desire to escape death, despair, and impermanence. He recalled the end of the dream. Knowing that it was impossible to hide, he had stopped running, and the screaming of the pursuing crowd ceased. Could the real enemy be his fear and pain, his yearning for an existence independent of the difficult conditions of this world? "Life brings us into the world and she buries us," Tanh thought. "There is no life without death, and no death without life. To accept life wholeheartedly is to accept both sides of life's reality." Tanh saw the little girl who had died in his arms, and she was smiling at him. What a miraculous smile! He saw that it was the same smile as Thi's. Yes, it was Thi smiling! The little girl experiencing the most horrible suffering and Thi with all his comforts, were the same child.

Though the war had ended five years before, and both uncle and nephew were living safely in a land of peace and democracy, the reality of Vietnam was alive within every cell of Tanh's body. The dream was not an illusion. It was as real as any physical object around him. He had climbed the steps and boarded the plane for France, but he had never left his homeland. He himself was his homeland.

Gently, Tanh came out of his meditation. He stood up and began walking slowly, making each step with the utmost care, as if he wanted to imprint his footprints clearly on the floor, on the earth itself. That morning, Tanh began a painting of little Thi standing next to a bouquet of peonies in full bloom. He worked all day and late into the night, only stopping for a piece of bread, an orange, and a glass of water. He then slept for four hours.

Early the next morning, after half-an-hour of meditation, Tanh turned on his studio light and continued working. Several times before noon the doorbell rang, but he did not answer it. He did not want to see or talk to anyone while he was painting Thi.

He worked until midday Thursday. The painting, he thought, was completed. Perhaps a touch here, a slight change there, but that was all that was needed. Tanh plugged in the spotlight on the south wall, focused the light on his painting, and sat down to look at his work. Thi's smile was clear and bright like the peony blossom he held in his hand. It was the same smile as that of the little girl Tanh had seen during his meditative sitting. He painted his nephew wearing traditional Vietnamese gray pants and shirt, which the little girl who had died in his arms years ago also wore. "She has come back," Tanh thought. "She now lives in Thi and in all the children who are alive and walking the ground of his homeland."

> *O, children, as you walk toward the future, take with you the thousands of small ones who were struck down. We adults who have been blinded by ambition and hatred must step aside and let you pass. Little Thi will never die. In him, the past is alive, and through him, all children, dead and alive, can go forth and realize the future.*

Tanh turned off the lights, closed the door to his studio, and walked up the staircase leading to the ground floor. He felt at peace. He wanted to eat lunch and take a short nap before putting the final touches on his painting, but when he passed his mailbox, he noticed an urgent message. It was from his sister: "I need you. Come right away. Tuyet." Tanh immediately changed into street clothes and headed for the bus stop.

By Wednesday, Thi's fever had climbed to 105 degrees and he began vomiting. His head hurt terribly, and he could not stop screaming as he desperately pressed his hands against his temples. Thi's cries wrenched his parents' hearts. Tuyet frantically tried to comfort Thi, and Doan called Dr. Peltier. The doctor told them to bring the boy to the Children's Hospital immediately and he would meet them there. By the time they reached the hospital, Thi was barely conscious.

Thi was put through a variety of tests, and the doctors found that he had a tumor on his brain, and that he was also suffering from an attack of meningitis. His life was in immediate danger, and they decided to operate to remove the tumor.

It was fortunate that the finest resident surgeon at the Children's Hospital was present. Preparations took nearly three hours, and Thi was wheeled in and put face down on a specially equipped table.

Tuyet and Doan waited in a small room outside the operating room. Time seemed to stand still. Tuyet chanted under her breath, invoking the compassion of Kwan Yin Bodhisattva. But Doan could not pray. His heart was on fire. The more he thought about Dr. Peltier's misdiagnosis, the angrier he became. Three times the doctor had underestimated the seriousness of Thi's condition!

The operation was completed by nightfall, and Thi was still unconscious. Doan was told that the operation had gone smoothly but that the child's condition remained critical. Treatments with various serums, antibiotics, and cortisone were being carried out, and Thi was expected to regain consciousness in about six hours.

The hospital allowed only one person to remain with Thi, and Doan decided that it should be Tuyet. He told her to telephone immediately if there was any change; otherwise, she should just rest. As her husband was leaving, Tuyet asked him to pray very hard, and also to send a mailgram to her brother Tanh.

Doan could not eat any supper. He drank a glass of milk and sat waiting for his wife's call. He could not sit still, as if a fire burned under his chair. He got up and paced about from the sitting room to the kitchen, back to the sitting room, to the study, to Thi's room, then from Thi's room to his, and to Tuyet's bedroom. Everywhere he walked, he felt on fire. He returned to the sitting room, sat down in his familiar armchair for only a few minutes before he stood up again and continued walking. His old, comfortable chair was totally enveloped in fire.

By eleven o'clock at night, there was still no call from Tuyet, which meant that their son was still unconscious. Doan began to panic. He wanted to be calm, but there was nothing he could do. He knew that at that moment his wife was praying for their son, and he wished that he, too, had such a pure and simple faith. But he could not bring himself to believe that invoking Lord Buddha's name would in any way improve his son's chance of survival. Tuyet had often encouraged him to pray with her, but he never could. Until his son came out of mortal danger, he knew he would not be able to rest.

The clock on the wall struck midnight. Doan put on his pajamas and got into bed, hoping he would just drop off to sleep. But he could not even close his eyes. Then, only then, did he slowly and clearly begin to see the true face of his inner disquiet. The image of Thi kept appearing before him. He trembled as he thought of his son's mortality. He tossed and turned, trying to find a position which might be more restful, to no avail. His bed was on fire too. He felt as if he, Tuyet, Thi, and their entire house, were floating on the ocean and could be capsized by a wave at any moment. It was the first time he realized how entwined Thi's life was with his own. He saw that if Thi died, he would no longer be himself. He would also die. Thi was more than just his son. He was Doan himself.

For years, Doan thought that providing security and comfort for his son was all he needed to do. He was like a gardener who, after planting a healthy tree and giving it rich soil and a windbreak, leaves it to fend for itself. Suddenly he realized that Thi was not just a tree. He was also the gardener, and the heart of the gardener as well. If the tree died, so would the gardener.

Doan's family lived on solid ground, not in a boat tossed about on the sea. France was a country at peace. Montpellier was a city with all the opportunity in the world to bring forth the fruit of his son's learning and abilities. Thi was surrounded by love and care from his parents, his school, his society.

Doan knew about the dangers that refugees who escaped by sea had to face, including hunger, thirst, storms, and pirates.

Just last month, he had read that fewer than fifty percent of all those who leave Vietnam by boat survive. He thought of the homeless and the destitute, the victims of the war, and he thought of himself. He was living in his own home, a charming house surrounded by trees and flowers, a house of love and tranquility. And yet, for a moment, he could see clearly that he, too, was bobbing up and down on the ocean. All his peace and security had evaporated, and his own fate was as uncertain as that of the boat people.

Doan's discovery was remarkable! Thi was not only his son, but Thi was Doan himself. Were Thi to die, Doan too would die. Even if Doan did not actually die, he would be only a shadow of himself. What a shocking insight! How could he ever fall asleep now that he knew this. He was like a man shot by an arrow. The shock, the pain, the reality of it all was so strong he could not even shut his eyes. Doan gave up trying to sleep. He went into the kitchen and made a cup of strong black coffee.

He knew that he had come face to face with a reality he had never faced before. His struggle for survival was as desperate as that of the refugees in their fragile boats. If he did not find a way to overcome his torments and worries, he too might drown. Tuyet had not telephoned and, he thought, if she did, it might be to tell him that Thi was still unconscious. All evening, Doan had been hoping for a call, and now he was afraid the phone might ring. But he had to stand firm, for the coming storm could bring them all down to the bottom of the sea. The night was only half over, and Doan imagined that his hair had turned white. He knew he had to fight. But with what weapons? Tuyet could pray, for she had her faith in the Buddha. Her brother Tanh knew how to sit quietly and meditate. Doan had neither Tuyet's faith nor Tanh's training. What about his scientific knowledge? How could it be of use to him in a time like this,

a time when fear and uncertainty were so huge that he felt ready
to burst into a thousand pieces?

It was now two-thirty in the morning. Doan had restlessly
paced from room to room, rolled over in bed, and sat down and
stood up hundreds of times. He had tried to read newspapers
and books, and each time he could read only one or two lines.
He asked himself who in the entire world would he most like
to have next to him to share some of his anxiety and fear. He
thought of his friends, and decided none of them would be able
to do that. No one could come into his lonely world and be
with him. He knew that it was easier to sit and face his torments
by himself than to be with someone who could not share them
with him. Then he thought of Tanh, and he realized that he
would feel less lonely if Tanh were sitting with him now, even
if silently. He knew that Tanh loved Thi as much as he and Tuyet
loved the boy.

If only Tanh had a telephone, he would call him right away.
However, he knew that Tanh was a free soul who might not even
be at home tonight. He then remembered that he had not sent
a mailgram to Tanh as Tuyet had asked him to do. He reached
for the phone, dialed, and dictated the message on behalf of
Tuyet, asking that her brother come over immediately. He set
the phone down, turned on all the lights in the living room,
and sat down again in his reclining chair. The phone message
would not be delivered until eight o'clock, so the earliest that
Tanh would arrive would be around ten. Doan knew that Tanh
loved Thi very much and that news of the boy's condition would
come as a great shock to him. But Doan could not imagine his
brother-in-law reacting with the kind of panic he himself felt.

The clock on the wall chimed three times. It was three in the
morning. Doan knew that his son was still unconscious, and
that his life was hanging by a thread. A frail, small body like
Thi's, how could it survive both a brain tumor and meningitis? If Dr. Peltier were here, Doan would not spare his feelings.

Doan knew that Thi's condition pushed the limits of medical science. Only last January his friend Binh had died at the Lariboisiere Hospital in Paris, even after successful brain surgery. "Faith in science is fine," Doan thought, "but in life one must also believe in miracles." He knew that his wife was praying now for such a miracle, invoking the names of the Compassionate and Healing Bodhisattvas. Doan desperately wished that he also could take refuge in such religious faith. But his interest in Buddhism was much more casual than the powerful faith of Tuyet or the practical and philosophical discipline of Tanh.

By now Doan was so tense that his brain felt as though it could explode. He stared at the telephone, wanting to call the hospital, but he knew it would be of no use. If and when Thi became conscious, Tuyet would rush to phone him. It was four in the morning. Doan lay on his bed with his arms and legs straight like a corpse. He got up, swallowed two aspirins with a glass of cool water, and went back to lie down, hoping the pills might calm his nerves. Half an hour later, his head was burning. He rubbed it with his hands for a while, then gave up. He went to the medicine chest and took out two capsules of Immenoctal, a powerful sleeping drug. After swallowing them, he turned off all the lights, even the tiny night-light in the bedroom, and went to bed again.

It was five-fifteen in the morning before he finally fell into a drugged sleep. He had frightening dreams, one after another. In the last one, he, Tuyet, and Thi were sitting in a small boat, being tossed in a rough sea. A wave as big as a mountain engulfed them. Doan screamed and woke up. He touched his forehead, which was drenched with sweat. His watch showed eight-twenty. He had slept for three hours, but he felt even more tired than before and his tenseness had not gone away. The more he tried to subdue his fears and worries, the more damage they seemed to inflict on his body.

The telephone rang. Doan's heart pounded in his chest. He ran to the living room. Yes, it was Tuyet. No, Thi was not yet conscious. Tuyet's voice was full of tears. Doan told her that he had sent a mailgram to Tanh, and that by ten he would be at their home. Tuyet said he should wait for Tanh, and the two of them could come to the hospital together. She promised him that she would call as soon as there was any news.

Setting the phone down, Doan realized that his son's condition was even more dangerous than he had feared. After speaking with his wife, his torment was even more devastating. When might they see any signs of improvement in Thi's condition? Tonight, tomorrow, the day after? Could he himself survive another day of this ordeal?

Doan sat motionless in his armchair. At this moment, his son was fighting for his life. Over and over, Doan muttered the same words to himself, "Keep it up, son, keep it up." Thi had to fight. And he, Doan, was fighting too. He did not have his wife's faith or his brother-in-law's meditation practice, and he could not borrow from them. What practice did he have that he could call his own? He thought about his vocation, his love of physics and mathematics. Was there anything in the research to which he had devoted years of his life that could help him now?

He asked himself that question, and suddenly he felt a strong urge to go to his study and sit at his desk. He went first to wash his face and put on a fresh shirt, and when he entered his study, Doan immediately felt rather relaxed. A pleasant feeling enveloped him as he again entered a world both physically and mentally familiar. He likened it to a snail retreating into its shell, or a spider crouching at the center of a web it had worked so hard to spin. "Am I taking refuge within my ivory tower?" he asked. "And is this tower strong enough to protect me from these torments?

"Last night was an eternity," he thought. "Time, time. My time, Thi's time, the time of electrons and mesons. Is the time of the physical sciences independent of the time of the human mind?" More than once Doan had pondered and talked with Tanh about the subject of time. They had discussed time in Einstein's Theory of Relativity, and Tanh had observed that time, space, and what we call physical phenomena have an intimate relationship with human perception. Tanh had said that only through the human mind do these acquire the forms and natures by which we usually know them.

Doan could almost totally agree with Tanh. Recent discoveries in subatomic physics had all but brought down the whole edifice of materialist physics, so that the very foundation of existence presumed since Democritus had lost its credibility. Scientists were unable to find anything that had a separate, independent existence. Whenever they conducted subatomic experiments, they were able to record only the entities' reactions, sometimes as waves, sometimes as particles. They could not locate a "self," only their own conceptions.

Doan knew that neither matter, space, nor time can be observed independently of the other two. He knew that a line between the past and the future, called the present, is normally assumed. But in his study of Relativity, he discovered that the span of the present varies with the distance in space between the observer and the phenomenon observed. The present might be a short span of time, but it can also be measured in years, or even tens of millions of years. Someone on the Earth watching a falling star may not know that from other points in the universe the star has not yet fallen, or it may have fallen millions of years before. The present is not a universal entity. It can also be identified with the past or the future.

Doan understood from quantum mechanics that there comes to be an infinite indeterminate with regard to speed and energy when one tries to specify the position of an electron. One cannot satisfactorily describe the actions and reactions of subatomic matter by mathematical formulas. In the domain of subatomic physics, the very nature of space and time becomes imprecise, so that one cannot always tell what is past and what is future. Some subatomic "entities" even seem to go in the opposite direction of time, in the reverse direction of the causal order itself.

Doan had the feeling he was moving from one dream to another. Thi had been a part of his world for almost eight years, and yet his son never seemed so real as he did now at the threshold of death. Doan could see Thi more clearly, thus he could see himself more clearly. His illusions of security and permanence had evaporated, and human life seemed as fragile and evanescent as a wisp of smoke. The past seemed like a dream. But what about the present, filled with anxiety and fear was it not also a dream?

Doan became aware of a new yearning within him. He wanted to awaken from his illusory dream world and enter the world of reality. He realized that time and space were a net imprisoning him. Thi's critical condition, a source of overwhelming anxiety, had become a doorway to Doan's liberation. Through the ordeal of his son's illness, Doan had come to realize that his world of scientific research was as valid as the world of everyday preoccupations.

For Doan, certain facts, perhaps amusing to most people, were primordial truths to be deeply contemplated. He would watch the bright red sun setting over the mountain, its rays warming his face, and realize that it had actually set eight minutes before—the sun one sees is never the sun of the present moment. He would contemplate the star that the poet speaks of "plucking from the firmament to fasten to his beloved's hair" and he realized that it may have exploded millions of years ago. His son Thi was born in 1972. "This fact alone, seen from different points in the universe, has different meanings," Doan thought. "From some places, Thi has not yet been born. In other locations in the universe, Thi will be very much alive, laughing and talking, one thousand years from now." By contemplating facts such as these, Doan realized that most human beings live their lives based on illusory perceptions which cause them untold pain and fear.

Now he understood the practical implications of knowing that electrons are manifestations of waves and particles. What he saw, heard, and touched every day were just so many phantoms. In the light of science, the most common assumptions about the solidity of things were proven erroneous. Doan suddenly comprehended that his anxiety about the possibility of Thi's death had been based on illusory perceptions. This realization burst in his mind like a flash of lightning.

Doan was totally aware of his son's critical condition, but he was no longer in a panic. All night, his state of mind had been too tumultuous to subdue or even to lull to sleep with pills. But his scientific understanding had come forward in a moment of need to offer him deep insight into the nature of existence. Scientific inquiry had proved to be his snail's shell and spider's web.

Doan sat at his desk, motionless and silent like a Taoist priest. If someone had asked him, "What is your innermost wish at this moment?" he would have answered, "To achieve total awakening." He did not wish to return to the dream of a son in perfect health and himself busily engaged in research and teaching. Although exhilarating, it was still a dream, and Doan knew that even beautiful dreams can be followed by nightmares, such as the one he had just lived through.

Instinctively, Doan caught hold of himself, and sat upright. He began to breathe slowly and deeply. Thoughts of birth and death arose. Doan knew that homo sapiens had evolved from single-celled creatures, and he smiled as he thought that life had been continuous from one little amoeba to himself. "Evolution is birth and death, but it is also nonbirth and non-death. The amoeba has never died, and neither have I. When was I born? Didn't I exist even before the first amoeba, in the very conditions which had made the creation of the amoeba possible? I have never died from the very beginning, so how can I die now?" Once, Tanh had said to him, "Birth and death are like stars in your eyes," but Doan had not understood.

Now he remembered that the French chemist Lavoisier had said, "Nothing is created, nothing is destroyed." Doan thought that the Lavoisier rule, intended to describe inorganic matter and energy, could be applied to the domain of organic matter as well. All creatures endowed with life are also beyond birth and death. Doan's life and Thi's life would continue uninterrupted. They were beyond destruction. Although a drop of water may become a cloud, rain, or a grain of rice, the river of life flows uninterrupted. Nothing is created, nothing is destroyed." "Nothing is born, nothing dies." How strange, Doan thought, that the language of science and the language of Buddhism are so similar.

Doan recalled the words of a philosopher. "I accept the limits imposed on my life in terms of space, so why shouldn't I accept the limits imposed by time? In the year 2000, only some of us alive now will still be alive, and none of us will be alive in the year 3000." Doan found this way of thinking mechanical and simplistic.

He knew that all phenomena are interdependent, that we are all part of the entire universe, and it is because we exist that other phenomena and the universe exist. "To live means to live with the entire universe," Doan thought. "Who can say that when I clap my hands, the sound will not, in some small way, disturb the entire Andromeda Constellation? Who can say that when I take a breath, the air that enters my lungs does not contain a tiny amount of air breathed by Julius Caesar centuries ago?

"To exist means to live in the totality of time with no beginning and no end. If there is no past, then there is no present or future. If there is no future, there is no present or past. Birth and death are conventional expressions, but they obscure the vision of a total reality which has never been born and will never die."

For over a year, Doan and Tanh had been having conversations on subjects like this, but suddenly Doan realized their real importance. "We are bound by our perceptions," Tanh had said. "It is our faculty of perception which divides reality into birth and death, one and many, permanent and impermanent, past and present."

Tanh had jokingly told Doan that his world of elementary particles was a world of ghosts. Now Doan understood that it was through this "world of ghosts" that he was able to see through the illusory nature of the ordinary world and grasp that the things we perceive through our senses are themselves illusions.

Discoveries in physics during the past fifty years have made it clear that things are not what they seem. Though Doan and his colleagues were all in agreement on this point, for almost twenty years scientists had been debating issues such as "wave and/or particle." Though hardly anyone would dream of describing the subatomic world by means of visual concepts, mutually contradictory notions like "particle" and "wave" remained. The scientist's perception was trapped within dualistic vision, seeing reality in terms of pairs of opposites. Although this vision had cracked with regard to phenomena whose very natures seemed to be in contradiction—matter and energy, inertia and gravity, time and space, space and matter, wave and particle— it remained intact concerning phenomena such as matter and spirit, subject and object. The arguments against a dualistic vision were not yet strong or clear enough to bring about its total dissolution. Otherwise, how could scientists acknowledge the non-dualistic nature of time and space, and yet continue looking for the ultimate beginning and limit of the universe? The Big Bang Theory, the talk of a universe that expands, or has definable limits, seemed to deny the oft-stated conviction that time-space is a nondualistic reality.

Recently Doan had heard a prominent scientist speculate about time inside black holes and within subatomic matter. Time and space were discussed as if they could be experienced locally, separate from subjective perception. The Theory of Relativity tells us that matter and space are of the same nature, and that time does not exist independently of space. Thus, all three phenomena—time, space, and matter—have the same nature. They do not exist outside of perception.

Some scientists have stated, "We can never know subatomic bodies unto themselves. We can only observe them through our own perceptions. As a result, any observation of the infinitesimal can only distort or change the observed object, and 'objective reality' remains unreachable." Doan realized that scientific observation is built on duality, that the objects of observation are regarded as independent of the subjects who observe.

Tanh had told him that in Buddhism, "observation" gives way to penetration. When you "penetrate" reality, the distinction between subject and object dissolves. Herein, Doan thought, lies the biggest stumbling block of modern science. Doan differed with scientists who believe that the language of mathematics is a solution to this problem. Doan regarded mathematics as a language of abstraction, born of the human brain, one which expresses human perception rather than the world itself. However far we humans go, Doan pondered, we only come face to face with ourselves.

If only Tanh were here, he thought, Tanh could offer insight into "non-discriminative wisdom," the Buddhist method of seeing reality nondualistically. Doan wondered what kind of language one might use when one reached that state. Obviously it would be one that did not divide reality into subjects and objects. In a sense, it would be an esoteric language because anyone who thought dualistically would find it difficult to un-

derstand a non-discriminative language. Perhaps notions conceived by Einstein such as "space-time continuum" and "four-
dimensional space," or a notion conceived by nuclear physicists
that a physical reality is at once "wave and particle," could be
used to destroy the old dualistic notions of reality.

Yet, Tanh had also told him that in Buddhism, to destroy the
dualistic vision does not mean to arrive at monism. If reality
can be one, it can be two, or three. The Buddha would not say
it is or it is not. Doan was ready to accept Tanh's explanation
wholeheartedly. Truth must be found somewhere in a middle
way.

Doan recalled some of Tanh's suggestions for ridding oneself
of dualistic notions: "Buddhism offers concepts such as 'interbeing' and 'non-self' to break down the boundaries which divide reality." Doan thought, "Aren't Heisenberg's 'indeterminate
relationships' also tools that could be used to wear down our
habit of describing reality by those 'determinate representations'?
Just as Buddhism has created its own language to help us go
beyond dualism, science too has to create new language in order to express its new understanding of reality."

Doan stood up slowly. Through the window he could see the
bright sun shining in the garden and dozens of birds rippling
through the foliage. He yearned to go outside and stand among
the strong, healthy trees. The worries and anxieties of the past
night were still present, but he felt calm and full of energy.
Doan's heart overflowed with tenderness as he thought of Tuyet
and her struggle through this intense night and day. Doan shuddered at the thought that, in the terrible storm, he had been
frail as a reed that could have snapped at any moment. He knew
the pain of loss would be tremendous if Thi did not win his
battle for life. But Doan had acquired a new strength and re-
silience which would help him withstand life's mishaps and give
Tuyet support from then on. Like Tuyet and Tanh, he too possessed deep inner resources.

Doan reached the garden. The lily-like fragrance of the peony blossoms saturated the afternoon air. Doan was aware that for years he had been so absorbed in his world of neutrons, mesons, and electrons, that he rarely found time to hold his son's hand and walk with him. Now, having journeyed far into the world of subatomic physics, he was able to be truly present in this lovely, cool garden.

Doan walked toward the chestnut tree. The doorbell rang, and Tanh was standing at the gate. Doan walked slowly, very slowly, on the gravel path toward his brother-in-law.

Tanh watched Doan closely. He had never seen Doan walk that way before—with such composure, such majesty. Tanh whispered to himself, "Something wonderful has happened to Doan!" For a moment Tanh forgot that he too had had a marvelous breakthrough during the night.

The two men looked deeply at each other, seeing the entire universe and all eternity. In that moment, their love and gratitude for an eight-year-old boy, now lying in a nearby hospital at the edge of death, was expressed. Thi had shot an arrow, and it had struck two targets at the same time.

About the Stories

∞

About the Stories

THE TEN STORIES in this book were all originally written in Vietnamese and published individually. They were translated into English by the following individuals in collaboration with the author. Background comments on each story follow.

∞

The Ancient Tree

THIS STORY WAS written as a memorial to Nhat Chi Mai, Thich Nhat Hanh's student who immolated herself for peace on May 16, 1967. For more about Nhat Chi Mai, see Chân Không, *Learning True Love* (Parallax Press, 1993). *Translated by Mobi Warren.*

∞

The Giant Pines

WRITTEN IN 1978, this is a creative retelling of the true story of a famous Tang Dynasty Chinese Buddhist monk who was an advisor to the King when he was suddenly struck by a disease. That monk is author of several works, including *The Water of Compassion That Washes Away All Wrongdoing*, a text on "Beginning Anew," practiced in many temples even today. *Translated by Vo-Dinh Mai.*

∞

The Pine Gate

WRITTEN IN 1960. The *me ngo* glass represents mindfulness. Even if you are a highly accomplished monk, without mindfulness and self-reflection, you can turn into a monster. The sword is the sword of Manjushri Bodhisattva, the sword that cuts through illusions. *Translated by Vo-Dinh Mai.*

∞

A Bouquet of Wildflowers

THIS STORY WAS written in 1978 to honor the author's friendship with Sister Chân Không on her birthday. The treasure of peace and happiness is hidden not in the ground but in the heart. The brother was looking for it but did not find it. The sister did not look for it and found it. The instrument used is not the intellect but mindfulness. Only mindfulness in daily life can reveal it. The poem, or *gatha*, is that of a famous twelfth-century Vietnamese monk, Tinh Không. *Translated by Dinh Nghiêm.*

∞

There Are Beautiful Eyes

THIS STORY WAS written in 1959, "for those who love their church too much." Church authorities may not want you because you love her (the church) so much. Even if you have brought her much beauty and radiance, her pride cannot stand your presence. *Translated by Thich Phap Canh.*

∞

The Bodhisattva on the Fragrant Mountain

WRITTEN IN 1983, this is a retelling of a legend known throughout China and Vietnam. This story was first told to the children of Plum Village, Thich Nhat Hanh's community in France.

Fragrant Mountain is located in North Vietnam, about four hours by car and one hour by rowboat from Hanoi, and remains a place of pilgrimage and great inspiration today. This story exists in a *chu nom* version dating back to the sixteenth century in Vietnam. *Translated by Tue Nghiêm.*

∾

The Stone Boy

WRITTEN IN 1979, this is a story about peace and, more importantly, a story about love. When we find true love, we care for all life, and we overcome suffering. The golden bird and the old man beneath the sea evoke the imagery of Vietnam's creation myth. See Thich Nhat Hanh, *A Taste of Earth* (Parallax Press, 1993). Accounts of attacks on villages, conditions in prison camps, and the plight of children searching for their parents are based on actual events the author witnessed or was told first-hand. The eccentric Taoist monk is based on the well-known "Coconut Monk," who kept a cat and mice who lived in harmony, and had a great bell cast from war shrapnel. During Stone Boy's incarceration, we are introduced to 300 Buddhist monks held at Chi Hoa Prison for their refusal to be drafted. The fast of these monks began on March 2, 1974, and continued for a month, when the monks were scattered to various prisons. If you are a Christian, the Stone Boy is Jesus. If you are a Buddhist, the Stone Boy is the Buddha. It is he who enables you to see things as they are. He and you may become one, if you practice well. *Translated by Vo-Dinh Mai.*

∾

A Lone Pink Fish

THIS IS A STORY about suffering, compassion, and wisdom. To attain the deepest understanding, we have to understanding suffering. The story begins with Dao drifting to a remote island,

and ends with her about to leave the island. This is much like the path of spiritual practice. We withdraw from the world for a period of time, but at some time we must apply the fruits of our practice and re-enter the world to help others. Hong, the pink fish, represents compassion and wisdom. The sea pirates represent greed, hatred, and ignorance—the three poisons. The boat people are in between. They represent those caught in the boundless ocean of suffering.

This story was written following the author's experience in the South China Sea trying to rescue boat people. The suffering was so great, the author felt it might be too much for people to receive if they were told directly, so he wrote it as a short story. He and several close associates were involved in a project to rescue and assist Vietnamese boat people adrift at sea, many of whom had been turned away from the shores of Thailand and Malaysia. Hong's descriptions of events were gathered from accounts told by these boat people. The Shantisuk was a real boat, chartered by Sister Chân Không for the rescue operation. Hong's tales of rape and murder, drowning and callousness, are based on the actual experiences of many people. For an account of this boat people operation, see *Learning True Love*, cited above. *Translated by Mobi Warren.*

∞

The Moon Bamboo

THIS IS A STORY about life in exile, being separated from family, culture, and homeland. The Bodhisattva of Love can transform herself into many bodies to take care of many people. If you are motivated by great love, you also wish to be like her, able to be here and there at the same time, for your many beloved ones. *Translated by Mobi Warren.*

∞

Peony Blossoms

THIS IS ALSO a story about living in exile, and is a journey into the awareness of "interbeing," the interconnectedness of life that can heal the agonies of separation. You do not need to be a monk to get enlightened. If you practice looking deeply into what you are doing every day, enlightenment will come, whether you are a painter or a scientist. *Translated by Vo-Dinh Mai.*

Parallax Press publishes books and tapes on Buddhism and related subjects. We are happy to offer this book of short stories by Thich Nhat Hanh. We have also published *A Taste of Earth and Other Legends of Vietnam* and *Hermitage Among the Clouds: An Historical Novel of Fourteenth Century Vietnam*, both by Thich Nhat Hanh. For a complete catalog of our books and tapes, please write to:

Parallax Press
P.O. Box 7355
Berkeley, California 94707

For a complete listing of Thich Nhat Hanh's books in Vietnamese, please write to:

La Boi Press
P.O. Box 3189
Walnut Creek, California 94598